Bruce Floyd
7-19-22

Praise for *Dead Souls*

"Mordant, torrential, incantatory, Bolaño-esque, Perec-ian, and just so explosively written that I had to stop and shake the language-shrapnel from my hair and wipe it off my eyeglasses so I could keep reading." —JONATHAN LETHEM

"As Brontë does so disarmingly in *Wuthering Heights* and Nabokov in *Pale Fire*, Sam Riviere gives a loquacious and pleasingly unreliable nobody the task of telling the tale of *Dead Souls*' true protagonist: Solomon Wiese, a recently excommunicated poet who seems to have been everywhere and known everyone. In long, sure sentences reminiscent of Thomas Bernhard, Riviere cracks open the administrative heart of the contemporary literary endeavor, finding it full not of hot air but of crowds of characters, a whole shimmering historical ecosystem—in short, the world as we know it, as mesmerizingly real as it is fictional."

—LUCY IVES, author of *Cosmogony* and *Loudermilk*

"If as I read Sam Riviere's wonderful first novel I discerned intriguing notes of Rachel Cusk's *Outline* trilogy and Thomas Bernhard's propulsive monologues, I also found myself thinking with pleasure of the intricate (and hilarious) book-world satire in Italo Calvino's *If on a Winter's Night a Traveler*. Echoes aside, *Dead Souls* is its own whip-smart, razor-sharp, wise-funny, highly readable animal, and I can't recommend it enthusiastically enough." —LAIRD HUNT, author of *Neverhome*

"*Dead Souls* is elegant, ambitious, very serious, and very funny—an enlivening burst of anti-anti-intellectualism."

—KATHARINE KILALEA, author of *OK, Mr. Field*

"Beautiful, intricately humane, and gut-wrenchingly funny; not so much cynical as a ruthless vivisection of cynicism itself. Reading *Dead Souls* feels like discovering the British Bolaño, and not just for the gleeful dismantling of the cultural ego: the restless, searching sensibility; the precise tuning-in to contradictory voices. I haven't been so excited by a debut novel in a long time."

—LUKE KENNARD, author of *The Transition*

"Sublime, legendary, delightfully unhinged. Sam Riviere's *Dead Souls* is a rare and brilliant pleasure, a coiling, searing fugue of a book that takes our deranged culture and pulls forth from it a box of stars."

—NICOLETTE POLEK, author of *Imaginary Museums*

"I absolutely adored *Dead Souls*. Reading it felt like overhearing the most exhilarating, funny, mean conversation imaginable—which is to say it made me extremely happy, and I dreaded it ending."

—MEGAN NOLAN, author of *Acts of Desperation*

DEAD SOULS

DEAD SOULS

A NOVEL

SAM RIVIERE

CATAPULT
NEW YORK

This is a work of fiction. All of the characters, organizations, and events portrayed in this novel are either products of the author's imagination or are used fictitiously.

ISBN: 978-1-646220-28-1

Jacket design by Na Kim
Book design by Wah-Ming Chang

Library of Congress Control Number: 2020943746

Printed in the United States of America
1 3 5 7 9 10 8 6 4 2

while I was lolling in a coach the novelty created such strange feelings that I coud almost fancy that my identity as well as my occupations had changd . . . that some stranger soul had jumpd into my skin

JOHN CLARE

It is the absurd ideas that are the clearest ideas, and the most absurd ideas are the most important.

THOMAS BERNHARD

The dominance of one sense is the formula for hypnosis.

MARSHALL McLUHAN

DEAD SOULS

I first heard about Solomon Wiese on a bright, blustery day on the South Bank. The man who told me about him, standing opposite me outside the Royal Festival Hall, within sight of the river, which could be observed heaving like horrible grey jelly, was the head of a small publishing company, and had mentioned the name Solomon Wiese in connection, I thought, with a literary scandal from earlier in the year. Before this happened I hadn't really been listening to the head of the small publishing company, although outwardly I was nodding, saying "Mmm," and even occasionally generating an entire sentence. There were two reasons that I hadn't been listening to the head of the small publishing company, apart from the obvious ones—that the head of the small publishing company was not a particularly enthralling conversationalist, for example, or the atmosphere of generalised boredom that mists these kinds of encounters, especially when they take place among a long series, as this one did, that closely resemble each other in tone and subject matter. The first reason was the presence, next to him, on my left, of his wife, who I remembered was a dentist, or in training to be a dentist, and like me had remained largely silent during the head of the small publishing company's discourse. As he spoke I had become increasingly aware of her, and her position relative to me in the small triangle we formed, standing on the biscuity concrete—I had been reminded of her name moments before but hadn't succeeded in retaining it. And although she had refrained from speaking almost entirely, and although I was able to prevent myself from sliding my eyes leftwards to look at her, the fact of her presence began to weigh on me more and more heavily, accompanied by a growing certainty that for seconds at a time she was staring at me, specifically at an area around my left shoulder, quite close to my neck. I was facing away from the water and it was possible, even quite likely, that the head of the small publishing company's wife was simply taking glances beyond me towards its surface, I thought, as the mouth of the head of the small publishing company continued to move. Without turning my head I could see the water, too, in the far reaches of my vision, registering as little more than a restless effect of the light—it was possible it was to this area behind me, where the river continued its dissatisfied heaving motions, that her eyes were drawn. It was possible, but it wasn't my feeling. That the head of the small publishing company's wife was uninterested in the conversation and seeking distraction in the view wouldn't have been difficult to explain, I thought, but I had met her two or three times before at similar gatherings, and if she had refrained from speaking more than absolutely necessary, she had at least always managed to give the impression that she was participating: her devices remained pocketed, and she faced the spectacle of literary society with an expression that wasn't bored or impatient, but carefully interested. If you looked at her during the conversation she would be smiling at a moment of mock obtuseness, or nodding minutely during one of the flat stretches. She had been to enough of these events, I reasoned, while the head of the small publishing company continued to speak, to have got far beyond wondering what she was doing at them; she no longer questioned their purpose, if she ever had, the literary events of her husband's professional world, with their warm hubbub, the haze of alcohol that clung to your clothes, the tired charades and the endless gossip—yet to look at her you felt that she *had* questioned them, in the past, perhaps in acid tones. That was all behind her now. She had become fully, numbly accepting of them, she attended unquestioningly, as a matter of principle, in support of her husband, who no doubt attended in a symmetrical way, I imagined, the social events around dentistry that surely took place from time to time, possibly in parts of the city very near this location, on the South Bank, the so-called cultural hub of the capital, and which she was obliged to mark in their calendar months in advance, so as not to spring one of these occasions on him without allowing him adequate time to psychologically prepare himself. It must be the same for her, too. Could it be, I wondered, that the wife of the head of the small publishing company had, during this conversation, reached a new plateau of boredom, so that she was on the brink of embarking on a course of action beyond her usual range? Or that she had become, despite everything, interested? I was forced to hold this thought at bay, as the head of the small publishing company's face indicated he required a response—he still had not mentioned the name Solomon Wiese—and I provided a statement neither so specific as to betray my inattention, nor so broad as to seem evasive, and in the opening that followed I took my opportunity and glanced at the head of the small publishing company's wife. It was as I suspected. Her gaze was not cast towards the grey surface of the river, or at the distant attractions arrayed on its far bank, but hovered instead in the region of my left shoulder, possibly around the collar of my shirt. All of this would have been enough to ensure that my attention to the head of the small publishing company, and the drift of his argument, as I understood it, on the noticeable lapse in quality of literary production over the past half decade, was thoroughly dispersed, but there was a further prelude to come, before his announcement of the name Solomon Wiese in connection with a recent publishing scandal. As the wife of the head of the small publishing company met my gaze with a frank expression, which seemed to herald a remark, the details of which I wouldn't discover, there was a movement to my right that drew my attention away from her and her husband. Who knows how it is that we can identify, in a large and fairly complex field of activity, the small events that pertain to us—the stare of a rival, or the movements surrounding a friend's departure. All I was really aware of at first was a faint, streamlined motion, and, dragging my eyes away from the head of the small publishing company, I was able to pick out the head of my ex-girlfriend, Genia Friend, in the company of her new partner, a burly, reticent South African named Piet Durcan. The angle was such that I could only see their heads gliding above a bar of speckled granite as they paced along a pedestrian ramp on the outside of the Royal Festival Hall, but I could guess from their trajectory that they, or perhaps Genia Friend alone, had already spotted me where I was standing in the relative calm of the riverside seating area, and without mentioning it had adjusted their passage through the crowd so as to avoid a meeting. Somehow I knew it was the last time I would see either of them. It was at this moment that the head of the small publishing company uttered the name Solomon Wiese. Something about the name, its melodiousness, its minor alterity, brought me back to the conversation, and, the heads of my ex-girlfriend and her companion having scudded from view, I indicated with an expectant expression and slight shake of my head that I was unfamiliar with the name, or the story he was referring to, or both. At least that was the impression that I gave to the head of the small publishing company—but in fact the name Solomon Wiese *was* familiar to me. As an editor at a mid-circulation literary magazine I made it my business—I was professionally compelled to make it my business—to stay abreast of all important and seemingly unimportant developments in the literary sphere: the prizes and grants, but also any deficit of prizes and grants, the reviews and mentions, but also the lack of reviews and mentions, the names that appeared in journals and magazines, and also their casual or calculated omission, the recipients of bursaries and residencies, as well as those who had been passed over, in other words all the appointments and expulsions, feuds and alliances, coronations, cancellations, deaths, debuts, all those who had been overlooked and all those who had been over-rewarded, not to mention the force and temperature of the various currents of favour and fatigue, and although I couldn't place the name Solomon Wiese precisely, as I waited for the head of the small publishing company to resume his explanation and reveal to me the pertinence of it, I was reasonably certain I had seen it featured on the tables of contents of several journals over the past eight or nine months. The aura of the name was that of a *new talent*, I felt sure, and which on a second or third sighting I had informally flagged, although not in a way I would describe as completely conscious. In any case, I wasn't familiar with Solomon Wiese's actual output, if indeed he was a writer worth investigating—the name had not gained sufficient shine for that—or of the difficult situation he was involved in, which the head of the small publishing company had just alluded to. The impression I gave to the head of the small publishing company, that the name and circumstances of Solomon Wiese were entirely unknown to me, was, then, only partly inaccurate, but the fact that I had volunteered my lack of knowledge so automatically gives some sense of my professional reflexes, and their essentially defensive or strategic function—if in doubt, at these kinds of events, I always claimed that I knew nothing, I shrugged, I waved my head, unless I forgot for a moment that despite the friendly, if unemphatic, tone of my conversation with the head of the small publishing company, we were representatives of rival organisations, meeting on the field of action with the purpose of exchanging tactical information. In other words, a game of incredibly low stakes was taking place, but in this case the lowness of the stakes only made the players keener and more ruthless in their conduct—this ruthlessness was a given, we both understood, a principle of the industry, and the centre that we vied around. It was wise of me not to betray any excessive curiosity about Solomon Wiese to the head of the small publishing company—my editor's autopilot was working correctly in that respect—unless he became aware, mistakenly or otherwise, of the value of the particular chip he was handling, and took it into his head to demand a higher price for its transfer. Either that, or he may simply have enjoyed toying with it in front of me, weighing it, withholding it—and if there was one thing I wanted to avoid during the course of my encounter with the head of the small publishing company, and which my slightly studied uninterest was calculated to circumvent, it was giving him the opportunity of extracting any more pleasure from the exchange than the bare minimum I could allow him. I had him where I wanted him, more or less—I had had him there for several years, and I wasn't interested in relinquishing a millimetre of my advantage. He had been the one to approach me, in the outdoor seating area on the South Bank beside the Royal Festival Hall, he had addressed me, he had done the talking, and I had listened, or feigned to listen, and I didn't plan on giving him anything more than he had come to expect. My indifference had to be more or less perfect. So I was careful how I treated his mention of the name Solomon Wiese, and while waiting for him to furnish me with the relevant facts, I tried to shore up my position by reminding myself what the head of the small publishing company had been saying while I had been preoccupied, firstly with his wife's behaviour, then the arrival and departure of Genia Friend and her companion, the taciturn South African, Piet Durcan, who I now remembered ran an artisanal business, roasting ethically sourced coffee beans. I should make it clear that we were gathered on the South Bank, next to the Royal Festival Hall, myself, the head of the small publishing company, his wife, and several thousand other participants in the arts, to celebrate the biennial Festival of Culture. Our formation of three was positioned close to the heart of the Literature Zone, adjacent to both the Theatre and Performance Zone, centred around the King George Hall, a hundred metres or so to the east, and the Visual Arts Zone, using as its base of operations the Hayward Gallery, which stood within eyeshot, through a crush of stairways and mezzanines set back from the river—it was in that direction that Genia Friend and her companion, the South African roaster, had disappeared. Hordes of people of all ages, enthusiasts and producers of culture both, moved through this scene at a dazed pace, taking their positions at pastel-coloured tables and chairs, where they drank coffees, teas, beers, juices and shakes, or ate tacos, hotdogs, soufflé pancakes, banh mi and bento from biodegradable packaging. Festival of Culture was here. A blimp turned faithfully overhead, with the new logo on it. There was some truth, I reflected, in the head of the small publishing company's earlier statement, that a crisis of confidence had emerged, here in the heart of the Literature Zone, so to speak, over the past couple of years: that a fever, felt only at the fringes to begin with, had swept in from those marginal, outlying territories of the art form, populated by antagonists and outcasts whose theories occasionally gained low-level support before being pitilessly extinguished by the rational majority—but in this instance the idea, or feeling, had taken hold, and gone on to infect the industry at large with a widespread, debilitating anxiety. This nervous mood had simmered away for months, increasing in potency, until it was reborn as a discreet but total state of alarm. Barely acknowledged within the sector's working environments, it nonetheless had begun to exert a powerful, unseen influence on the day-to-day choices of its operatives. This heightened atmosphere was one of uncommunicated insecurity, even paranoia, meaning that beginning from the bottom, with the junior editors, slush pile readers, publisher's assistants and reviewers for mid-circulation journals, belief in the established standards and practices of the industry had begun rapidly to wane—many literary agents and editors ceased, almost overnight in some cases, to vouch for their own judgements, and when these key negotiators turned for support to their colleagues and associates, or to such benchmarks as provided by their previous deals, or other trade success stories, which usually could be counted on to have a steadying effect, those cornerstones, rather than meeting them with reassurance and solidity, turned out to be entirely insubstantial, their elbows passed straight through, and down they went. Of course, these individuals, the assistant editors and up-and-coming junior agents, the interns and first readers, were confident young men and women, employed to an extent on the basis of their capacity for certainty, and products in many cases of elite educational institutions—if they trusted in anything at all it was in their own faculties and their ability to make judgements. They had always known what they were looking for, or they had known it when they saw it. But now a fissure of doubt had opened, and they were no longer certain they knew what they were looking for, whether they would recognise it when they saw it, or if they had missed it, and it had already passed them by. They began making tentative enquiries to their colleagues and associates, and were relieved to discover, having endured a certain amount of pretence, that their colleagues and associates found themselves in a similar predicament. It was simply not believable, they felt, that their gifts could have deserted them—the fault must lie, they felt, when they met to talk about this, as they began to, on high stools at city pubs after work, sliding their microbrews and almost spherical glasses of wine agitatedly on the table tops, with the material itself. The problem had to be with the material they were handling, they decided—something had changed, something fundamental—and so they passed it on: they passed it up, in other words, to higher stations, to the floors above, the inboxes of senior editors, to offices with tall windows and views of the grey and green squares of the city, to persons whose names were debossed on paperwork and on metallic signs above the brown brick doorways. They knew that the owners and senior actors of these companies were not as assured as was widely believed—they appeared that way when they were glimpsed in the windows of a restaurant, having one of their famous lunches, or lifting a pen behind an antique desk, but in reality much was projection, much was illusion. The circumstances of these appointments were labyrinthine, concerning many disparate, interested and invested parties, the result of delicate, shadowy calibrations, and frequently passage to those high-ceilinged offices did not lead through broad daylight. Once their junior staff, tier by tier, had begun to furtively evade responsibility in the decision-making process, which often required only a touch of finessing at the final stage, once deprived of those systems of consensus, whose key posts they started to find unresponsive at the moment they appealed to them, many of those at the pinnacles of these companies panicked. A flurry of rash decisions followed—some stalled, entering a state of paralysis from which they didn't emerge, even as the floors below them descended into chaos; others attempted to deflect the blame, and became ensnared before long by their own duplicity; still others embarked on strategies to protect the public face of their interests, and insisted in all dealings on presenting the semblance of control. It was this last tactic that led to the worst disasters, in the form of a series of discoveries, staggered over two or three weeks in the spring, during which the story dominated all platforms as it entered an annihilating spiral that was willed to completion by various orders of the commentariat, that two of the main commercial houses had been proven to have released several *fixed books*, that is, to have sold, as new, publications that were revealed to be reprints of earlier publications, with minimal changes implemented to disguise this fact. Typically locations and names were switched, titles and authors were of course replaced, while the rest of the content and structure remained intact. The supposedly culpable parties, when they were unearthed in their buildings, admitted before the banks of media that they had undertaken this admittedly extreme and reckless course of action only to tide things over while the market endured its most troubled and unpredictable period in recent history. These hastily summoned apologists, with their calm willingness to shoulder the blame, were regarded as unconvincing and inadequate sacrificial offerings by most onlookers, and so, on an unforeseen scale, every aspect of the industry's architecture came under intense scrutiny; every major player in the field received challenges to redress and redesign, as shockwaves moved up and down the once proud edifices of publishing, shaking loose careers and reputations. Heads, like they say, began to roll—the heads of the highest-paid agents, for example, and the heads of company heads—heads fell from the windows of the Big Four—from the top of the tree, for weeks, it rained heads. Finally, those that were left in the emptied towers of the once great houses began to regroup, to organise themselves. They met after dark in curtained rooms, for hour after hour, and eventually they mounted their response. The reading public—they wrote in a collection of statements, echoing each other, and released simultaneously by representatives of all the implicated bodies—the reading public was exhausted and frustrated by the whole affair, they were bored, in fact, by the tiresome continuation of the crisis beyond a point that was meaningful or helpful. Terrible mistakes had been made, but it was now time to draw a line under this regrettable period and to start afresh. For that to happen, in a way that would begin to rebuild the reading public's trust, to allow them to read with confidence, certain of the industry's integrity, measures had to be taken. What they proposed was this. They—and by "they," they meant a panel selected by a coalition of the main publishing houses' PR departments—had been working in collaboration with a team of software engineers on a technological solution to the crisis. The team of engineers was nearing the completion of a programme that they—the select panel—believed would have wonderful, recuperating effects on the devastated marketplace. Working from the latest developments in plagiarism detection services, the team of engineers had constructed a tool that made all previous plagiarism detection services resemble child's play sets—that was the claim. Not only would this programme be able to recognise and match any extended sequence of words and phrases in the submitted document with those contained in an existing publication, but, using quantitative analysis and comparison of a sophistication hitherto not imagined, it would be possible to identify such features as the machinations of plot, the structural dynamics of narrative and perspective, the balancing of metaphor and the density of descriptive language, tactics of rhetoric such as repetition, assonance, anaphora and apostrophe, the intersecting arcs of major and minor characters and the patterns of their outcomes, the pacing and delivery of dialogue, the physical laws of fantastic worlds, chronological distortions, and even the biologies of imaginary creatures. They also had in their sights that most elusive quality, the *style* of the work, which would be objectively defined at last, locked down, taking into account the frequency and emphasis of specific words, the frequency and emphasis of specific sounds, and perhaps even—the engineers refused for now to be drawn on this point—the indivisible emotional components, below the surface, underpinning everything. So that what the programme would arrive at, by logging all of these variables and myriad others, over a plethora of categories and sub-categories, was a complete taxonomy of every literary publication in the language, graphed every which way, testable through any metric, readable along any axis, displayed in colour-coded charts or sharp monotone grids, as the viewer preferred. A friendly dialogue between two sworn enemies. Business failure prompting a descent into criminality. Children who die in the first twenty pages. Descriptions of the light in western Scotland. Easter as the story's climactic and final date. Friendships resulting from traffic accidents. Giant plants. Historical figures crossdressing. Isolated pieces of luck. Junkyards as hideouts. The knocking-out of the narrator by an unknown assailant. Lavish descriptions of feasts. Mythical creatures malevolent in appearance yet well intentioned. Northern European cities as honeymoon destinations. Open wounds infested with maggots. Purple garments. Questions directed to an artificial intelligence. Risky bridge captures. Sex in bathrooms. The betrayal of a king by his nephew. Uses of time travel to investigate ambiguous parentage. Visions of the Christ child. Worlds with three or more moons. Xenophobic shopkeepers. Yellow-haired villains. Zoo as principal setting. And so on. We are able to apprehend, the statement continued, for the first time, an absolutely individual fingerprint, the *soul* of the book, and with this wonderful tool we will strive to ensure that no work is brought before the paying public that runs the risk of being exposed as a sham, a copy, on any level a fraudulent document. This kind of deception is at an end, the originality of the author enshrined, placed once again at the centre of the enterprise which we each still live to serve. Signed, yours faithfully, etc. Further to this grandiose announcement, the replacement heads of the large publishing companies, in their wisdom, opted to house their plagiarism detection programme, or a visual representation thereof, in a highly visible city location, in fact on the site of some disused cash machines along the Strand, making it a kind of monument: a reflective metal globe with serrated discs, lit up inside a glass box, to serve as a reminder, they said in the press release, for the industry and all its employees. The effects of this were easy to predict, and indeed were predicted by many invested outlets and individual commentators—having gathered up the blame, the strange nervousness and fear of that time, as if into a dark cloud of apocalyptic width, the old houses and agencies were now able to cast it down, like rain, upon the authors. The uproar was immediate. Criticism and condemnation rose on all sides. The new measures meant *authors* would be punished for the mistakes of the publishers. *Authors* were to be made scapegoats for the incompetence of editors. *Authors* would be victimised by this rigorous programme of testing, while the industry evaded responsibility. Piece after piece was written on this theme, the plight of the authors. But the data analysts were not as clunky or literal in their endeavours as many would have guessed. They had anticipated the reaction and were ready with their counter-argument—a manuscript, they said, would not be purged by publishing's new oracle for simply quoting an existing work, obviously. Neither would it be penalised for making use of the deep structures of a mythological source, or the rhyme scheme of a forgotten poem, or deploying many of the popular devices of literature widely considered available for use—choices that no lawyer versed sensibly in copyright law would be willing to prosecute. This had all been factored into the programming. Anyway, it was clearly not in their interests to seize up literary production for any longer than necessary. An agreement was reached that a submitted document must achieve a score of ninety-six per cent or more, across its listed categories, in order to qualify as unacceptably derivative. This sounded high to everyone, and was duly confirmed as the new industry standard. It was against this backdrop that Solomon Wiese's predicament had to be understood—events that still loomed large enough for everyone in the industry to be preoccupied with them. The fallout hadn't much affected the head of the small publishing company, who, like me, was a long way down the food chain. But as a poet still at the start of his emergence, months before either myself or the head of the small publishing company had heard or uttered his name, Solomon Wiese had been *directly penalised* by the recently implemented machine testing, in the freezing first weeks of the year, for the submission of a manuscript, a poem of some length, if the head of the small publishing house was to be believed, to some or other peer-reviewed journal. It had returned a score of ninety-six, on the nose, was rejected by the system, and the name Solomon Wiese subsequently *grey-listed*, in other words recorded in the annals that were accessible only to employees of the main houses and agencies, who now received log-in details the morning they commenced their employment. Solomon Wiese's long poem was not the first literary work to be found in breach of the introduced standards, as even in the extreme infancy of compulsory machine testing, its confidential files were crammed with names of would-be authors and the details of their infractions, their *crimes against originality*. It may seem bizarre, to those uninformed of recent developments in literary publishing, that a poem was subjected to such intense scrutiny, when the commercial return on such a product was ordinarily so slender—but one outcome of the industry-wide crisis of confidence was a wholesale re-mapping of the landscape, an unanticipated side effect of which was the surprising rise in stock in works of poetry—the reading public turned to them, it seemed, as if they harboured some innate form of truth that works of fiction, or drama, or even biography and autobiography, were unable to convey. Faith in these popular genres had been eroded to such a point, I reminded myself, that *even poetry* had become preferable to them. In this assumption the reading public was of course gravely mistaken, as poetry possessed precisely as much, or as little, direct relation to the truth as any commercially produced memoir or openly fantastical fiction—perhaps it was actually less truthful, in that its producers were by and large aware of the misconception of its new audience, which gathered in droves to purchase and read aloud from their publications, and did nothing to correct it, but instead traded on this expectation in the most cynical way imaginable. I state this as an enthusiast of the form, who has benefitted directly from its change in fortunes, in that the little magazine I run is concerned mainly with the state of the eldest of the literary arts. It will sound astonishing, perhaps, to those unaware of the vicissitudes of literary fashion, its tenacity when it latches on to a trend, but in these altered conditions, poets were making real money. Poetry was flooding the market. There were *rich poets*, suddenly—to some this was a terrifying prospect. I should clarify that when I stated that the likes of the head of the small publishing company and myself were not much affected by the fallout from the crisis, that is not entirely accurate—clearly we were caught up in the public mood, we were as susceptible as anyone to the highs of righteous accusation, the exhilarating prospect of seeing old oppressors toppled, and positioned in the lower rows were well placed to enjoy the spectacle. When the changes came, we were jostled slightly by the shifting ranks above us, but more important, when we looked around, we realised our worth as editors had grown in ways we couldn't have anticipated, as the reading public flocked to our publications and back catalogues for a dose of whatever indefinable thing it was they felt they'd been denied or cheated out of. Perhaps this makes it more understandable why Solomon Wiese had been drawn to poetry as his medium of expression, and why he was willing to risk his burgeoning reputation by submitting a manuscript of questionable origin, knowing the stringent procedures it would be subjected to. Anyway, the consequences were serious for anyone who found themselves in his position—a *grey-listed author* wasn't prohibited from publishing exactly, but was treated with caution by those with access to the ever-expanding spreadsheets produced by quantitative analysis and comparison. This information was supposed to be restricted to the few with a professional interest, but the social life of the industry being what it is—there were promises to decentralise post-crisis, but it is still concentrated in a small quarter of the capital—the results were broadcast across face-to-face networks without restraint, effectively becoming an open secret. Most likely, this was why I had recognised the name Solomon Wiese when the head of the small publishing company had mentioned it. The frequency of the leaks became widely known, and at around this time requests were made for the technology to become available to all—in short, that is what transpired: for a small fee, anyone whose lack of access to the quantitative analysis and comparison system (QACS) could be demonstrated to unfairly disadvantage their editorial practice would be granted a one-use passcode upon request. In reality this meant the doors were flung open, as the prospective user required only the most perfunctory reason—a claim to be researching an article was sufficient—and even this safeguard was relaxed as the profit-making ability of the system became apparent. Solomon Wiese had, in the meantime, adapted his approach, as the head of the small publishing company continued to explain to me. He had gone quiet in the wake of his humbling by the industry's new defences, and when he re-emerged some months later, at the start of this summer, he was no longer presenting his work in the form of written manuscripts at all, or submitting them to this or that literary journal, and therefore exposing them to the scrutiny of the quantitative analysis and comparison system (QACS). No one had seen so much as a page of writing attributed to Solomon Wiese since his penalisation at the start of the year, nor would they, despite the levels of notoriety he went on to achieve, the head of the small publishing company continued. Solomon Wiese's significant innovation, when he re-emerged from his informal period of exile, was that he appeared onstage without notes, and simply began speaking—speaking spontaneously, he insisted, not according to a memorised script like an actor, or from a series of prompts scrawled on his hand like a comedian, or from a pre-prepared piece of rhymed doggerel—no, he simply began to speak, sometimes pausing for longish periods, the head of the small publishing company said, then continuing in a distinct although soft and restless voice; he would speak for about ten minutes, and the things he said, the head of the small publishing company believed, having attended one of these recitals only a few weeks ago, were in every way definable as *genuine poetry*. Didn't I feel, the head of the small publishing company suddenly enquired, with a quiver of excitement in his voice I hadn't heard before, that for a long time now, since before the crisis perhaps, there had been *no poetry*, as it were, *in* the poetry? That it was possible to believe, when we swiped through the pages of the journals and magazines, or studied an image of a book jacket that a friend had posted, or browsed a table of contents full of names we recognised, that we were in the vicinity of poetry, that we were in a *poetry area*, but on almost every occasion it turned out that there was actually *no poetry* there after all. Like a smell, it was either there or it wasn't, the head of the small publishing company said. For a long time now there had been *no poetry in the poetry*, that was his view—there we all were, standing around expecting poetry to be served to us through the usual outlets, but instead we were served up some kind of imitation of poetry—we were served faux poetry, we were served *fauxetry*, the head of the small publishing company said. We had been left unsatisfied, we could admit, surely, by this thin material that was served up to us in the name of poetry. Surely we could admit to each other now that the so-called poetry of the last five or ten years had only left us confused and disappointed, the head of the small publishing company said. Even if what the head of the small publishing company claimed was familiar to me—and in some senses I actually agreed with him—there was nothing I could do at this point except gently demur. Agreeing with the head of the small publishing company would mean losing a fraction of my advantage—so I explained to him with a certain meticulousness that, on the contrary, we had to admit, surely, that everything was relative, and that a compelling or even life-changing poem to one reader was quite possibly a worthless piece of drivel to the next, and that our endeavours as editors were directed only towards making the possibility of that compelling or life-changing experience available to our readers, not because we underwent it with every poem we selected for publication—very far from it—but because we sensed, somehow, and this was our special expertise, the potential for it in the work—it was like intuiting the depth of a body of water, or the altitude of an aircraft, it was almost instinct by now, and that was what we were paid for, wasn't it? That is what I said to the head of the small publishing company, and I impressed us both, I thought, with the force of my contention. Perhaps it wasn't surprising that for us, I went on, reading as we did endless reams of works of such varying interest and quality that they blurred like the surface of a road into a kind of sameness, for long stretches of time, perhaps for years, we operated entirely on this hunch without really understanding or feeling anything towards any of the pieces we were choosing for wider distribution—we simply *tapped* them, as one would *tap* a vase one was considering for purchase, or as one would *tap* a section of wall where one was considering hanging a picture, to see if they in any way resonated—and this was enough, this was all that was expected. Then I said to the head of the small publishing company that I thought he sounded disillusioned, partly to recover my poise, as I felt that I had veered towards impassioned over-explication, possibly. Having re-emerged at the start of the summer, Solomon Wiese had quickly gained notoriety as a performer—rather than responding, the head of the small publishing company simply continued with his narrative as if I hadn't said anything—his audiences in the capital were enthralled, the head of the small publishing company said, whether at the literary soirees or rowdier cabaret evenings, and some went to see him night after night, telling anyone who'd listen that no two performances were identical or even similar, and though some particular phrases might recur, some said, this seemed unpredictable, even exhilarating. It wasn't an improvisation act or anything so crass, these new enthusiasts of Solomon Wiese's poetry insisted, really it was a new order of creativity. It was another beginning, unconfined by the genre divisions that had riven the literary community time and again, year after year, the enthusiasts of Solomon Wiese's poetry said. The head of the small publishing company had his own theory, which he offered to share with me, if I thought I'd find it interesting—I made a gesture of acquiescence—that Solomon Wiese's ascent to prominence on the literary and performance circuits over the summer was precisely *due* to the fragmented condition of the arts, their splintering into mutually hostile encampments that sought only to determine their own sovereignty after the painful moment of separation. These divisions had resulted in several open channels, the head of the small publishing company had hypothesised, which would allow certain practitioners to proceed rapidly along the lines of breakage, towards maximum exposure, if they discovered a form or medium with the necessary ingredients for transit. One could speculate on the specifics, but a degree of populism seemed to be necessary. The head of the small publishing company had theorised all this previously, he said, but until recently he had never seen it happen. Discovering this hidden trajectory would endow the artist with a sort of irresistible speed, he said, and this was connected to the expedients of fame, probably. The breaking apart of the arts, the head of the small publishing company continued, had reached a point where each discipline had become a lonely, self-defining island, governed by a spirit of insularity, floating without moorings in little or no relation to its siblings. This isn't how things were in the classical periods that had produced the great, lasting works, he said, and for him the market was to blame. It was down to the atomising logic of the economy, he thought, regrettably. Occasionally one of these islands passed within sight of another, but even that event had become a rarity. Now they had drifted apart so far that the gaps between them had reached the stage of becoming navigable pathways, a kind of no-man's-land, cleared of any traffic—this is how he visualised it, the head of the small publishing company said, he hoped I didn't mind but he had ended up using a kind of shipping metaphor. Large vessels could now be steered along these routes, drawing crowds from the banks on either side to marvel at their progress—if I could envisage what he meant. Solomon Wiese had located just such a pathway, the head of the small publishing company thought, between the disciplines, and had attracted just the sort of cross-party support he would have predicted, had he known how to set his theory into action. But people, at least people in this country, can't stomach too much acclaim, the head of the small publishing company added. It doesn't take very long at all before any earnest attempt to celebrate a writer and their work draws its gang of detractors, who insist on spreading doubt and cynicism among the audience. They move intently through the crowd, brandishing their message, and soon they begin to influence small groups, who in turn affect the opinions of larger, looser groups, and then even casual observers, who, in their innocence, might admit to *quite liking* the work of a specific performer, would witness the expressions of their friends darken sardonically—no more needed to be said. Like an army abruptly changing allegiance, the colours of the spectators thronged along the banks, moments ago held there in admiration of the otherworldly music emanating from the passing craft, switched to their opposite, they showed their backs or jeered, their fond excitement not even a memory. But, in reality, they had only cheated themselves, the head of the small publishing company reflected sadly. They had crushed a small, sputtering joy that only the true, spontaneous artistic expression could have coaxed to life within them, in just a ten-minute window, in a dim room above a pub, for example, filled for the most part with people who had just finished shifts at the surrounding offices, in their jobs at tech start-ups, advertising agencies, at design companies, in marketing and public relations—an upstairs room with grimy lamps, in the heart of the content sector. His lament had reached a natural pause and the head of the small publishing company looked past me for a moment, towards the city, I supposed, or across the river, where panels of colourless light had settled, fluctuating with the current, as the afternoon wore on. His wife had relented and was stroking the screen of her phone. Obviously people had taken the opportunity to record Solomon Wiese's performances, the head of the small publishing company continued, whether out of sincere enthusiasm or with entrepreneurial intentions, these days it was hard to distinguish, and either way it was unavoidable; probably several hundred recordings existed of the thirty or so performances given by Solomon Wiese in, say, a nine-week period over the summer, all backed up by now in the data cloud, thereby leaving their indelible trace on the cultural record, and retrievable for the rest of history—barring a large-scale technological disaster, the head of the small publishing company added wistfully. Somebody, or a group of people, had begun compiling footage of Solomon Wiese's performances, he said, perhaps for the enjoyment of viewers outside the capital, or perhaps a few of his followers had got together and decided they wanted to compare each of his performances in depth, to see how much they differed from one another. This compilation of thirty-plus performances, which showed Solomon Wiese appearing before the audiences of the literary and performance circuit, in a series of similar-looking event spaces, always unencumbered by notes or devices, was posted and widely shared, and at some point soon afterwards the montage was transcribed in full, perhaps several times, resulting in a document, or several documents, differing according to the transcription software used, or the diligence of the transcriber. These were also made publicly available through file-sharing services, each version representing a slightly mutated rendering of the source video—and after *that* happened, it was probably only a matter of time before somebody was willing to stump up the fee, perhaps out of simple curiosity or perhaps out of a sense of mischief, to submit one or more of these documents to the quantitative analysis and comparison system (QACS), either sharing the results themselves, or passing the key data breakdowns on to someone with more of an appetite for public intervention. It had all come out ten or so days ago, the head of the small publishing company said—ninety-eight per cent derivative, that was the verdict. The response from the creative community, which had tended towards a more understanding or forgiving attitude when the revelations dispensed by the quantitative analysis and comparison system (QACS) were restricted to industry insiders, this time was acrimonious and immediate. Now that the tools of exposure were in the hands of the consumer, even on a pay-per-use basis, they felt outrage in earnest, on their own behalf, rather than half-heartedly, on behalf of the monetisers. Many felt they had been cheated, misled, duped, exploited, deceived, personally wounded and so on, and the excitement around Solomon Wiese, his relatively mild claim to innovation, was transmuted instantly into its inverse—it was as if on a given day a single voice, resonating with inner fury, began to speak, passing its condemnation upon the poet, its steely tones replicated in the commentary of all who weighed in—and there were many—as they demanded apologies, response, recompense, consequences. Exactly what form these reprisals should take created energetic division among the commentators, all of whom were incensed by Solomon Wiese's activities, either because they had attended his performances themselves and issued recommendations to their friends and listeners, and now had been made to appear ridiculous or undiscerning, or because they felt indignation on behalf of those who had, the head of the small publishing company assumed. All agreed the punishment should be tailored to fit the offence, and each suggestion that emerged was more ingenious in its irony than the last, vengeance was succeeded by ever more refined vengeance, focusing and refocusing, until the public voice of condemnation formed a perfect needle of instrumental hatred, which hovered, trembling, over the name Solomon Wiese. Curiously, a relatively small number of those who voiced these opinions, among them the most avid campaigners for specific penalties to be visited upon Solomon Wiese's person, seemed particularly interested in or even aware of his previous successes, the head of the small publishing company said. But it was the *lack of respect* and *callous manipulation* of his supporters by Solomon Wiese that they objected to, and—they were quick to point this out—they would have pounced on this kind of behaviour wherever they observed it. In this fraught atmosphere, the actual infringements of Solomon Wiese's work were all but forgotten—that was what interested me the most, rather than the specifics of Solomon Wiese's fate, which the head of the small publishing company probably imagined he was detaining me with. I almost expected him to break off his narration before revealing that crowning detail, in fact. Although our mutual antagonism had remained veiled, I'd noted his growing confidence, and I anticipated an ambush of some kind before we parted. It was getting late. We had both missed opportunities to connect with other figures from our networks, some of whom had been hovering nearby at various intervals during the afternoon, and I had to leave soon for another appointment, so I risked asking the head of the small publishing company about the details of Solomon Wiese's infringements. The monologues appeared to have lifted entire passages verbatim, completely uncredited, he said, from several authors, but these sources were not at all well known—in fact, most of those involved in the public remonstrance had disregarded this information when they realised they had no idea if the wronged persons were living or dead, but—and here the head of the small publishing company drew his head closer to mine—mostly they were living. They were mostly living authors, obscure, yes, old in some cases, yes, but in most cases very much *still around*. Requests for comment had been made, the head of the small publishing company said. It was time to make my excuses. I registered the head of the small publishing company's pained expression—I was leaving without hearing the conclusion of the affair, but at that moment it didn't interest me what specific punishment was currently being demanded for the poet Solomon Wiese, and my refusal, at the final moment, reset our relationship to its proper imbalance. He couldn't touch me. I said goodbye to his wife and left owing him nothing. My route took me eastward, along the river, the same unresponsive grey, despite the late sun angling its thick beams from behind me. I had been invited to the twenty-sixth Festival of Culture to fulfil a number of duties, and the most pressing now lay ahead of me: the recital of some poems, in translation, by the Ukrainian poet, essayist and broadcaster Zariyah Zhadan, before an audience of several hundred at the King George Hall. Zariyah Zhadan had been booked to recite her poems in the original Ukrainian, and her animated performance style was to provide the conclusion to the evening, which featured a number of other controversial or politically sensitive writers, paired with authors and editors who had either translated their works or published them in English—which is what I had done, selecting five of Zariyah Zhadan's poems for appearance in the spring issue of *Casement*. The event had been thrown into disarray by news I had received earlier in the afternoon from the organisers, via email, that Zariyah Zhadan would be unable to attend, as she had been detained by authorities at Heathrow early that morning, for reasons that couldn't be specified, word of which had only just reached them. So I would be reciting the poems of the outspoken Ukrainian poet *alone* onstage at the King George Hall, where I would be expected to in some way embody the work's political efficacy, in front of an audience of close to a thousand spectators, who were eager to soak up statements of political dissent, particularly when targeted at a regime that is portrayed across our media as violently repressive and dangerously corrupt, in this case that of the Russian government. What purpose did it serve, I wondered as I passed a food stand selling savoury Brazilian pastries, to read out these works—undoubtedly deeply felt, terrifying and hilarious works of poetry—first in translation, so lacking the reference points and natural medium of their own language, and second for the applause of a comfortable audience, on a clement early autumn weeknight, in the centre of London? A trip out to a thoroughly respectable cultural event and a glass of wine afterwards—wasn't this kind of thing simply assisting our own complacency and impotence, I thought as I shouldered through a group of teenagers carrying skateboards on the South Bank, dramatising in the guise of a worthy literary event a power struggle from the seemingly distant arena of post-Soviet politics, and basically celebrating our distance from it, thereby completely ignoring our own situation? Might this spectacle just as well be completely made up, set on Mars, for example, featuring a race of reptilian humanoids, for all the impact it would have? Hadn't the poetry of Zariyah Zhadan been converted, in these palatial buildings, with their lighting rigs and sound systems and multilevel restaurant and bar facilities, seamlessly into inoffensive, or even officially mandated, entertainment? I didn't know, and I didn't really care—I recognised these thoughts as displaced anxiety about the performance. But it was true that I had considered them earlier in the day, too, running over several possible critiques that could be mounted of the event, a habit I'd formed years ago, like many in the literary sector, of having to imaginatively justify my activities to a zealous and politically astute cabinet of observers. Certain friends, certain acquaintances and certain enemies sat in this imaginary boardroom. They presented the facts about the occasion, interpreting them in terms of my personal gains, weighing this against the benefits to others and the larger community, often zoning in on aspects of the situation that precisely *appeared* to benefit others and the larger community, but in actuality benefitted mainly myself, not least through contribution to my public image as someone sensitive to the predicaments of those less fortunate, in the creative sphere, at least. When a critique of this sort came from one corner of the imaginary council, it would be met with something like the following, from the opposite wing: to a person actuated by self-interest, any attempt at altruism, that is, at assisting others or the larger community, however indirectly, will always appear self-serving and performative, in the final analysis—and the real tragedy was that this cynicism was itself capable of thwarting *genuine* attempts at assisting others or the larger community, out of fear that such an action would be interpreted only as cynical, performative and self-serving by the host of onlookers whose attention we could take for granted. Then a third voice would speak up, from somewhere in the middle of the boardroom, pointing out that this cynicism, if it could fairly be described as such, was clearly not as effective a deterrent as the last speaker insisted, as everywhere one looked there were advantaged idiots with nothing but the best intentions, in other words the *appropriators of worthy causes*, who whatever their aspirations always ended up controlling the agenda in the most clueless way imaginable, dominating the discussion and transforming it into a dialogue fit only for idiots and poseurs, so that in the end with their sheer cluelessness and idiocy they did far more harm than good to the cause they thought they were supporting—because anyone they were unable to dictate to, in other words anyone not prepared to be ruled by blind idiocy, was quickly driven away by their sheer cluelessness. In other words it was of no consequence how genuine or well-meaning these people were, the third voice went on, as that in itself was no guarantee of the virtuousness of their actions. These people had started out as astute and insightful commentators, in some instances, but as soon as they had achieved a certain level of visibility and success it was as if their stances on these issues, however legitimate and well-meaning, were revealed overnight as being misguided or deluded versions of themselves. Now that their opinions were no longer remarks made from the side-lines, the third voice continued, but were examples of established opinion, which had never had to withstand the sort of critique they themselves in the past had aimed at other examples of established opinion, it turned out they were not particularly resilient or well-formed after all, and a multitude of inconsistencies were immediately exposed by the first salvos of their opponents. So the question remained, in the imaginary boardroom—namely, was my publishing and reciting of poems by the Ukrainian poet and political commentator Zariyah Zhadan *objectively speaking* in the service of others and the larger community, *or* was my publishing and reciting of these poems merely in service of my own reputation—in which case I was doing nothing but appropriating Zariyah Zhadan and her works in the fortifying of my own egotistical brand? And this I couldn't answer. I had already admitted to some scepticism about the event itself, with regard to the composition and receptivity of the audience, and so I couldn't pretend to myself that I was acting entirely in the service of the public good, that is, in the interests of others and the larger community, and the idea that I *could* pretend made me extremely uncomfortable. Because if I allowed myself to believe for a second I was acting for the public good, it was as if the taint of egomania became even more unbearably apparent—as if by denying personal gain as the reason for my actions, it was suddenly revealed as the decisive element. Pitted against this suddenly—from a new voice on the back row of the imaginary boardroom—came the idealistic possibility, often cited by poets themselves, of there being in the audience *one* listener on whom the poems did their work—the archetypal *one* young person, appearing at the ideal moment of ripeness and impressionability—as surely the possibility of inspiring such a person would justify everything. But I had to accept that the steep price of the tickets made this an extreme unlikelihood. The audience would be mainly in their fifties and sixties, their responses dulled by rich food and wine to a low-level brain murmur, so the words of Zariyah Zhadan in English translation would become abstract patterns even as I spoke them, dissolving into the air as soon as they were registered. In all probability, the event would attract to Zariyah Zhadan's writing no new readers. The attendees would remember little of the evening other than a warm feeling of *having listened*, forgetting the deep boredom they experienced as it was actually happening. And Zariyah Zhadan herself wouldn't be there to soak up the applause for the sake of her own enjoyment either. But equally—came a supportive voice from an area near the front of the imaginary boardroom—the disagreeable nature of the ordeal now in front of me, that is, of standing up in the spotlight and announcing Zariyah Zhadan's words, rendered satisfactorily or perhaps not-so-satisfactorily in English, would seem to discount the possibility I was acting mainly out of self-interest, with an eye on inflating my self-esteem and public profile. I was honestly dreading the performance, and took no pleasure in appearing in the public eye. Wasn't I, then, in my willingness to sacrifice my own emotional well-being, devoting myself in a real sense to the poet herself? Wasn't I forgetting my own reputation and my own discomfort to honour with a defiant gesture of support a writer from a foreign state, engaged in a significant conflict—and didn't this basic integrity underlying the event have some bearing on the value of my actions? But I had to admit I didn't seem to care about Zariyah Zhadan very much at all, on a personal level. I hadn't spent more than half a second considering her detention at Heathrow, whether she was at that moment facing interrogation in one of the small bright rooms at airport security, and if so whether this was distressing to her or a predictable inconvenience that she was overly familiar with. So that wasn't it either. The only answer I could come up with, for my imaginary inquisitors, and it wasn't an answer at all, more of a shrug, was that I seemed to be doing just what was required of me, given my station and the limits of my resources: this seemed to be about right. It was roughly *what I should be doing*. As I replayed this sequence of thoughts, which it seemed to me I had retrodden to almost exactly the same state of impasse—at which point the boardroom didn't respond by shuffling its papers, or by darkening theatrically, but merely by *pausing*, as if it were an episode of a drama I would return to the following evening, but for now was too tired to continue with—as I replayed my thoughts, I also visualised the scene as it had appeared to me earlier in the afternoon, sitting with Zariyah Zhadan's poems on my tablet in a seating area on the fourth or fifth floor of the Southbank Centre, with several men who may or may not have been homeless sleeping on the benches around me, looking out of one of the enormous windows facing the river, windows that, deliberately or not, had similar dimensions to those of a cinema screen, so it was hard to avoid the impression that you were looking at crisp video footage of central London, such as you might see at the beginning of a high-budget documentary film, rather than at central London itself. I had watched the little flags fluttering over MI7. The stamped angles of the bridges and walkways. The shifting waters, composed of pooling black and white shapes, at that time, from that vantage. A fleet of drones in holding patterns around an elevated charge point, on one of the poles of Hungerford Bridge. A military aircraft roughly the size of a paperclip, which took a full minute to traverse the scene—below that, a jumble of buildings like the clutter of appliances in a junk shop window: hulls of outmoded computers, dismantled vacuum cleaners, speaker casings, scaled-up radio components, pieces from anonymous board games, and several plain cuboid constructions, arranged like a minimalist fireplace. The historical fragments of the city had been entirely lost from sight, the forked spires and castellated turrets, like an antique fungus, were now hidden in crevices between the sheer planes of the redevelopments. I had observed this view contentedly for several minutes, entirely as an image, without questioning or even really absorbing it, realising I had no way of accessing its real functions, or the network of its wider meanings. From ground level even that insight had been concealed, I thought, walking beside the river—packed away inside the neat formula of the skyline, behind the faces of the weekday restaurants and office blocks that fronted the water with the impersonal availability of a newly minted typeface. But I couldn't distract myself from my commitments any longer. Arriving outside the King George Hall, I followed the directions to a fire door below an echoing rampway, where I was met by one of the floor staff, a young woman dressed functionally in black, with a chunky piece of technology hanging out of her ear, who punched at the keypad and provided commentary in a brisk, relaxed tone—did you find the place okay, it's a bit of a maze down here, we'll just get you miked up—as she led me along a series of corridors lined with what I presumed was audio and lighting equipment: heavy-looking black boxes with LED displays, behind which ran webs of cabling and ducts. It struck me, not for the first time, that these cultural institutions were mainly giant *back-end facilities*—underground storage units, kitchens and laundries, corridors and lifts, connecting various media hubs lit by screens for surveillance, screens for broadcast and interior display, each with their teams of assistants, technicians and security staff—all working to manufacture the tiny, bright pinnacle of visible activity above ground, in the venue itself. Perhaps the entire city was no more than a giant *back-end facility* at this point, I thought, as a battery pack was clipped to my belt, and a radio mic attached to my head—given over to enormous zones of pre-production and post-production, while the shrinking public spaces were vacated for a constant flow of visitors, the blurry observers who recorded absolutely everything. We were creating a deep layering of recordings, I thought, as I had thought many times before, the city's central locations were preserved as if by a protective wrapping millions of video streams thick. The footage had embalmed the streets and buildings, I thought, making them impossible to access even when you were standing in front of them, they were encased in a kind of transparent shroud, like the mummies in the British Museum. I rarely went into the city any more anyway, and when I did I had often found the parts that were still recognisable to me blockaded by foreign film crews. My recital of Zariyah Zhadan's poetry lasted twenty-five minutes, during which time I was able to remain more or less oblivious of the audience, invisible in the near total darkness and silence that appeared like a curtain in front of the wide, bare stage, its only features a pair of spotlit lecterns, the one to my left occupied, it seemed to me, by Zariyah Zhadan's accusatory absence. As I read from her poetry in its English translation, to the surrounding and near total darkness and silence, I was able, I thought, to discern a meaning of some kind gathering around me—I was able to see how I appeared to those watching, from inside the near total darkness. And I appeared, it seemed to me, basically as a pained, beleaguered figure, straining to lift the name that I appeared beneath—literally, as the name of Zariyah Zhadan was projected onto the backing screen with accompanying Cyrillic script. I could offer only a kind of fried connection to the absent poet, who that morning had been *denied access* to these islands, it had been announced to a ripple of interested discovery, and therefore to her own recital at the Festival of Culture. The audience had seemed profoundly grateful for learning this fact, I had thought as I waited in the wings with a pale young man with a walkie-talkie: it was something to latch on to, something in which to carry the meaning of the occasion—the poet was *denied access*, they would enjoy saying later when making their report of the evening, she was *detained* at Heathrow. They were excited by the prospect of being able to speak these words, it seemed to me, although sadly, of course, as they would say, they weren't surprised by them. I even thought that this statement, which was made during the introduction of the recital by an unseen announcer with a flutey voice, was intensely gratifying to the majority of the audience members, and it was clear to me then that my own presence, and the presence of Zariyah Zhadan's poetry, would simply slot alongside this piece of information, which the audience members immediately recognised as the only worthwhile thing about the evening. It was all that they would remember of it, and for the next twenty-five minutes it was all that the poems would cast their light on, and in turn be lit by, that is, as *authentic missives from a suppressed artist*. There was safety in this meaning, that the poems were immediately broken down to fit, and which the audience held on to, I could feel, with the passionate gratitude of people clinging to jetsam in the aftermath of shipwreck. When I had almost finished the reading, having resigned myself to the incontrovertible and flattening effect of this information, when I was on the second-to-last poem, I heard something from the area of near total darkness and silence in front of me—I heard a sound that I assumed at first was feedback from the microphone, a high-pitched hum with no obvious origin. It continued steadily, and in the gap between the second-to-last poem and the final poem I looked around for a second—it seemed to be coming from the audience, or rather the area of near total darkness and silence before me, this low whine, or high-pitched hum—I recognised it then as the sound made by someone running a finger around the rim of a wine glass. A resonant, unmodulating tone, the precise location impossible to pinpoint. I continued with the last poem, sensing some distraction in the audience, who probably dismissed it as a technical fault—but by then I was certain, it was the sound made by a moistened finger circling the rim of a wine glass—it went on for the remainder of the recital, until it was drowned out by the applause, which was loud and extended, but also unemphatic, adequate, completely formulaic. As I walked offstage, I realised that the tone from the wine glass had come almost like a warning, a signal intended to draw the audience's attention to something, and that inexplicably it was a feeling of *being caught out* that the sound of a finger running around the rim of a wine glass had provoked in me. There wasn't really anything wrong with what I had been doing, I thought, as I made my way to the green room in the company of another assistant, there was nothing to really warrant this feeling—in other words, there wasn't anything wrong with my reading out the poetry of Zariyah Zhadan in English translation in front of an audience of close to a thousand. Besides my own microanalysis of the ethics of the situation, which despite the amount of time and energy I seemed to expend on it, I regarded basically as a private entertainment, I couldn't think of anything—and if there wasn't anything *obviously* wrong with my actions, then why had I had this feeling, of *being caught out*, as I put it, when I had heard the resonant, unmodulating tone produced by a finger circling the wetted rim of a wine glass? It was certainly an antagonistic gesture, I thought in the green room. It was not a gesture undertaken by someone appreciating the event, who was absorbed in the poetry I had been reciting—on the contrary, it was a statement of boredom, of disrespect, of *extreme* disrespect even, expressed in a playful or childish manner, similar to the way malicious children might disrupt a class they found tiresome, or when they didn't like the teacher. It was also completely fearless—there was no fear of reprisal or of recognition—the other audience members sitting near the culprit must have been aware of what he or she was doing, and which made them, the, say, five to ten audience members sitting in close proximity to the person running their finger around the moistened rim of their wine glass, complicit in this action, or at least partly complicit. It seemed to me that no one had tried to prevent this behaviour either. They had allowed it to continue, for a period of two or three minutes, which in reality is a long time to keep up disruptive activity of this sort—two or three minutes of sustained disruption, caused by the running of a finger around the rim of a wine glass, to some extent ignored and to some extent covered up by the ten or so people surrounding the culprit. Perhaps more. Perhaps more members of the audience had become aware of the intentional disturbance, and with their silence came close to sanctioning it, to acquiescing to it, at least—perhaps part of them secretly *approved* of the disruption, because they had detected something in the event, namely in my recital of Zariyah Zhadan's poetry in English, that was deserving of this kind of response, that in a certain way invited it. They had sat there with all their worthy feelings about Zariyah Zhadan's poetry, perversely enjoying the disruption of the recital by a finger circling the rim of a wine glass. But even if this was the case, why had I been so struck by it, why had the sound, when I had recognised it, caused me to react with something close to horror? Was it because, despite my misgivings about the recital, I had undertaken it with a kind of complacency? Even though I was sure there was something not quite right about it, something self-congratulatory, I thought, in terms of its staging and production, I had, through necessity, managed to convince myself that this didn't matter, and then I actually managed to dismiss it from my mind completely—but I had realised, when I heard the tone produced by a finger circling the wetted rim of a wine glass, that I myself was the form of that congratulation, that my recital of Zariyah Zhadan's poetry was *how it was articulated*. An interchangeable part: that was how I had viewed myself, I thought in the green room. If it wasn't me reciting the poetry of the revolutionary Ukrainian poet in English translation, then it would have been somebody else, I would have reasoned before the event. Before the event I would have argued that my identity was beside the point, that it was incidental, beneath consideration, that it *didn't count*, but all of that melted away once the tone produced by a finger circling the rim of a wine glass had cut through the air, making it clear that somebody else—an observer—regarded the event in a different light. Because at that moment, I—me personally—became the target, and the fact that it was me and no one else reciting the poetry of Zariyah Zhadan was suddenly of the utmost importance. The person using a wine glass to sustain a resonant, unmodulating tone had either attended with the intention of pointing this out, or it had occurred to them during the course of the recital, and they had spontaneously chosen to communicate what they knew—that the event was an expression of a culture capable of taking a dissenting sentiment such as that found in Zariyah Zhadan's poetry, and utilising it for its own purposes of self-congratulation. I had assumed, I thought, on some level, prior to hearing the note caused by a finger circling the rim of a wine glass, that my motivations were in some way separate from those of the *culture at large*, and that my personal reservations, despite the fact they were heard by no one, observed by no one, somehow counted for something. I had thought that such a thing as the *culture at large* could be said to exist, even, in any meaningful way as something that encompassed my actions and relieved me of responsibility. Somebody else present at the recital had made it clear they didn't agree with that assessment, I thought to myself in the green room. They had also made it clear that what I called my *microanalysis* of the situation had merely been a kind of game, an insurance policy that I could take comfort in, having anticipated, or so I believed, every interpretive facet of the event and essentially ignored my own conclusions, which remained safely in the abstract realm of argument and counter-argument. But even as I was experiencing this horrifying feeling of exposure, which my thoughts seemed to slow down or extend in duration, so it could be experienced in agonising detail, and the maximum yield of information extracted from what had just happened, part of me was aware, sitting in the green room in front of an array of herbal teas that were offered to performers free of charge, that after a certain amount of time had passed I would be able to reduce these feelings to their correct proportions, to view them as a semi-irrational response to something that, even if it was malicious, was hardly the major derailing it had seemed for the minutes directly following it, and which I was currently living through. It would shrink to the dimensions of an amusing story, part of me already hoped. But there was something else about the resonant, unmodulating tone produced by the wine glass that was bothering me, I thought, and which became more apparent as its immediate impact began to fade—because it had happened before, I realised, during a poetry recital I had given more than a decade ago, when I still regarded myself as a young poet, and was determined, with all of the egoism and unshakeable self-belief of a man in his mid-twenties, who has been granted certain advantages and spared certain realities, to make an impression on the poetry readership, or indeed any available audience. It seemed to me then that I had some precious, irreducible nugget lodged inside me, which required only the correct formula to be extracted and converted into works of poetry whose worth would be self-evident to all. I was in tireless search of this formula, and I shared my personal conviction with several other young men—there were four of us—who formed what we regarded as a miniature movement of the art. To us, our work was of obvious immediate and lasting significance, and if our efforts, in the form of poetry recitals and a series of self-produced publications, were met with indifference or uninterest, as not infrequently happened, we were genuinely puzzled—it was inconceivable to us that the value of our enterprises was not objectively apparent, and therefore equally impressive to anyone who encountered them. As well as wishing to inflict the products of our creative labours on our peers, and indiscriminately on other members of the local artistic community—this was before any of us moved to the capital—we were possessive of our chosen art form, in and of itself, and if any of us heard of another writer of verse who lived in the area—unless they were one of the few older poets we admired and had sought out as mentors—or was of a comparable age to us, or had had some precocious success, we would trawl the popular platforms of the day, and, meeting in our private messaging group, demolish through sarcastic quotation and pedantic critique what we had found. My proprietorial instincts were keen enough that if I noticed someone in a café or on a train writing in a journal or on a laptop in a way that suggested their activity was literary—I became expert at spotting the clues—I was seized by a jealous rage, and would attempt if possible to glimpse what they were working on. Sometimes the screen revealed a spreadsheet, or the tablet showed a sketch, and my murderous anger would subside, but at other times I caught sight of what looked like a work of fiction, or worst of all, the stark lineaments of a poem, and, dismissing it as unquestionably substandard work, or as irredeemably misguided work, I would return to my own projects with renewed anxiety and aggression. During this period, my opinions on poetry and art were entirely determined by my interactions with my friends, that is, the three other young men I lived with, for three years in total, the three years of our undergraduate studies, during which time we spent every available moment discussing poetry and fiction and music and art, three years of basically relentless discussion while talking and drinking in the pubs of Bury, talking and drinking in the rooms of friends, talking and drinking as we walked between pubs and houses, and as we talked and drank to excess, rather than becoming incoherent, we became increasingly *coherent*, we became adept at anticipating and rebutting one another's opinions, at *attuning* ourselves towards or against one another's perspectives. No sooner would I assert a particular perspective on a particular poet or poem, a dislike of poem *x* or poem *y*, or of poet *x* or poet *y*, than one of my three friends would express the contrary opinion, that is, he would immediately launch into a convincing case *for* poet *x* or poet *y*, as if he had foreseen my statement and prepared in advance a counter-statement, so before long I would find myself coming around to his point of view, to the extent that I would actually *take on* his point of view, as if it were my own point of view, in some sense actually *believing* it was my own point of view, that my affection for said poem or said poet preceded my hearing his opinion, when this was precisely not the case—I had simply subsumed his position into my own, or more accurately I had simply *replaced* my point of view with his point of view. It always seemed to me, after hearing my friend's opinion, that he had just expressed *my* opinion, and I would even go on to hold a slightly more exaggerated or emphatic version of his opinion than he himself appeared to hold. Then, some time later, as would usually happen, during some further talking and drinking session, I would hear that this same friend had now cooled on said poem or said poet, and so I would instantly respond, and I, too, would cool on said poem or said poet, but my cooling off would happen in a faster and more emphatic fashion than his own cooling off, so I would end up beating him back to my initial position of scepticism about or open dislike of poem *x* or poem *y* or poet *x* or poet *y*. These discussions and disputes were the methods by which my friends and I manoeuvred ourselves and one another in and out of our advantageous or disadvantageous positions—because the truth was that, on some level, I wanted to see them destroyed, my friends, the three other young men who I lived with for three years, drinking and talking more or less constantly, just as I knew that they wished on some level to see *me* destroyed, and two of them in fact eventually *were* destroyed, and while their destruction did not happen at my hands, I was able to observe it—in other words, I was able to make sure of it. My remaining friend escaped destruction, due to his circumstantial advantages, which mirrored my own—he had allies and resources that he deployed secretively and intelligently, so that he managed to escaped the negative whirlpool that towards the end of the three years living together threatened to consume us all. I also managed to escape this negative whirlpool, by relocating to London. I managed to escape the psychological demolition site that our friendship group had become, just before my remaining friend could properly destroy *me*, and he managed to escape it just before I could properly destroy *him*. It was not surprising, from a certain perspective, that it was myself and my advantaged friend who eventually managed to extricate ourselves from this psychological demolition site, and that it was my other two friends who succumbed to it, as my friend and I shared by virtue of our backgrounds an inventory of weapons, comprising financial support, sympathetic parents, industry connections, escape routes in the form of friends or family who already lived in the capital and so on—weapons that my two friends who *were* in fact destroyed did not have access to, so could not make use of in aiding their escape, and so they did not escape. It had been years since I had seen any of them, or since I last took it upon myself to compose a poem, and these passions and rivalries now seemed very remote to me. Or perhaps they had simply been relocated to another order of productivity—this thought had occurred to me, too—because it seemed to me that I never relinquished my ambitions exactly, or failed in my aims, despite to all appearances having renounced the art I was at one time devoted to, turning away from the modest success I was able to achieve there. It felt more as if I had transcended the limitations of those goals, and that my sights became focused on larger, more durable rewards. Doubtlessly this was connected to my slow and reluctant acceptance of the *deadly relativity* of literary judgements, and the *deadly relativity* of the value of literary works, as well as the undeniable inconsequence of practically all of the literature being produced, its worth being directly and inversely proportionate to its excessive quantities, pouring out as it did from institutions and writing programmes in an unstaunchable, undifferentiated torrent, at the time I began to practise it. An argument made by some at that time was that *the more writing produced the better* for the culture in general, that *more writers equalled more readers*, that *more writing* equalled a healthy *writing culture*, and while not being unsympathetic to this angle for a period, I came to violently reject it. There were more readers, perhaps that was true, but they were readers on the hunt for ideas, for workable models, for styles to crib, for plots to adapt—predatory readers with the eyes of trophy hunters, in other words, always seeking to measure one book against another, to assess everything steadily next to their own creation, calculating the favourable attributes that they had in common, or noting the disagreeable features on display that in their view were unnecessary or unaesthetic. In short, they read with an interest only in what they could *make use of*—a sickeningly pragmatic approach that was antithetical, in my view, to the project of literature and the artistic tradition itself. I had recognised this tendency in my own habits of course, and in my case it was a pronounced attitude, with a special ugliness all of its own—once I had caught sight of it I couldn't dispel the image that I read only as a rival producer, in other words as a cynic, an opportunist. When I left these concerns behind to become an editor—or when I became an editor and left these concerns behind—I realised that a poem was actually a pathetically fragile excrescence, hardly existing at all. Its grasp on reality was only a temporary stay from oblivion—that rather than a sturdy brick, baked to indestructibility, its formation was uncertain, provisional, a crystal growing out of a daydream, so easy for me to shatter with my little mallet—with my "I regret on this occasion . . ." Suddenly, rather than wanting to stamp them out of existence, I wanted these larval forms to survive the light I turned on them. Of course, most of the time I was bitterly disappointed by what landed in front of me. But in other respects the compensation was great; if I had left behind my own artistic pretensions in the most direct sense, I had also scaled up my project, elevated it—I was now an author of artistic destinies, of careers, of *real-life trajectories*. The act of composing a creative work came to seem almost vulgar to me, from this perspective—in some way too obvious. And in retrospect, my first intimations of this shift away from poetry came, as a nameless suspicion, the first time I heard the resonant, unmodulating tone produced by a finger caressing the rim of a wine glass, as it cut through the close silence of a poetry recital, like a subconscious alarm. One of the three young men I lived with in those days had an old school friend from the deprived rural areas outside Bury who visited us over the summer. Basically indistinguishable from countless other medium-sized English towns, at the end of a train line, with only its low rainfall statistics to recommend it, Bury was seen as something of a graveyard—many had been buried there, the joke went—but for Christian Wort—that was the name of my friend's old school friend—it was as close to the metropolis as he'd been. In his own way he was a writer too, far better read than any of us, especially in history and poetry, which were apparently the only books he could get hold of from the second-hand emporiums in the long-declined ex-farming towns where he came by most of his reading materials. He still read books in their entirety, which shocked us a little, and declined to engage with the contemporary discourse, or what little of it was accessible outside the paywalls. All of this added to the old-world atmosphere that surrounded Christian Wort; to us, with our micromanaged profiles, thread wars, network expansions and subscription packages, he seemed like a relic from another era, and his private perspective mystified us to start with, born as it was from his largely solitary reading and thinking. There were other alarming aspects of Christian Wort that we learned about soon after he alighted at Bury coach station, with the night birds still chattering, for his stay of six or seven weeks, during which he slept under a stained quilt on the floor in the unfurnished box room off his old friend's bedroom. If you went into the bathroom after him, we learned, you would find the soap and basin inexplicably blackened, as if by soot; his clothes had a characteristic mildewy smell; he had a problem with one of his feet, which leaked at all times a clear pus, meaning he kept it wrapped in what can only be described as rags, inside his boot—when at home in the country, he told us, the family dog loved to *lick the juice off his foot*, of an evening. Once he had acclimatised to town living, as he referred to it, he would disappear on nocturnal excursions, entertaining us with stories the following morning that sounded unbelievable, but which if pressed he calmly insisted on—he would claim to have walked twelve or thirteen miles during the night, or he'd say that he had spotted a will-o'-the-wisp floating in the upstairs window of a terrace house, or he'd swear he'd discovered a large factory or industrial facility on the outskirts of the town, its windows lit, and emitting a sub-auditory hum, which didn't appear on satellite maps. Christian Wort was also in possession of an old-fashioned chivalrous temperament, a romantic sensitivity *when it came to women*, as he put it, and his overt brand of heterosexuality was a regular source of embarrassment to the rest of us on nights out, where it came across as either alarmingly dated or slightly threatening—over that summer he *fell in love*, as he put it, easily and often, while viewing our lukewarm hook-ups and casual, cautious relationships with bewilderment, or perhaps envy. His new surroundings made him perceive his relative innocence for the first time, I thought, and this became most obvious when his direct, well-meaning advances were met with either terrified retreat or open mockery by the girls he attempted to corner at parties or on nights out. All this confused Christian Wort—he was unaware of codes everyone else was fluent in—he never worked out our flirtations rarely happened face to face, but consisted of a range of light touches landed over various media, a careful abstinence from curiosity. His lack of tact and fluency unnerved us too much to feel sorry for him; despite his sensitivity, he seemed dulled and immobile, and finally it was too amusing to witness and recount his frequent humiliations. The incident I remembered, in light of the interruption of my recital of Zariyah Zhadan's poetry, must have happened quite soon after he arrived—we had organised a recital in the basement of a sports bar that didn't charge for room hire. Even if he hadn't been interested, Christian Wort had nowhere else to go, but poetry, as he put it, was *close to his heart* and he was touchingly eager, I thought, before the evening unfolded, to see what the *poets in the town*, as he put it, were up to. I had selected a long poem to end the first half of the event—long poems, it is my shame to admit, were my speciality—and I had been about midway through when I became aware of the high-pitched hum or low whine, followed by a scattering of laughter, from the audience of twenty or so fellow students—plus one or two writers in their forties or fifties, whose approval we were vying for—uneasy at first, but laughter that spread as the tone of the wine glass went on unabated, if anything getting louder as Christian Wort's finger—it was him—warmed to its groove. Outwardly I took it in good humour, but the half-apologetic smiles of my three friends took a place in my memory, their half-guilty amusement that turned to open hilarity as the resonant, unmodulating tone from the wine glass seemed to grow in volume, and laughter proliferated in the basement room of the sports bar. I received it in good humour, but my pride had received its first serious blow—the formula of my *long poem* had once again failed to locate the material I felt sure was hidden, like some inscrutable nugget, inside me. What's more, I couldn't tell if Christian Wort had been making it clear that he thought my long poem was a dreary and pointless linguistic exercise that no one wanted to listen to, or if the disruption was a way of announcing his own spontaneous temperament to those assembled in the small basement below the sports bar—if he simply desired to be seen and heard, an impulse I would have recognised and understood, and forgiven more easily—and if *that* was the case, had he chosen to interrupt me more or less randomly? Was he just drunk? In the end I never found out—I never had the honest exchange about poetry with Christian Wort which at that moment I probably regarded as inevitable—an exchange that I imagined would begin with jokes and mutual derision, become heated, then reconciliatory, finally requiring difficult inner adjustments from us both, bringing us closer together, perhaps even connecting us deeply, as our opposed stances were reflected between us and transformed into a valuable resource—retaking my seat in the basement below the sports bar, perhaps I had anticipated something like that. As it happened, I took my revenge on Christian

Wort instead, without setting out to do so—revenge came to me of its own accord, and it was only later, when I noticed its reviving qualities, that I decided to make it more of a *theme*. Of all his romantic causes, the one that preoccupied Christian Wort most was a girl called Jessica Lake, who didn't study at the college but had her own flat on a narrow lane in the town's mediaeval centre, above the vintage clothes shop she ran with her friend Phoebe Glass. The first time he had set eyes on Jessica Lake, as Christian Wort often recounted at the height of his infatuation, she was standing next to a mannequin in the window of her shop, Lake Clothes, carrying an old picture frame for the window display, an old picture frame that framed her face like a real-life portrait, Christian Wort claimed, making the abundance of bead necklaces, coloured boas and scarves in the shop window part of her frame as well, and then the street itself, quiet and ridged with early morning sun, also became part of what framed Jessica Lake, as she stood in the window of her shop, budging a mannequin in velvet trousers aside with her hip. On display in the doorway there had been a sign, in Jessica Lake's precise, slanting cursive, half-seriously or half-jokingly calling for "boyfriend applications" to be handed in at the till, a wildly hopeful or wildly hopeless experiment it was hard not to be struck by, one way or the other. All five of us ended up writing one of these applications, initially in a spirit of solidarity with Christian Wort, who by this time was self-conscious about displaying his interest, and although initially buoyed by our support, his attitude quickly turned to one of jealousy and suspicion, fearing that Jessica Lake, whom he was yet to exchange a word with, would select one of our flippant compositions over his more intense proposal, a mini-epic in prose in which he more or less flung himself at Jessica Lake's feet. At our suggestion he had attempted to brighten the piece with humour, and the result was strange, but as a group we thought it was possible, just about, that Jessica Lake would glimpse Christian Wort's genuine warmth, stripped of its alarming industriousness, and if it wasn't her thing, then at least she would be spared the romantic onslaught that he had threatened to embark on, and from which we actually had to restrain him, pacifying him instead with an arm-wrestling contest, which he won emphatically, the night after our applications had been passed over the till, straight-faced, to Jessica Lake's best friend, Phoebe Glass. In the end, Jessica Lake went out with each of us once before making her decision, whereupon Christian Wort's fears became a reality, and I was revealed as the front-runner for her affections—receiving a text message inviting me to her flat above the shop for drinks at the weekend. My total lack of interest in Jessica Lake must have been misinterpreted as mastery of my desires, I decided later, and it was only the inevitability of wounding Christian Wort, when it occurred to me moments after receiving the text message, that guaranteed my attendance at the little flat above Lake Clothes on Saturday night. I would never have gone out of my way to cause Christian Wort the emotional distress that I undoubtedly did cause him, but it became possible simply by allowing the sequence of events to play out in an order that seemed predetermined. The incident in the basement below the sports bar still lived in my memory. It had retained its vividness, its heat, and I didn't reject the opportunity that had fallen into my lap to redress the balance, if only in my own mind—no one else suspected I still harboured a grudge for the interruption of my recital, it was dismissed as one of Christian Wort's idiosyncrasies, and had been succeeded by other examples. Perhaps there are no coincidences. During my dalliance with Jessica Lake, which lasted a month or two, we often went drinking with a mixture of friends at a pub at the end of the narrow lane where she had her shop, and on these evenings Christian Wort would usually excuse himself, supposedly due to a lack of funds, but, I learned later, mainly because of the anguish he suffered seeing my hand entwined with Jessica Lake's. At that time, or perhaps at all times, Jessica Lake used a pair of crutches when walking more than a few metres, as she had a problem with cartilage in her knee that had required keyhole surgery, I remembered, and on our way back to the little flat above her shop I would become aware of a shuffling gait behind us, stopping and starting to keep pace with our slow progress—a combination of drunkenness and Jessica Lake's limp—and I would know that the sound was Christian Wort. This was the moment of my victory, it seemed to me. The detail of Jessica Lake's limp, I remembered in those moments, had endeared her all the more powerfully to Christian Wort, as he had perceived some kind of *poetic association* between her leg and his foot, as if these imperfections, as he put it, united them in some way. I had even suggested this once to Jessica Lake, when we had some reason to notice Christian Wort's behaviour, and she had found it ridiculous, perhaps even mildly insulting. But she wasn't insensitive to his feelings either, and on at least one evening, when his agony became irrepressible, she had talked with him for ten or fifteen minutes outside the bar, where he'd been waiting in the cold while we'd been drinking inside surrounded by her friends. I'd stood some distance away, smoking, before she joined me, swinging over on her crutches, rolling her eyes, and we went back together to her little flat above Lake Clothes. For some reason I have no memory of what went on between us when we got back to her bedroom, which was directly above the shopfront, after another night of drinking in the pubs and bars of Bury. I do remember, though, the steep view from her window onto the lane below, and that her room was opposite a small church, and as the buildings on the narrow lane leaned towards each other on the upper floors, its stone wall was so close that you could open the window, reach across the lane and touch it. Perhaps once or twice, to try to stir my feelings, I suggested we do certain things in bed together, but what I had in mind put too much strain on her knee, she told me, when we tried. It came to an end soon enough, after yet another poetry recital, which Jessica Lake had agreed to come to, under a small amount of duress—I don't get poetry, I'm only a shopgirl, she had said, grinning yet half-serious when I brought it up, eventually attending with a nervousness I found surprising, but after the recital, in the bar, she was more forthcoming and said that she had liked it, or had liked some of it, and even offered an interpretation of one of the poems the visiting poet had read, a poet we all admired. At first I didn't understand what Jessica Lake was saying, and the truth was I'd never heard anything quite like this interpretation of a poem before, but once I thought I understood it, I said I disagreed with her, finding it to be an amateur's view, disregarding literary allusion and focusing only on the poet themselves, who was still present, drinking in the bar, but when another person at our table asked the poet about it, the poet we all admired actually confirmed that this interpretation, that is, the interpretation of Jessica Lake, who openly admitted she didn't like poetry, was the correct one, and was remarkably perceptive, and they, the poet and Jessica Lake, proceeded to have a long, involved conversation, which I felt gradually excluded from, eventually walking home by myself, not to the little flat above the clothes shop, but to the house I shared with the three other young men, to resume our constant discussions of poetry and art. I saw Jessica Lake in Bury barely twice after that, and a year or two later I noticed that the shop on the narrow lane had closed down. Now I wondered, finishing my cinnamon tea—I wondered about Christian Wort, and specifically I wondered about the resonant, unmodulating tone that had interrupted my recital of Zariyah Zhadan's poetry half an hour previously, as I exited the green room, still wearing my guest pass on a piece of blue cord around my neck. I found myself on the cavernous ground floor of the Southbank Centre, its central bar flanked by four distinct but borderless zones: a restaurant towards the front, ticket offices and seating to the sides, and the bar and performance area to the rear. I scanned the tables, which were moderately busy, picked out randomly by ceiling spots, the rest of the space dim or even dark, until I caught sight of a figure standing alone, where the floor began to dip towards an area sometimes used as a stage, which was empty and unlit. A little more than an hour later I was walking across Waterloo Bridge. The river had transformed from the sluggish, heaving body I'd watched earlier into a black, pellucid surface full of flares of gaseous light; it looked somehow active, connected, and at the same time dormant and inert. The streams of night traffic on the adjacent bridges appeared as halting blocks and dots of light, intermittent, as if unable to load, blinking as they struggled against the counter-rates of pedestrians and cyclists. I was heading for the Travelodge on the far bank, where many of the poets who had gathered in the capital for the biennial Festival of Culture were staying, and had arranged to meet for drinks *en masse*—the Travelodge just off Waterloo Bridge, as unbelievable as it sounds, being the only establishment in the area with a twenty-four-hour alcohol license. A stupendous amount of poets had assembled in the capital for FOC. They had spent the entire day attending recitals or giving recitals, listening to lectures or giving lectures, chairing panel discussions or participating in panel discussions, giving interviews or conducting interviews, buying poetry collections or signing poetry collections, asking long, meandering questions in the Q&A or attempting to answer long, meandering questions in the Q&A, and now they were ready to drink. Almost every poet I could think of who would be in the Travelodge bar shared the same infantile dependence on alcohol, especially when coping with a gathering of this magnitude, or else they completely abstained, in which case they were most likely indebted to some less-traditional stimulant or medication, but in all cases something was necessary, I thought, to overcome their innate awkwardness, and the bitterness of their resentments, and present an acceptable countenance to the rest of the poetry community, if only for an hour or two. The truth was that I had avoided practically everything on the exhaustive programme of recitals, lectures, conversations, panels and interviews, restricting myself to my small set of obligations, and although the participants of these events were always careful to scrutinise the audience and note any conspicuous absentees, such was the density of the scheduling that it was always possible to claim to have attended some other event happening simultaneously, as a prior obligation, which provided everyone with an automatic excuse, thankfully, I thought, crossing the river. My dark secret was that before tonight I had managed not to attend a poetry recital for close to five years, after an epiphany during the course of a particularly punishing event one winter, when, bored almost to tears and needing desperately to urinate, I had realised that not a single person in the audience of the poetry recital actually wanted to be there. The violence of my desire to leave—which I was unable to act upon, as it would have meant rising from my chair and stumbling to the end of the row, causing the seven or eight people sitting there to get up and file out to let me past, before walking towards the door at the front of the poetry recital and practically brushing shoulders with the poet themselves, mid-spate, on my way out—had revealed this to me in a flash of insight. Everyone in the audience, I realised, wanted to leave with an urgency that was no less intense for being a *psychological* desire to leave rather than a *purely physical* desire to leave—my *purely physical* desire to leave had merely made me conscious of my equally urgent *psychological* desire to leave, which I immediately realised was shared by everyone in the audience. Everyone in the audience, I realised, was there out of a sense of obligation, almost a sense of duty, the threat of which was carefully hidden, as if by mutual agreement, and although the audience members attended with an outwardly cheerful, hardy demeanour, occasionally their masks slipped and the strain of endless poetry recital attendances could be glimpsed, revealing that their true mind-set was one of grim resignation, and their feelings were as far removed from the pleasurable eagerness with which one attends a concert or film as it was possible to get. They were only attending this particular recital in case *their absence was noticed*, I realised, or they were attending to break up a string of recent absences, to push up their average, in other words, because they knew that otherwise, in a kind of passive retaliation, their next recital or panel or Q&A would be furnished with empty chairs in return. Of course, not every person in the audience was directly involved with the production of poetry, and while it was hard to guess the motives of those who weren't recognisable figures, and therefore compelled to attend, it was as if they had been lured there on some misunderstood pretext, and were constantly on the verge of discovering their mistake. The longer I was able to go without attending a recital—it extended to months, and then, I noticed with a light-headedness not far from joy, to years—the more focused the shape of a recital became in my mind, for some reason. I was able to view it as if from above, with a kind of geometrical impersonality, and to make out the skeletal form that lay beneath all recitals: the form of the *ur*-recital. And it seemed to me that every poet who appeared on stage, at the apex of the diagram, was reduced instantaneously to a single attribute—this poet was funny, for example, this poet was deadly serious, this one had once been a manual labourer, this one was a fey intellectual, this one wrote about their religious beliefs, this one their nihilism, this one their chequered sexual history, this one their marriage, this one their children, this one their parents, this one their background of economic deprivation, this one their background of emotional deprivation, this one sarcastically, this one sincerely, this one descriptively, this one directly, until it seemed that the only way to circumvent this effect would be to somehow embody *all or none* of this multitude of possible attributes, and appear as a sort of excessive blank—to occupy the central point of the recital somehow deprived of your specificity—in other words, to appear not as a poet at all, but *as something else.* Maybe this was why the person who stood up at the start, all too briefly I thought, to read out the biography of the person about to read their poetry, to list their publications, and provide comforting information about where the fire exits were located, and when the interval would be, was usually the most enjoyable part of the evening. This person alone knew the job that they were supposed to be doing, and was able to accomplish it with a degree of honesty and integrity, I had often thought. Actually, I was always in some small way *moved* by the efforts of this individual, their unassuming devotion to the task they had been allotted, and I made sure I thought of them when I applauded, slowly and dutifully along with the other applauders, at the end of the evening—at the end of another poetry recital evening, which amazingly I had managed to avoid for close to five years. It had reached the point where I found this fact impressive enough to feel tempted to blow my cover and start telling people—purely to see their reactions—but I mustn't do that, I thought. I mustn't ruin it. It seemed to me too that the poets themselves were well aware of their dependency—they were aware of their reliance on the single trait they were reduced to. They knew what it was, and they played upon it consciously, in conversation they even knowingly referenced it, I thought, but somehow *this knowingness evaporated* when they took to the stage. Once there, under the hot lights, they inhabited the role they had expressed sceptical awareness of moments before, but with no embarrassment or discomfort whatsoever. Which, then, I wondered, was the truer presentation? The acknowledgement of the poet—typically before or after the recital, but sometimes even in their introductory remarks, which typically went on for longer and were better rehearsed than the poem that followed—that their appearance onstage meant their reduction to a single attribute, with which they had learned to manipulate their audience into a state of compliant reception? *Or* was their real statement the high sincerity of their poetic labours while they recited their work onstage, overpowering whatever convenient social platitudes they might have uttered before or after the event? When it was time for the poets to perform I had noticed a complete shift in their attitude, I thought, a kind of imperviousness descended onto their shoulders, or perhaps an *obliviousness* to what they were about to do—it was as if this new person, perhaps a dangerously deluded person, abruptly cut themselves off from the seemingly ordinary person you had been speaking to a second ago, and they now *refused to meet the eye* of that earlier person, whose very existence reduced their chances of so-called poetic communication. But did one of these roles underpin the other, I wondered—was there a hierarchy? Because if the sincerity of a poet as they recited a poem represented their true feelings, then the modesty and knowingness they displayed before and after the recital was simply a performance—it was the *real performance*—a mask that despite its more natural and convincing appearance disguised the immoderately high value the poet placed on their own words. *But* if their modesty and knowingness were the genuine expressions, I thought, then that made their poetry nothing more than a fully contrived project of mass manipulation, behind which there was no feeling, just the cold-minded deployment of the attribute that a given poet had been allotted within seconds of opening their mouth, and that experience had taught them to ruthlessly exploit. Or was it possible that both attitudes were held in a kind of suspension, with no mental overlap, I thought, making the reciting of poetry at best a kind of willed insanity? Because it seemed to me that the poets were only able to pretend to themselves they believed in what they were doing *while they were actually performing their poetry*—it was only then that they really believed in the value of their attribute—their sense of humour or their deadly seriousness, their astute political critique or their demonstrations of devoutness, their flat vowels or their soft consonants, their ability to capture the smell of their grandmother's greenhouse or the sound of a moorhen taking off from a lake, their experience of desire or their desire for experience—to the extent that it actually needed to be recorded for the benefit of people outside their immediate circle. Strangely, it was only in the company of those people, that is, their immediate circle of friends and family, that they were able to admit to the strange purposelessness of their actions, and show that they understood the ridiculousness of their situation, I thought. This part of themselves appeared only *in the presence of others*, I thought—the rest of the time it was sealed off completely, as if behind a sheet of glass. And yet this part of them was still able to observe the *ridiculous actions of the poet* with total clarity, while the poet carried on with no awareness of this hidden perspective on themselves—it was forgotten as soon as they were standing under the hot lights, addressing a microphone. There was no communication between them, these two parts, I thought. One acted in a ridiculous manner, and the other looked on, in horrified fascination, as may be. In this sense, the attribute that the poet was assigned, that they subsequently recognised as their *talent*, and which their poetry followed from, was a crude misrepresentation, but perhaps the kind of misrepresentation that one can wholeheartedly believe in, and that is revealed in the end as unwittingly, devastatingly accurate. Yes, they ended up being pinned down by it, they ended up *serving* it, I thought, as I opened the door to the Travelodge bar, which was already full of the din of poets in conversation and dispute, the air heavy with a full day's worth of conference sweats and stale exhalations of coffee and tea, and the Travelodge bar's own strong undernotes of carpet and cleaning products. I swung my eyes around the room, taking in the array of poetry world faces, the array of poetry world outfits, listening to the sound of the poetry world talking to itself; it was a real who's who, a roster of the great and the good, and I stood there for a few moments, paralysed, waiting for one cluster or another to relax its ranks and draw me in. To my left, as I entered, I saw Alex Warrington, author of *The Good Son* and *Giving Grace*, latterly editor of *Albion Poetry*, in conversation with Bea Fielding, author of *Visiting Songs*, winner of an Ern Michaels Award and the Simone Horowitz Award, whose back was almost touching the back of Claire Cluny, author of *Back to La Mancha* and *The Harbourmaster's Ruin*, also winner of an Ern Michaels Award, who was talking animatedly to Daniel Wake and Esther Foley, authors of *Wide World* and *Limn*, among other publications, and winners between them of Ern Michaels and Preface awards, who parted to allow Frankie Tipton through, author of *Mirage Property*, which was shortlisted for the Shaw, Preface and Matlaske prizes, who had just left a conversation with George Corley, author of *Five to Eight Chipmunks*, Hannah Peach, author of *Quick Fix*, and Isobel Berger, author of *Marquee Croquet*; behind them I could see the back of Jake Clemence's head, the author of *sadder* and *my problems are slowly becoming your problems*, which was winner of a Playhouse Award, and, in profile, Kacey Brathwaite, author of *Sea Chart*, winner of the Preface Award, and *A Tune Below*, among other publications; to their right, in a tight circle, I spotted Lindsay Stonebridge, whose collections included *Fire Milk* and *Hear/Say*, and who had been nominated three times for the Matlaske Prize without actually winning it, Matthew Fairbrother, author of *The Life and Times of Mrs. Peacock* and *Big Deal*, Neerja Sajid, author of *Tidings*, *eXtinguisH* and *Deeper Cuts Deeper*, Oliver Bolter, author of *Now, Never* and *The Insidious Bleartax Heresy*, for which he was nominated for a Trailerbox Prize and the Shaw Prize, and Pia Credo, author of no full-length as yet, although it was eagerly awaited, but a host of poems in magazines and journals including the *Poetry Centre Quarterly* (PCQ), *The British Poetry Bulletin* (BPB), *The Poets' Chronicle* (PC), *Crescent*, *//*, *Papaya*, *The Versifier* and *Trough*. There was a small gap, where it looked like several drinks had been dropped and covered with a pile of paper napkins, and then in a looser and more mobile formation, I made out among a youthful contingent the faces of Quentin Moody, Rachael O'Regan, Shivani Raina, Thom Goji, Uma Coombes, Vincent Dermer and Wendy B. Knox in rapid succession. I kept moving, past Xing Golding and Yasmine Wilbury-Rice, who were locked in a kiss, before discovering a kind of empty buffer zone before the bar, which appeared unstaffed, and at which only two people were seated, a man and a woman, facing away from the throng. Confronted with so many living representatives of the poetry community, I returned for a moment to my thought of the limiting attribute. That there was more at stake in this designation for some was obvious, I thought, as I waited either for a barperson to materialise or to be absorbed into one or other social cluster, as there would always be some attributes that would weigh more pressingly on the bearer, because like everyone poets did not live in a utopian society—if the poets *had* lived in a utopian society, then they wouldn't have been poets, it wouldn't have occurred to them to be poets, and in fact poets as we understand them wouldn't exist—so rather than misleading themselves about this, I thought, it was preferable that instead all poets were made to inhabit the *most reductive and obvious categories imaginable*. Rather than alleviating the oppressiveness of the attribute, the oppressiveness of the attribute should be *amplified*, I thought, especially on those who were fortunate and felt it less keenly. The attribute's confining force should be brought to bear on all, I thought, its oppressiveness increased to the maximum for *all*—not better for some, but *worse for all*—everyone should be *brought to their knees* before their attribute, the advantaged should bear the same load as the disadvantaged. It was the duty of the audience, I realised, to categorise and reduce everyone with *equal remorselessness*, and that rather than being discouraged from doing so, they should be urged onwards in this tendency. I recognised the idealism of these sentiments, as I cast my eyes around the Travelodge bar. I recognised the powerful appeal of these sentiments as the result of my being aligned, politically speaking, from early adolescence, or even before, with the red team, who for me embodied the values of fairness and justice, as opposed to those of unfairness and injustice—in effect the good rather than the bad, I would be forced to state, if asked. And although I would have struggled to answer, if asked, where my unshakeable allegiance to the red team had come from, I reflected in the Travelodge bar, it seemed highly probable if I thought about it, which I seldom had reason to do, that it was due to my being born into a family of a particular social class and sensibility, and that if I attempted to be even more objective about it, my loyalty to the red team was a direct consequence of the circumstances of my birth, and after that my education, to a large degree. In this sense it was possible, I thought in the Travelodge bar, to regard my conviction that the red team was right, and the blue team wrong, as basically a *predisposition*, such was my lack of decisive input in arriving at it—in other words, it was difficult or even impossible for me to imagine having a vantage on events on the national or international stage *other* than that shared by the red team, barring, perhaps, a situation in which I suffered some kind of extreme misfortune that had the effect of uprooting my position, and altering it to the *exact opposite* position—altering it to the position occupied by the blue team—which would be taken up as a kind of revenge against my previous worldview. I couldn't say for sure when my hatred of the blue team had hardened into the impervious certainty that it now enjoyed—I knew that nothing short of an extreme intervention would ever interrupt my untrammelled disdain and sense of moral outrage when it came to the blue team, politically speaking, though most of the time I was unable to admit that there was an element of arbitrariness to the position I had taken, which I shared, naturally, with every one of my friends and acquaintances, or so I assumed. There was really no other choice, when it came to red team and blue team, *than* red team or blue team—there was no rose team, beige team, mauve team, turquoise team or olive team, unfortunately, and the occasional doomed attempts to imagine such a team only reinforced its conceptual impossibility, I thought. We, the red team, had to uphold our end of the polarity, because they, the blue team, were holding up their end of the polarity, and they had to hold up their end of the polarity because we were holding up our end of the polarity. Really I had for many years been relentlessly dominated by my unwavering, unreflective allegiance to the red team, I thought, circulating aimlessly among social groupings in the Travelodge bar, and part of me had actively enjoyed my total domination by the red team point of view, and the sense of moral authority that the view from the red team corner afforded me, which was no more or less keen, I had to concede, than the moral authority claimed by representatives of the blue team, in the opposite corner. I appreciated, too, the trouble that this saved me, I thought, from otherwise having to investigate the complex and contestable historical accounts of every occurrence and proposal that ventured onto the national or international stage without any support or insight or specialist knowledge, when as it was I could happily fall back on the position prescribed by the red team and enjoy the certainty of being correct in my assessment, as well as the deeper comfort of having obeyed the imperative my allegiance asked of me. Of course, these days the red team position was more often than not called into question by those *on* the red team, who saw an opportunity to shuffle the order to their advantage, but in reality this further choice always turned out to be a further inevitability, I reflected in the Travelodge bar. It was simply a matter of waiting to see how things played out, as the position that the majority arrived at was always claimed in the end as being at the core of the red team ethos, and never really in doubt. But it was important not to let oneself become too *embroiled* in this frequent wrangling, I thought, just as within the poetry world, reproducing as it did the political power structure *in miniature*, it was important not to get too *embroiled* either—to cling too rigidly to any central figure or institution, in case you were demoted or felled alongside them, when they found themselves on the wrong side of public opinion, I thought, looking vaguely around the Travelodge bar. Although in recent times it was true that it was more and more difficult to remain uninvolved in these internal, internecine conflicts, I reflected, and especially not to become *emotionally embroiled* in them, I had largely succeeded in doing so, I had succeeded in keeping my distance, that is, *as was my luxury*. I was fortunate that I was not obliged to become too directly involved in these conflicts, I was not *victimised* by any of these conflicts, though I had sympathy, completely useless sympathy I should add, for those that did suffer under that obligation, and who were victimised. But, I thought, I would never resent or begrudge anyone who exercised their right to turn away from these all-consuming conflicts, who prioritised their own peace of mind over participating in these pointless conflicts, and in doing so deprived these pointless, all-consuming conflicts of the fuel they required to sustain themselves, and so wreak further havoc on all those they came into contact with. My sympathies would always be *with the deserter*, in other words, my sympathies were with those *fleeing the field of battle* without a backward glance, I thought as I waited for the bar staff to return from wherever they were and serve the customers in the Travelodge bar. Looking around, I found it strange to see so many producers of poetry in one space, it made the air feel oversaturated, despite the fact there were probably fewer than seventy people in the large, low-ceilinged and excessively bright Travelodge bar—the gathering was too replete with interpretations, like a recording overlaid too many times, I thought, or an object given too many perspectives, every chance pairing made by my eye-line producing a prospective alliance, every disintegration of a small group suggesting a potential schism. Who, for example, was Zelda Green, a poet I was suddenly forced to engage in conversation, as I hesitated in the empty buffer zone before the bar, which remained unstaffed. Perhaps more of a media entity than a writer, I was surprised to see her here, as her particular expertise over the whole complement of media platforms had allowed her to rise clear of the concerns of the poetry world and forge a legitimate career as a full-time cultural commentator. She published literary pieces, too—a poem by Zelda Green would multiply by some dizzying expedient the sales of any journal—but they seemed like by-products of the main work, which was her own fine-tuned, responsive presence, so really it seemed that Zelda Green was the work of another, anonymous individual, who perhaps did or perhaps did not share the physical form of the person standing in front of me. In fact, there were long-running rumours that Zelda Green was in reality a company or small collective of individuals, headhunted from the orders of advertising, poetry, contemporary art, fashion blogging, linguistic programming and modelling, by an unknown *poetry world svengali figure*, in order to sculpt a live public narrative—the only public narrative worth the name—a tale of swift rise to cultural relevance, followed by disaster and, some speculated, death. The person standing in front of me, according to the rumours, had been cast as the most likely candidate to capture a niche public imagination based on the raw materials of demographic, delivery and demeanour, all of which could be optimised almost out of recognition by the Zelda Green team's assembled skill sets. In any event, I thought, the fact that she, or the group of individuals comprising her, had chosen to attend a fringe FOC event was a conspicuous PR move—conspicuous for all the wrong reasons, outwardly—as to most observers Zelda Green's appearance at something this far below her usual grade of associations would indicate that something was badly awry with her story arc. There would be a plethora of explanations offered among the commentariat for this apparent misstep, I predicted, and of course, depressingly, I thought, her appearance might be nothing more than a ruse to attract heat to the Zelda Green narrative. It was remotely possible that Zelda Green's attendance at FOC was a genuine attempt to consolidate her presence within the literary communities, however, meaning that she had been unable to find the artistic velocity that the project aspired to, or more likely had simply run out of backing, I thought as I looked at Zelda Green's face and wondered if the rumours were true. The only evidence to the contrary I could come up with right then was the noticeable lack of links between Zelda Green and any other industry figures in a romantic or sexual capacity, which would have been too poignant and lucrative an avenue for most image and narrative management agencies to resist. But there had been one report, I remembered, a summer or two ago, from a young boy-poet, who claimed to have been offered a contract by the organisation behind Zelda Green to write a series of love poems to her, with the aim, the boy-poet claimed, of sparking a trend among other boy-poets, and augmenting Zelda Green's brand with simulated fandom. This claim had gathered some support before the tide of opinion turned the other way, after the boy-poet's additional revelations that there was a darker endgame planned than most would have pictured, in that the organisation behind Zelda Green was actively looking for young suicides to attribute posthumously to an infatuation with Zelda Green. The boy-poet's statement wasn't particularly coherent, and he was forced to add that he wasn't suggesting that the organisation behind Zelda Green was actually offering to pay someone to kill themselves, but that it was considering—and it was only an idea at this stage—approaching the families of young suicides with an offer, which if accepted would involve intervention in the subject's media history, and basically the insertion of a Zelda Green infatuation. This had proved too much for most observers to stomach, and the young boy-poet had been decried and effectively ostracised in the wake of his new claims; all sympathy for him had dried up soon after, I remembered, and he had, in fact, been found dead a few days later. A suicide. No one had raised the possibility of Zelda Green's status as an industry fiction for the rest of the season; it had also coincided with her most prolific and visible period, during which she became an object of fixation, mainly among teenagers with journalistic aspirations, who downloaded her new Locket app in their tens of thousands—her position as a minor literary celebrity must have seemed assured. The moment had faded, though, I thought as I made one or two non-committal noises in response to Zelda Green, and again pressed the buzzer to summon the bar staff. She had dropped from sight, and was now at a low ebb, whatever level of fiction or reality she was operating on—which still only partly explained why she was talking to me, in the Travelodge bar off Waterloo Bridge. What exactly had gone wrong for Zelda Green, I wondered—why had the light faded from her name? Even the most well-financed idea, in the hands of highly trained personnel, can simply lose momentum and coherence, I thought, and while the continued wait for a reveal had been tantalising, the most feverish interest had exhausted itself: the moment been and gone, uncapitalised on. Peak Zelda Green was behind us. At her height theories had proliferated wildly, I remembered. The most shared, that Zelda Green was the brainchild of this *poetry world svengali figure*, had been embellished with a subplot that the *poetry world svengali figure* was themselves a failed poet with enormous private wealth, who had set up the venture as a vanity project, to experience the poet's rise vicariously—in this version, Zelda Green's works were actually the works of this failed poet, who intended to prove a theory that the reception of a poem was determined entirely by the image of the poet, I now remembered. Others thought that Zelda Green was most likely the creation of one of the media platforms she had helped popularise by association, Weibo or Basket. But the most plausible explanation I'd heard was that Zelda Green was really no more than an image consultancy experiment, with no firm wager in the poetry sector or apps market beyond aiming to prove they could be manipulated at will—part of a broad drive to amass data on the dynamics of small arts scenes, but mainly a case study used to impress prospective clients with the depth of the firm's reach and its experimental edge—it wanted to attract the kind of clients who would enjoy being in on the joke, I thought. Whatever the truth of the situation, there was nothing I could do for Zelda Green at that moment, a fact she seemed to remember a minute or two after she started speaking to me, her expression glazing over fractionally. She spun away towards another cluster, leaving me at the bar, in the empty buffer zone that had formed around the two people I'd spotted earlier, a man and a woman, who sat facing away from the throng. The pause allowed me to take a long look in the mirror behind the bar and examine the two faces reflected there. The woman on the left I recognised from my Bury days, with mild curiosity, as Phoebe Glass, while the man, in his early twenties, wearing an unseasonable dark coat threaded with a lighter weave, was familiar to me from other poetry events—I used to see him attending recitals on his own, where he'd usually sit at the bar on a high stool, wearing his dark coat threaded with a lighter weave, unseasonable or not, as he was doing now. I knew at this point that he must be Solomon Wiese, or I knew it without knowing it—it had simply become obvious that every development pointed in that direction, that the familiarity of his face mirrored my recent awareness of his name, that they matched, so it was no surprise to me that when I took my place at the bar beside him and Phoebe Glass, who I greeted with a nod, as I once again pressed the buzzer to summon the bar staff, he identified me at once and introduced himself. His voice was soft but perfectly audible above the clamour of the bar—it seemed to come from *below* the clamour of the bar, in fact, to address me privately—I was quickly mesmerised by this voice, which although soft was rapid and precise. As I looked around for the bar staff, who were nowhere to be seen, I mentioned the name of the head of the small publishing company, and said he had told me something about Solomon Wiese's current predicament; Solomon Wiese repeated the name of the head of the small publishing company in his soft voice, before asking if I knew the head of the small publishing company's wife—I remembered for a moment the persistence of her gaze—and did I also know that she had recently given the head of the small publishing company one more year, *not a day more*, to make a financial success of his small publishing company, or they were moving to the Near East, where her father was involved in a large rare-earth mining corporation, which the head of the small publishing company would work for, probably in an administrative role of some description, for a lot more money. This would mean the wife of the head of the small publishing company wouldn't have to work as a dentist, which Solomon Wiese had heard from a reliable source she had no desire to do—she hated looking into people's mouths, she hated inspecting the granular textures of tongues and the disgusting protuberances of the browned and yellowed teeth, and she especially hated seeing the little nodules of food that were caught there, Solomon Wiese's source had heard—she found it all completely disgusting, she had decided, and so had informed the head of the small publishing company that unless the financial situation improved dramatically with regard to the small publishing company, which he had run for something like nine years, they were moving to the Near East, where he would work for her father at the rare-earth mining corporation, that was the long and the short of it. I said it was news to me. At this point the barman, who had finally materialised, placed a pint of lager on the bartop, which I had already noticed was sticky and smelled strongly of synthetic fruit. As I swiped my thumb on the scanner he held out, I remembered the head of the small publishing company's pained expression earlier in the afternoon, when I'd left before hearing the conclusion of his story about Solomon Wiese, and felt a pang of something, pity perhaps, as I would miss the head of the small publishing company, in a way, if he were to vacate his post in the literary sector, which now seemed like a certainty, as the idea that he would transform his small publishing company into a highly profitable organisation, despite the recently increased returns on poetry, was frankly laughable, knowing what I did of the head of the small publishing company's business acumen and general efficiency. I also felt the stirrings of a renewed interest in Solomon Wiese's predicament, which I felt sure was connected to the presence of Phoebe Glass; Phoebe Glass, the friend of my once-girlfriend Jessica Lake. I suddenly recalled Phoebe Glass's largely silent presence during my days at Lake Clothes, the sense of steely observation from her corner of the shop, and her tendency towards intense negativity, as expressed, I had thought at the time, in her exacting frown and the *forward tilt of her head*—this was in contrast to Jessica Lake's equally intense positivity, and her tendency to *toss her head back* when she laughed, I remembered. In Lake Clothes, Phoebe Glass would sometimes launch into detailed attacks on her and Jessica Lake's acquaintances, people who were unknown to me, extended verbal assaults or in-depth character assassinations that Jessica Lake would recklessly throw her head back to laugh at. Jessica Lake's essentially *postitive* charge seemed balanced out, in the atmosphere of Lake Clothes, especially as she tossed her head *back*, with Phoebe's Glass's essentially *negative* charge, as she tilted her head *forwards*—and where Jessica Lake's positivity had a permanent undercurrent of sadness, I had always thought, Phoebe Glass's negativity had had a permanent undercurrent of joy. I'd never worked out what she thought of me—we had left Bury at roughly the same time, I remembered; later she had become an avid cultural commentator, with a reputation for merciless, categorical, not to say humorous and incisive social critique. She had stayed pointedly quiet during Solomon Wiese's description of the wife of the head of the small publishing company's ultimatum, I noticed. But we're not like that, are we, Solomon Wiese was saying in his soft voice, retrieving my attention with a glance: he was referring to the head of the small publishing company's imminent departure from the scene. We're in it for life, aren't we, he said, turning a bottle of beer in front of him, not looking at me now but seemingly at himself in the mirror behind the Travelodge bar. And if it's easy to be in it for life when you've made use of certain advantages, it's also no longer your choice to be in it for life, it becomes inevitable, Solomon Wiese said to me, turning the bottle of beer on the bar, there's a real inevitability to it. In it for life—that's how it works for people like us, he said. Our eyes met in the bar mirror, and then the eyes of Phoebe Glass joined them, and there was no antagonism in her face, but a gentle, almost sympathetic expression, which hovered there, in the mirror, over the backdrop of jostling bodies of increasingly drunk poets who now filled the Travelodge bar. I wondered briefly about her and Solomon Wiese. I don't know if you believe in the destiny of the poet, Solomon Wiese continued, looking down at his beer bottle with a small smile, and although it was a ridiculous statement I was instantly alarmed by it, because the statement was also an accusation, I thought, an allusion to my abandonment of poetry, even though there was no hint of this on Solomon Wiese's face or in his tone of voice, which remained soft, and so I couldn't fully explain the uneasiness I felt, as I sat at the Travelodge bar, at the biennial Festival of Culture, facing away from the throng. We start off believing that we're special, don't we, Solomon Wiese went on, but we keep this knowledge secret, unaware at first of the mundane reality that our private and innermost belief is shared by everyone who also shares our supposedly unique aspiration—the thing that we believe makes us unique, we later discover, is the thing that is shared by absolutely everyone, and everyone desires the same things that we desire—yet we are still convinced that we possess a *unique ingredient*, no matter how much we protest against it later, and we hold on to this hidden piece of information, never admitting it to anyone, but the fact is it powers our pursuit through life, and it justifies our actions when we capitalise on every natural or unnatural advantage, every vagary of fortune. Outwardly we learn to renounce it, Solomon Wiese said, there comes a time when we even forbid ourselves to think of it, we dismiss it as the illusion of ego and the lottery of birth. Because on the surface, in your case, Solomon Wiese said, with his small smile, turning his beer on the bartop, it would have seemed quite remarkable, almost an achievement, if given the circumstances of your upbringing, your socialisation and early education, you had failed to find success in your field in some way or another. Raised within easy reach of every cultural hub worth knowing about, and, I can state without having to enquire, within a liberal family who valued above all the artistic accomplishment. We can, both of us, repeat to ourselves and to others versions of this statement over our whole lives, that it is all down to circumstance, that it is a matter of luck, and at times we almost come to believe it, we come within inches of believing it, and it seems to us that we believe it. And to further convince ourselves, we scorn any explanation other than the purely material one. But from deeper within, a counter-assertion is always waiting to tip us back the other way, isn't it, Solomon Wiese said—back to the lodestone of our secret knowledge, with the lightest of touches. It is a dark, ulterior impulse that steadies us, that reassures us of our basic imperative—like a hard, cold hand that emerges from behind a curtain, reaching out, gripping us, whenever we start to turn too far away from our inheritance. *You don't really believe that*—this is what the hand says, silently, said Solomon Wiese, as his own hand reached out of his dark coat and gripped my sleeve, or it says, *we know differently, don't we*, back here, behind the curtain of appearances, where our secret knowledge sits untouched, like treasure, away from all this talk. As Solomon Wiese was speaking he produced a vaporiser from the pocket of the dark coat he had kept on, despite the airless and oppressive atmosphere of the Travelodge bar, and the mist he exhaled had a sour, musty smell I couldn't identify. I know you're going to ask me what happened, Solomon Wiese said without pausing, through a cloud of vapour. As soon as I saw you come in, I knew what you were going to ask me. I watched you in the mirror, he said, gesturing with his forehead, as you wandered around, waiting for you to come over here and ask me what happened. And I knew what I would say to you when you did, I imagined it, as I sat here, playing out like this—exactly as it has, he said, expelling sour, musty vapour from his nostrils. I sat here and imagined you standing here next to me, as you are at this moment, as I told you what I'm telling you now. I knew exactly what you'd ask me, the minute I saw you, and I knew what I'd say in reply, he said, glancing to his left at Phoebe Glass, who didn't speak. I took a sip of my lager and eyed him in the mirror, noticing again the empty buffer zone that had formed, apparently of its own accord, around the spot that he and Phoebe Glass had taken, and where I now was also marooned. As I listened, I kept thinking that I should get away from this situation—you should leave at once, I thought to myself, leave immediately, before this goes any further, before you become *embroiled*, emotionally or otherwise, but for some reason I made no attempt to leave, I continued to wait there, and if anything I leaned more deeply against the Travelodge bar, erasing the condensation on my glass in vertical strips with my thumb. For as long as he could remember, Solomon Wiese said, more slowly now, as if satisfied that for the time being I was trapped, he had had a desire to disappear. Even as a small child. He could remember his earliest attempts at disappearance, his dreams about it, dreams in which a scene played out before him, completely neutrally, like a surveillance tape, a scene of his family in the car, for example, and although he wasn't there, in the car, he wasn't missing either—it was simply as if I never existed, Solomon Wiese said. When he was seven or eight he had decided to hide somewhere, because of this idea, he thought; he had hidden in a tree in the corner of the garden of the house where he grew up. He had climbed up high in the tree and, staying incredibly still, he had watched and listened—he listened for the first sounds of his disappearance, for his name when it sounded from inside the house. There was no definite moment when his absence was noticed, he realised, and though he heard many voices and sounds from up in the tree, it was hard to understand their meanings, he wasn't sure if the sounds contained the sound of his name—then he heard a voice calling him distinctly, and he saw his sister come out into the garden, walk towards the tree where he was hidden, look around, then turn back towards the house. The air calmed around him, and the house went quiet for what seemed like a long time, I saw the sun had changed its angle, Solomon Wiese said, and that it was nearly evening. After waiting even longer, he could almost imagine that the house in front of him was *any* house, he said, it was gradually emptying of its familiarity, it was a house that looked so ordinary he began to wonder why it was he was looking at it—why this particular house, he had wondered, and not another house. He stayed very still in the tree, and now it was as if he were somehow *inside* the tree, looking out through its branches—it was a holly tree, covered with prickly leaves that he had had to move through carefully when he took his place in it, and the leaves hid him from view completely. He imagined what it would be like if he had staggered out of the woods that were behind the house, if he had no memory, and the back of this house was the first house he had ever seen. He almost began to believe that he *had* staggered out of the woods, that he had no memory, and that he was waiting patiently in the tree, watching the first house he had come to, waiting for dark to fall—that is what would happen next, he realised, if he stayed in the tree. Darkness would fall, and at intervals the windows of the house would light up. Despite his absence the lights inside the house would be turned on. He would see his family moving around inside the kitchen and the living room, but for some reason he didn't imagine them panicked, making calls, trying to discover where he was, but going about their evening completely normally, it was like in his dream of the car, he imagined them serving up hot food onto plates and sitting down to eat. Eventually, Solomon Wiese said, he had gone back into the house—he knew this must have happened, although he didn't remember it, and he didn't remember being punished or questioned by his parents, he only remembered the hours in the holly tree, where he had stayed almost motionless, and he thought later that it was as if some part of him *had* come out of the woods and climbed up with him in the tree, and watched the house as the sky had changed to a deeper colour. Things changed while he was in the tree, but not at a rate you would notice, only at some point you noticed they *had* changed. It sounded more dramatic than it really was, but since then he felt as if he had always carried a small amount of the nothingness he had experienced, waiting in the holly tree, watching his family home until it became unfamiliar, a kind of nothingness that stayed alongside him, in such a way that he always knew where it was—he knew where it was in his bedroom, where it waited while he brushed his teeth, and how it followed him around at school. There was no characteristic at all he could give to this nothingness, that was what made it a nothingness, it was nothing threatening or frightening and nothing comforting either, it was simply there, like a water outline left on paper that had once had something spilled on it. Probably the nothingness had always been with him, Solomon Wiese said, but the day he climbed up inside the holly tree was the first time he had noticed it. Later on, he found the nothingness could be used as a receptacle of sorts—if he wasn't sure why he had done something, it sometimes seemed the answer was contained in the outline of the nothingness, or that he could perhaps place it there. He tested this, in a quiet way, without telling anyone about the presence of the nothingness, out of embarrassment partly, and the fact he didn't know how to articulate it, of course, being seven or eight years old. He had probably given a particular image or flavour to the nothingness simply by using the word "nothingness," that was in fact inaccurate; he hadn't conceptualised it this way when he was seven or eight years old, he had actually hardly thought about it, he was merely aware of it, in the same way he was aware, for example, of a discoloured area of wood inside a cupboard in the spare room of his family house, that was roughly the size and shape of a face. The nothingness, it was fair to say, did seem connected to other things of this type that he could think of, when he looked back, but it was hard to tell if he was forcing the connections. There was a picture he remembered that had looked like a pinkish watery smudge to him for most of his childhood, he had never noticed more about it than this, and it had become associated with the idea of the nothingness, due to its indistinctness, its slightly out-of-the-way placing on the stairs, until one day he looked at it and saw a hill—a distant hill and a line of trees, completely clearly, and there was no room for nothingness in the picture anymore. Then there had been times when the nothingness had swum into the foreground, become more obvious—specific occasions when, looking back, it seemed to be there more distinctly than usual. He remembered, for example, playing football on the playground at primary school—they were playing, he remembered, with a squishy miniature football, and during the game the squishy miniature football had deflected off his foot and flown straight into the face of the teacher on break duty—Mrs. Hewitt, who at that moment had been raising a mug of hot tea to her lips, which the miniature football, for all its squishiness, had smashed to pieces, covering Mrs. Hewitt's face with scalding tea, and giving her a fat lip and a bloody nose—he remembered the unbelievable sight of Mrs. Hewitt bowing to eject blood from her mouth and nostrils. Mrs. Hewitt, the elderly teacher of the first form, for five- and six-year-olds, who was the kindest of the teachers, and had treated Solomon Wiese with a special affection, it had seemed, when he had started at school. Gasps went around the playground. Everyone had seen Mrs. Hewitt surrounded by pieces of ceramic, still clutching the handle of the shattered mug, her blouse and cardigan darkened with tea, as she spat strings of blood from her nose and mouth. The accident, to Solomon Wiese's amazement, was treated as malicious by the other staff member on duty, a bearded man who emerged as the main witness and claimed that Solomon Wiese had *intentionally* kicked the ball at Mrs. Hewitt's face at the moment she was raising the steaming cup of tea to her lips—the expression on little Solomon Wiese's face was portrayed, in this second teacher's account, as being filled with malicious intent, and to this several other pupils added they had seen Solomon Wiese laughing immediately afterwards. He was laughing about it, they said, and the image of little Solomon Wiese's face contorted with glee was instantly transmitted to all the staff and pupils of the primary school. In the face of the accusation Solomon Wiese tried to remember the moment his foot had made contact with the squishy miniature football, and he began to wonder if he hadn't experienced a moment of recklessness, and if in this rush of exuberance he hadn't directed the kick, as his foot came into contact with the miniature football, towards Mrs. Hewitt, where she stood around the halfway line, at the side of the playground. An unfocused exuberance that had momentarily spilled over into aggression, he thought, a flash of almost joyful recklessness, submerged as soon as it was experienced, which had caused him to direct the football, as far as he was able to, at Mrs. Hewitt's head, with its helmet of grey hair, as she raised the mug of tea to her lips. That was how it had seemed to him, when he thought about it, as an eight- or nine-year-old, although of course he would have struggled to describe it—and with this thought he became aware again, suddenly, of the nothingness. Listening to the bearded member of staff's accusations, which this member of staff seemed to exult in for some reason, Solomon Wiese found he was able to instantly deposit both possibilities, that is, his complete innocence of any wrongdoing, of which he was certain, and his joyful, reckless wish to cause harm, which now also appeared certain, *inside the nothingness*, where they cancelled each other out, returning, he thought now, Solomon Wiese said in the Travelodge bar, to a kind of raw potentiality—they reverted to this state with a tiny visual adjustment, like a lens refocusing, somewhere in the nothingness's non-shape. The effect was that the young Solomon Wiese was able to accept the blame for striking the ball in Mrs. Hewitt's direction with no sense of outrage or ill-feeling: he immediately ceased his tearful protests, he endured his punishment of being kept indoors during several subsequent break times unquestioningly. Perhaps his parents had noticed a change in Solomon Wiese's disposition at around this time, the emergence of a kind of passivity, a broad, unemotional acknowledgement of things as they were, which could seem at times like indifference, odd in such a young child, Solomon Wiese said, but nothing that concerned them unduly. His recourse to the nothingness soon became part of his internal behaviour, part of his habits of thought, at least that's what I would say now, Solomon Wiese said—it slowly sank from consciousness and became a reflex, with no external indicator. For the rest of his childhood and through his teenage years it stayed hidden from view, only recurring in certain periods, which he would always forget about soon after—but somehow whenever he experienced the nothingness again, all of its previous appearances rose into sight too, down the years, like bubbles grouping together against the curvature of a bottle. For example, after he had learned to drive, aged eighteen, and would borrow his parents' car at night to do laps of the ring road of the town where he grew up, sometimes until early in the morning, alone, listening to music and drinking caffeinated soft drinks, he remembered pulling up at a red light, the road ahead completely empty, the pristine surface with its banded markings extending into the darkness, waiting for the lights to change, and becoming aware of the nothingness beside him in the passenger seat. And then all the nothingnesses, rising into view like clear balloons. The point was that apart from those times, which were rare, the nothingnesses remained out of sight, Solomon Wiese said. It was this nothingness that had attracted him to poetry in the first place, without his realising it, he thought now. The literal nothingness on the page, invading from the right margin, threatening to wipe out meaning entirely, and the nothingness he experienced when he had begun to write, after finding volumes filled with this nothingness in charity shops around town—rather than *making* something, Solomon Wiese said, the writing of poetry was far more like *deleting* something, it was like pointing at something to make it disappear. It tapped into his deep desire for disappearance, Solomon Wiese said. He had recognised it immediately, on some level, the first time he set eyes on a poem—the presence of the familiar nothingness, he thought now, it had been almost reassuring to him, unlike most people, who when they set eyes on a poem reacted with incomprehension and annoyance. Prisoners and lonely children reacted in a similar way, he said, they got it immediately. The encroaching absence. The blank space invading the pathetic structures that were built to hold it at bay, the complete futility of those structures, and the chance to see them overwhelmed at last. Even reading a poem was like watching something retreating—it was like watching a worm disappearing into a crack in the wall, and poetry in general was working its way, like a worm, slowly but undeterrably, towards its removal from life. He had felt this instinctively, and when he read about the poets from the past, he took note if they had ever said similar things, which sometimes they had—a poem was the removal of a thing from the world rather than the addition of a thing to the world, Solomon Wiese said, poetry was the gradual *replacement* of things in the world with their absence, and to write a poem you had to want this to happen, it required a certain vengefulness. You had to be fixated on it, on helping the edge of nothingness eat away at the world of objects, like acid, until all of it, you had to hope, would dissolve one day, it would all be vaporised into a meaningless poem that no one could read, because they had been vaporised too, Solomon Wiese said, jetting sour mist from the side of his mouth. Right from the beginning, with the first poems he wrote, he had treated it as a project of eradication, he said, without quite realising it; for him poetry had become a kind of *pest control for stray thoughts*—in fact, for him poetry became one big *extermination project*. Writing a poem, for him, was a way of hunting something down, of cornering it and destroying it, isolating it, boxing it in with words, essentially, nailing it to the ground and then drumming it out of existence. Repeating it until it was worn away, and only a smudge remained, a meaningless smudge—that was the desired result. Rather than a form of meditation, or a method of understanding or empathy, or a means of communication, as he had sometimes heard it described as he sat in the audiences of poetry recitals, his heart full of loathing and scepticism, it was at bottom a way of *stopping* thinking about something, of *preventing* it from continuing, Solomon Wiese said. His head at that time was full of the words of older poets, dead poets and poets still alive but older than him, who may have known the truth about poetry at one time but had since made themselves forget it in their bid for endless productivity and validation, Solomon Wiese said. His head had been buzzing with their words since he first became interested in poetry, when he began collecting sand-coloured paperbacks of all-but-forgotten poetry, these all-but-forgotten poems had taken up all the room in his head, so when he came to write his own poems, he had wanted to expel them, to wipe them from his memory, and so he had effectively regurgitated these words, words that no longer had any associations to him, but were like pieces of rubbish lying around in places where people had long since vanished, with voices and feelings that had also long since vanished. He wanted to regurgitate all this meaningless rubbish that he'd accumulated, just by reading poetry, so he had simply thrown it up onto the page to make it disappear, because it was making him sick, he thought, and he wanted to get rid of it—he wanted these old poems *nothinged*, in effect, Solomon Wiese said. Poetry was his way of evacuating poems from his system, of disowning the useless thoughts he couldn't stop thinking—he had to write them down to get them out of his head. After that he didn't care what happened to them—the pretence of writing a poem simply allowed him to expel them from his mind, once and for all, Solomon Wiese said, in the Travelodge bar. The promise of publication was just an excuse, a ruse, I may not have realised it then, but it was merely the pretext for the act of purging myself of these useless thoughts, from hundreds of all-but-forgotten poetry books, he said. So when at the start of the year, still taking his first tentative steps as an emerging poet, he had received notification of the penalty, that is, the email that informed him a poem he had sent to a small journal had returned an infringement score above the acceptable threshold, that in other words he had failed the now-notorious quantitative analysis and comparison (QACS) authenticity test, it was as if he'd already known, he said. He'd known something was wrong, and that all this time he had been operating under a basic misconception. He didn't react with any surprise, as when he read the email from the service people at the quantitative analysis and comparison system (QACS), it was as if he already possessed an identical piece of information, and so there was no painful moment of realisation. He had already known it, on some level, even though he hadn't realised it prior to reading the email, deep down he had expected it. As soon as he'd read the email he had remembered that he already knew. He didn't question the verdict, and he didn't return to it later, privately, to absorb it, because he was already aware of it, he realised, he had just suspended this awareness somehow. He didn't hate them any less for this fact, the people at the quantitative analysis and comparison system (QACS), Solomon Wiese said, he hated their appalling neutrality, even if it was all automated, even if the email had been sent out automatically, *especially* then, because there was nonetheless a tone to the automation, a personality, the automated response was still the work of a person, or a group of people, and he could sense them behind the contrived informality of the missive he had received—the informality that although supposedly amicable was utterly impersonal. But it was also impersonal in such a way that was profoundly revealing about the poverty of spirit of its creators, Solomon Wiese had thought, he said. He envisaged a work space teeming with programmers, their positivity and pragmatism, their office pranks, their coding jokes, their wrist supports, their special juices, their memes, their shortcuts, and their determination to frustrate his project of removal, no doubt because the only thing that made sense to them was to *accumulate*, he said. To gather more and more—more information, more processes, more hardware, to necessitate more invention, more activity. A roomful of proficient and soulless *machine operators*, against the anguished spirit of the poet, that was how he pictured it, he must have been distraught—he had visualised himself as a solitary figure adrift in a landscape that could never understand him.

That was the image that he conjured up, in the wake of his penalisation at the hands of the newly armed publishing industry, with its quantitative analysis and comparison system (QACS), Solomon Wiese said. He had allowed himself that indulgence. For a while he was sure that it was over, he said. It was a complete waste of time and energy, anyway, poetry, and now it was over; he could stop writing poems. He deleted everything. He went through his hard drive and wiped it all, every draft, he deleted all back-ups, he trashed it, he released it back evenly into the void. There was a real satisfaction to it. It was only now that he began to realise this was what he'd been trying to do the whole time, when he was writing poetry, that it was what he had been aiming for all along. His intention was only revealed to him as he systematically deleted everything he had ever written—that the real purpose behind his writing was literally to *get rid of it.* Only this wasn't possible, of course. Not only because he had to have created something in order to delete it—he sensed as he was doing the deleting that this was a one-off, that it wouldn't work if he did it knowingly; if he wrote something with the intention of deleting it, it wouldn't work, because in reality he would be deleting nothing. But *getting rid of it* also wasn't possible in a more direct sense, because there were back-ups, back-ups beyond the back-ups, back-ups that he couldn't access, preserved forms of his poems that had been cast deep into the petrified chambers of the data cloud, where someone with the right tools and expertise could locate them; it was simply not possible, anymore, to erase something completely, a trace always remained in the multiversal maps of communications history. Sitting at his monitor he had felt a longing for earlier times, when you could simply burn something. You could take a match to something and burn it and it was gone, there was no chasing around after ghostly older versions that hung around him, yet were out of reach, like spots on a mirror. The nothingness was there with him, he realised, as he thought about this, and it was the first time he'd really felt it as an adult, or that he'd thought about it directly. All its previous appearances bobbed into view, as they had before, but this time they remained on the surface, and he found he could recall them at will; as memories they seemed extraordinarily well preserved, untainted by repeated recollection, and not wanting to dull them he refrained from thinking about them too often, he was happy to let them float around him, with their rich, weightless emptiness. The future critics of culture would not be wasting their time with poetry anyway, he told himself, after he had deleted everything as far as possible, and began resigning himself to long-term artistic inactivity. The recent spike of public interest in poetry, in the wake of the industry-wide publishing crisis, was only an illusion, a distortion, Solomon Wiese said, and soon that illusion would be dispelled, revealing poetry to be in an even weaker condition than before its artificial revival. Then it would be divided up and absorbed by the more popular, commercial disciplines as their borders expanded, Solomon Wiese said. The current situation was a kind of dream that poets would be abruptly awoken from, sooner or later, that is what he had told himself, Solomon Wiese said—he compassed with a fluttering hand the increasingly loud and intermingled cliques of poets standing around us, in loosening bunches, in the close alcoholic fug of the Travelodge bar. For a long time poetry had been existing in a kind of afterlife, and it had failed to become aware of this fact, he went on, because it had been superficially reinvigorated by a series of short-lived innovations, the rapidly turned-over fashions of zonal poetry, or yellow hammer poetry, or xxx poetry, or wicca poetry, or velvet poetry, or uvular poetry, or triumphalist traditionalist poetry, or sloomy poetry, or ritualistic poetry, or quiet poetry, or pylon poetry, or optical poetry, or nostalgic nationalist poetry, or macro poetry, or literal poetry, or joke poetry, or icicle poetry, or house of horror poetry, or grey poetry or green poetry, or fey poetry or fugue poetry, or evil poetry, doom poetry, civil service poetry, bed poetry or automated poetry, but these were little jolts of life that could never sustain it for long—poetry was like a branch that had been snapped away from the trunk, and was slowly being drained of its last resources, Solomon Wiese said. Inside it was already hollow, and its sporadic signs of life were actually caused by the rampant decay already in progress below the surface. Its intermittent, anaemic growths were merely the reflexes of a corpse, expending the last of its spastic energy—it could perhaps extend its pale half-life into the next decade, before it suffered a complete internal collapse, and its remaining parts were farmed out to younger and more vital art forms, Solomon Wiese said. These remnants would be grafted onto new cultural movements, engorged and reanimated as part of the new traditions, and they would be thoroughly corporate, commercial traditions, if he was being honest, not artistic traditions, and if there were apparent similarities, upon closer examination the actual purpose and value of these resurrected remnants of the latest dead art form would have been completely altered. Their former uses would be forgotten, their once fresh inventions would become routine formulas in the emergent corporate, commercial media culture. Artistic electricity would be remade as corporate, commercial grease for the synapses, basically—or so Solomon Wiese told himself in the bleak spring, as he began adjusting to his life as a non-poet, in the wake of his penalisation by the quantitative analysis and comparison system (QACS). The disadvantage of giving up poetry was that he found he was unable to stop thinking about all the things he had previously been able to expel from his mind *through* poetry, he said, the circular thoughts and repeating phrases that had plagued him since he had started reading and writing poetry four or five years previously. It might not seem like a particularly long time, Solomon Wiese said, but you had to remember that in the early stages of growth a year is a *whole era of development*, a complex history with subsidiary phases and changes of dynasty, whereas later, for someone like you, he said to me in the Travelodge bar, that becomes hard to believe, a year is barely breathing space between projects, it's a minor lull, an afternoon, a chance to regroup, he said. But for me, four years was almost like four lifetimes set end to end. I lived through whole artistic movements in that period, I survived their deaths, he said, and I saw them resurrected a century later, in their new lives, while you were probably staring at your socks, or peeling a banana, or waiting for the bill in a restaurant, he added. I didn't respond to this portrait of myself. I realised, though, that my movements of impatience and anxiety had gradually ceased, and that the three of us had unwittingly moved closer together, our heads tilted towards one another, as if in conspiracy, at the Travelodge bar. I momentarily met Phoebe Glass's eyes again in the mirror, pinched in amusement or scepticism, I couldn't be certain. The density of time is different in those early periods, Solomon Wiese said, but perhaps you don't need to be reminded of that. The density of information that you encounter really *determines your experience of time*, and in this sense time *is* information, Solomon Wiese said. There was nothing original about this as an observation, but the experience of it was actually novel, when you grasped it for yourself, he said. When he stopped writing, the experience of time became smooth and frictionless, it became hard to tell how fast it was moving, as to all appearances it had more or less slowed to a complete standstill, despite the fact that time was actually *accelerating*, Solomon Wiese said. Months were passing his windows in a pale flicker. He was trapped with his thoughts again, there was no way to discard them, and immediately he had become morbidly preoccupied with a particular question, a question that had been frozen in his mind when he had first opened the automated email and received his caution from the quantitative analysis and comparison system (QACS). He couldn't determine, when this had happened, he said, if he had been caught in the *act of hiding*, that is, in the act of concealing himself behind the words and ideas of others, when he had regurgitated the secondhand phrases that comprised his poetry—*or* if he had been caught in the *act of exposing himself*, that is, in the act of revealing the thoughts and ideas he couldn't stop thinking about, that were painfully personal to him, and which he had to free himself of by writing down. This thought had arrested him at the exact moment he had opened the email from QACS. Concealment or exposure. Hiding or revealing. Both seemed equally shameful. Around and around it went, in Solomon Wiese's head, especially at night. At first he tried to be methodical—he visualised a series of doors—that was how bad it got. The first door represented a simple interpretation: he had copied the work of others, to increase his standing as a young poet, and he had been caught in *the act of hiding*. He passed easily through this door, which was so large it was hardly a door at all. The second door represented his defence, and was a much smaller, person-sized door—his thefts, it said, although blatant, couldn't really be described as calculated, as there had been an involuntary aspect to them, to the point that he hadn't been aware of what he was doing—it was all mixed together, his language and the language of others, it was like pulling a sock out of machine-load of wet washing, he couldn't be expected to know who it belonged to. But Solomon Wiese had to admit that it wasn't random either—it wasn't as if any random line had been sucked undiscerningly into the industrious whirlpool inside his head. In this sense his selections, however disorganised, were *an act of revealing*—the poem he had served up to the literary community was like a nest his brain had sat in. He passed through the second door. The third door was small, close to the ground, you had to get through it on hands and knees. This door was a justification: it proposed that he, Solomon Wiese, had memorised only items that were connected with things that he *wanted to disappear*. The third door showed his recycled poetry as a version of a prisoner's wall markings—a list of things that stood between him and the broader aim of disappearance—they were connected to him only in the sense that they helped to confine him. His *act of exposure* was carried out in *order to hide*. He crawled through the third door, and immediately found himself facing the fourth door—actually two narrow doors that you could pass through only by turning to your side—its dual nature seeming to represent a question. Through these doors he could see a fifth door in the darkness ahead, made up of four low, revolving doors, like slots, which he would have to roll through, and an overwhelming sense of futility washed over him. At this point he would often start to dream, Solomon Wiese said. A particular dream had remained with him, and he had even had the dream recurrently, he thought. He was spending the night with an old friend, in a house near the train station, but late in the evening it became clear that he couldn't stay there after all—nothing serious, but he went out to find a hotel. He had two large suitcases, which his friend said he could leave behind. He walked the dark, empty streets around the station, it was very late, and eventually he found a small hotel on a street beside the river. Sitting on the bed in his room, about to remove his shoes, he had heard voices through the wall—the voice of a young woman, as if asking a question, then the voice of an older man, as if providing an answer. Suddenly Solomon Wiese became convinced that the voices were coming not from the adjoining room, but from the cupboard—he opened the cupboard door, but instead of a man and a woman, or an iron and an ironing board, he found a passage with walls of unfinished brick and wet rock, which he followed for what seemed like a long time, until he appeared back inside his friend's house, emerging from behind a curtain in the kitchen. Everything was the same as when he'd left, except his friend had spilled something red onto his shirt, and, Solomon Wiese saw, his friend's face now had a strange silvery tint to it. When he looked more closely, his friend's skin was of a colourless tone that reflected the light almost in the manner of a metallic object. He tried to retrieve his suitcases from the bedroom upstairs, but his friend refused, not recognising him, and no amount of explanation or effort to remind him of who he was had any effect. Drawing rapidly and repeatedly on his vaporiser, Solomon Wiese continued to give his account of the dream's ending, but now I was only half-listening, as a detail had reminded me of my encounter with Christian Wort earlier in the evening, which until then I had managed to avoid thinking about. After spotting his figure by the deserted stage area, a couple of hours previously, on the cavernous ground floor of the Southbank Centre, noting that he was holding the glass of wine with which I presumed he had disrupted my recital of the poetry of Zariyah Zhadan in English, I had approached him—he greeted me without enthusiasm, and said he was waiting for someone. Over ten years had passed since we'd last seen each other, and Christian Wort was much changed—he was virtually unrecognisable, in fact, it was only his posture that gave him away. He was smartly dressed, like the typical man of the city, a dark suit and white shirt with a large, stiff-looking collar. I saw a cufflink glint as he lifted his hand to shake mine. He still carried his weight mainly on one leg. Despite his attire Christian Wort didn't look well, though, I thought, as I voiced some meaningless platitude about how good it was seeing him again, after all this time—he looked dreadful, I was thinking, as I said how good it was to see him, and as I uttered the words *it's good to see you* I realised their obvious falsity, and actually how terrible he looked, though it was difficult to pinpoint what it was about him precisely that gave that impression. There was an air of sickliness about him, I had thought, of late nights, of work involving abstract sums of money, of overlit offices, a flat overlooking a train line, or on reclaimed land, new carpets, the same solitary mind I remembered but now fully adapted to the corporate, commercial environment, filleted of its sentimentality, that was for sure—I pictured Christian Wort's windowless bathroom, I pictured him ironing his tie with the news on in the background, the long hours polishing his mental tools: a life of competition and cultivated, professional hunger. Or at least that is how it appeared to me, on the cavernous ground floor of the Southbank Centre. He spoke very little—whatever I had imagined saying to him as I approached was impossible, and it was hard to be certain if it wasn't an effect of the lighting and my general sense of foreboding, but I remembered thinking that his skin had looked almost grey, that it even had a kind of metallic lustre, as if his cheeks had been shaded in with pencil—that was more or less the effect. A silvery tint—I had glanced at my own hands for comparison, but they appeared normal under the lights, and I had been on the point of scrutinising him more carefully, I thought, but I had forgotten about it, after he had made his request. Of course I wondered now about the identity of Solomon Wiese's friend, in his dream, as I drank my drink and surveyed the debauchery taking place behind me, in the mirror of the Travelodge bar. The buffer zone was intact, separating us from the throng; I was still stranded. Phoebe Glass was drumming at her phone. I wondered again if I was ready to call time on the encounter—I disliked the implication of Solomon Wiese's claims about destiny, or whatever he chose to call it, the poet's lot, it sounded suspicious, unsavoury, when I returned to it now, basically dubious, I thought, as Solomon Wiese continued to describe the ending of his dream—too close to some sort of occult theory of natural superiority. I had rejected all that when I gave up on my poetry aspirations and became an editor, but even as I thought this I made no move to leave, I simply went on standing there, or rather leaning there, at the bar, making no attempt to disengage myself. The dream had had a profound effect on him, Solomon Wiese was saying; it had had significant consequences, because the dream had made it clear to him that he was an imposter in his own life, or in both of his lives, if you prefer, in his life as a poet, where he was clearly an imposter in the most literal sense, and in his life as a non-poet, where he could only listen through the wall to his other life, now foreclosed—only leaving one life for the other had allowed him to see this, he said. He had had to leave in order to return, like in his dream, and perceive the hidden reality of his situation, a reality in which his friend had a stain on his shirt and silvery grey skin, and wanted to keep his property from him. What is a friend, precisely, at this juncture in history, Solomon Wiese said, turning to me—in fact, where are *your* friends? I mean friends you could rely on, regardless of the mistakes you might make, friends who wouldn't distance themselves due to some work-related embarrassment, for example, friends who are not also colleagues or professional acquaintances, who are not associated first and foremost with your activities as an agent of the cultural sector, and as such loyal to you only in terms of your actions in that capacity, Solomon Wiese asked me, blowing sour vapour across the surface of my beer. I watched the cloud coast towards the mirror, and chose to remain silent. It was true, though, that none of my acquaintances had approached me since I had been stationed at the bar, I thought. I had given up attempting make eye contact with anyone who drifted within range, when it became apparent I was being actively avoided—that I was being *blanked*, in other words, due to my choice of companion, by the poetry community. Friendship is an *invention*, Solomon Wiese was saying, and it is a *convention* that has outlived its usefulness, in the current climate. We are correct to speak of colleagues, associates, connections, acquaintances, networks, this formality is entirely more honest, entirely more dignified, and entirely more moral, he added, than speaking of friendship. Because what is a friend, apart from a person who has no definable function, and to whom you have some kind of obscure, outdated obligation? This is the first thing that my dream showed me. The difference of this dream from so many others that seem important and prophetic, only to be revealed as ridiculous seconds after you wake up, is that this one only became more solid, it hardened, and it reached into real life, Solomon Wiese said. I wrote to several of my so-called friends the week of the dream, Solomon Wiese said, I wrote to them in formal language, notifying them of the termination of our connection. *Termination of friendship notices*, I called them. These were people who had failed me in some small way at one time or another, or who could have helped me in some small way or another but didn't, or who I had helped somehow and they had not reciprocated; and none of them of course had helped me when I had been exposed by the quantitative analysis and comparison system (QACS). No doubt this sounds ruthless, or stupid, or both. But really it was just another way of convening with nothingness, Solomon Wiese said, and truthfully it has made certain pathways available to me that would never have been opened up otherwise. He still felt his exile from the world of the arts keenly, at this time, Solomon Wiese explained. He had regarded himself as an outcast; there was an intensely romantic dimension to this that I now find unforgivable, completely ridiculous, he said. It was pure egoism, he said. He would see himself as if from afar, he explained, as he walked around town completely aimlessly, with an escalating sense of panic in his chest. After a while, this *distancing mechanism* had become habitual, and he could view himself at will as if from a few paces behind, as if he were seeing himself from *inside* the area of nothingness that continued to accompany him wherever he went, Solomon Wiese said. The sensation was basically that he had begun to spy on himself, he said, to watch himself going about his daily activities, in his oval of romantic isolation. There was pleasure in it, of a kind. He fantasised about meeting someone who was similarly afflicted, Solomon Wiese said, they could have spent the days watching over each other, through the windows of cafés, from station bridges, nothing more than that, he said, but the other people he passed on his walking circuits, many of whom seemed to wear their loneliness or desperation plainly on their faces, gave him an almost exaggeratedly wide berth. It couldn't last, this romantic trance he had put himself into, and he began to experience interruptions—he would notice his exterior vantage on a scene from *within* the scene, Solomon Wiese said, he would become aware of himself as an observer, with the effect that the distance he had created would collapse, and he would instantly perceive his affectation, he would appear at once as a kind of hideous puppet, performing in the most preposterous way imaginable. It was a physical sensation, he said, like having a rubber band twanged at the centre of his forehead, an unpleasant, almost vertiginous feeling of release and return, whereby Solomon Wiese would find himself squarely back behind his eyes, deprived of the broader aesthetic frame that had made his situation tolerable. He would notice himself watching himself walking across an overpass, for example, and it was as if he glanced up and met his own eyes—that was all it took for the scene to dissolve, and with it the mild, abstracted enjoyment he had been sustaining himself with since the intervention of the quantitative analysis and comparison system (QACS) in his life as an emerging poet. In this manner he managed to sabotage the secret habit that had allowed him a modicum of pleasure while wandering the boroughs of the city. Confined again to his own skull, he became oppressively aware of the limits of his awareness; he began to recognise his responses to his surroundings as inadequate, reflexive, barely responses at all—it was like occupying the brain of an animal, Solomon Wiese said. He had no grasp, for example, of even the most basic facts about the areas he passed through, who they were inhabited by or why, the city was as if without history for him. It was as if it had all been created yesterday, in a fully operational state. On some level he even began to believe something like this, he began to feel that everything he saw somehow *came into being* alongside him, that the limits of his knowledge described the limits of the world, and this gave his days a further air of unreality; sometimes he would look up from the pavement or down from the sky and have no idea where he was. He was able to access the mental distance which had provided him with some relief only fleetingly, then it seemed to disappear altogether, until once, during an especially long and unrewarding afternoon trudging pavements in the rain, he had glanced up at a girl wearing headphones. She smiled past him, probably at what she was listening to, but a frame enlarged around them, Solomon Wiese said, he saw himself walking away from her, he saw the purpling gradient of the clouds above him, the oval around the moment made by trees that lined the road. After a few seconds he had turned around and followed her. She walked quickly, no one took any notice of her, mentally she was in the next part of the day, he remembered thinking. He had watched as she jogged up the stairs of a building, then vanished through the revolving doors. It was a library. He had joined on the spot, taking a seat among the bowed ranks of silent readers, all seemingly passing the time, all waiting for something—it was if they had been sitting in this room for years before he had made his entrance. He looked at some books on local history, but he couldn't connect the information and images in them with any place he recognised. He didn't see her to begin with, spotting her only after a while at a bench on the other side of the room, headphones on, laptop open—he had looked away, tried to read, unsure what he was planning to do, but feeling somehow calmed—he immediately felt more in touch with the world in her presence, Solomon Wiese said. He felt able to observe himself again, he said, and with his head bowed he could mentally sketch their postures, the space that had opened and, he thought, been made articulate between them. After a period of time in this pleasurable daze, a man in vaguely military attire had sat down next to him. He took his time getting settled, arraying his technology on the desk, items with a utilitarian bulkiness and khaki palette that suggested to Solomon Wiese distant combat scenarios. His laptop was unbranded and partly metal, his bag had military webbing and a desert camo design. He was dressed in what might be called civilian clothes, but their looseness suggested concealed layers, further equipment; his shoes were heavily rubberised, the tops hidden by baggy stone chinos. Solomon Wiese had felt the man scanning the room—the frame of his daydream was gone, demolished, but he could feel the man's gaze exploring its ruins, as if he detected some prior set-up and wanted to probe it, to analyse it. Eventually the man's eyes came to rest, with a terrible inevitability—Solomon Wiese could feel it happening before it happened, he said—on the girl with headphones, across the room, sitting behind her laptop. The man's stare intensified, Solomon Wiese said. He didn't have to be looking at the man in order to know this, he could feel it, and across the room the girl with headphones felt it too, she straightened, her eyes may have darted towards the desk where Solomon Wiese sat, to the right of the man with the military-style backpack. He felt terribly exposed, Solomon Wiese said, sitting with the book on local history that he had been unable to summon any interest in, as the man with the military-style backpack sat next to him and stared at the girl with headphones—it was as if he were *a part of* the man's staring, Solomon Wiese said, it was as if he were *adding* to the weight of the man's stare by virtue of the fact that he had been staring in exactly the same direction a minute or two previously. He now wanted to disown that stare, to detach himself from it completely, and side with the girl with headphones, to shield her from it, if necessary. But he was positioned near the point of the stare's origin, and it was possible he may even have been attributed as the *source* of the stare, if the girl with headphones had not looked properly, but sensed that the stare came from this area of the library. It was almost as if the man with the military-style backpack was the *personification* of a stare, the personification of *Solomon Wiese's stare*, Solomon Wiese thought wildly, it was as if his stare had become tired of his unwillingness to deploy it properly and had set up its own operation. Because Solomon Wiese would never have stared in the uninhibited, blatant manner in which the man with the military-style backpack was continuing to stare at the girl with headphones, Solomon Wiese said. Solomon Wiese would have *sneaked the occasional glance*—that was much more his style. The occasional glance, scattered among other glances to other parts of the room. A limit on the length of the glance of no more than a second or two. A harmless glance, and that was the truth, there would be no harm in it. This stare was something else entirely, Solomon Wiese thought as he sat in the library, he said, here was a stare whose power was if anything deepening by the second, and surely, Solomon Wiese thought, eliciting some kind of response. Action was required, Solomon Wiese thought, even more wildly, something had to be done to force the man with the military-style backpack to cease aiming his crazed stare across the room—a thought occurred to him, and a moment later he had done it—Solomon Wiese had let out a sigh, a deliberate, long, almost theatrical sigh. He felt the sigh soak into the room. It had introduced possibility, but more was required. He sighed again, just as theatrically. There could be no doubt, he thought, that this was a sigh designed to communicate something, that there was intention behind this sigh—it would be clear to anyone who heard it. He sighed again, recklessly, to ensure the change—this risked a total breakdown of the situation. Someone cleared their throat, a few looks flashed towards him. Next to him, he sensed the stare had been interrupted, and then, as the silence was replenishing itself, unbelievably, Solomon Wiese thought, the man with the military-style backpack *yawned*—certainly not a genuine yawn, but an openly fake yawn directed at the person to his right, Solomon Wiese could only assume. He felt light-hearted suddenly, the situation seemed of no consequence, the whole thing was ridiculous—he sighed again. The man yawned. He sighed, shudderingly. The man yawned, finally, an outrageous yawn, the yawn of some digesting predator on the savannah, and smacked his lips. At this, any sense of order in the library was finished—several people tutted, someone got to their feet and approached the front desk. Feeling happier than he had for months, Solomon Wiese shut the book and fled. His elation had lasted until the following day, when, heading to the library again, he had seen the man with the military-style backpack on the steps outside, talking to the girl with headphones, which were not in her ears this time but dangling at her neck. They walked in together. Solomon Wiese found out soon after that the man with the military-style backpack's name was Christian Buch, and the girl with headphones, who was actually thirty-four, was called Amalia Albers. They were independent academics, and were married—he had discovered this when Christian Buch started talking to him in the locker room of the library, a couple of days after Solomon Wiese had witnessed the to-him-depressing sight of the pair in friendly conversation on the steps of the library. Solomon Wiese had yawned, accidentally, which Christian Buch had taken as a reference to the yawning and sighing with which they had demolished the tranquility of the library a few days earlier. Christian Buch's genial tone had caught him off guard, as the to-him-threatening and predatory way that Christian Buch had targeted the girl with headphones with his stare was still clear in his mind. Christian Buch's behaviour was revealed in its full character in the short conversation that followed, when it became clear to Solomon Wiese that the girl with headphones was in fact his, Christian Buch's, wife, and he was forced to rearrange the troubling and farcically resolved episode from the previous week in his memory. He now assumed that Christian Buch had simply been trying to get the attention of Amalia Albers, or that the stare was part of some private dynamic he didn't understand, or even that he had *imagined the stare*, though this seemed impossible. Amalia Albers and Christian Buch were the first people Solomon Wiese had met since his informal expulsion from the poetry world, and their expertise, specialising in something they described as *ahistorical distribution strategies*, was far enough removed from Solomon Wiese's previous milieu for him to relax in their company. Amalia Albers and Christian Buch seemed to think and act almost as a single entity, he soon realised. Together, they told him, they regarded current literary activity as a bemusing and largely pointless after-image of the significant artistic periods of the past—to them the question of cultural production was closed, they viewed history as basically complete, as of a century or so ago, with everything coming afterwards being essentially a reorganisation of the existing materials, essentially *archive work*—which is what they were preoccupied with. Solomon Wiese was evasive about his prior activities as a writer, and even the word sounded faintly absurd to him in the presence of Amalia Albers and Christian Buch. As their friendship developed, he became intrigued by the couple's research, and bit by bit they initiated him into their *operation*. In reality, he discovered, the independent academic label was a front, and Amalia Albers and Christian Buch made a living from data piracy; as well as memberships at every library in a fifty-mile radius, they possessed multiple identity cards for each, and they often visited in disguise—Christian Buch had been disguised, in fact, when Solomon Wiese had first encountered him—he called that invention "the grey man": a militaristic prepper with sidelines in habitat conservation and avian disease. Both Amalia Albers and Christian Buch spent most days reproducing by covert photography the content of as many books as possible, the more specialised the better, uploading the resulting files to an invitation-only site with subscription figures in the hundreds of thousands; revenue was generated by non-invasive advertising and the sale of specialist contact lists. The proceeds were substantial, but they wouldn't be any more specific. They lived in a large, run-down house in its own half-acre of derelict land inside a maze-like housing estate that had seemingly been constructed around it. They existed frugally—Solomon Wiese intuited there was another dimension to their activities that they weren't ready to reveal to him yet, and he imagined a sealed bunker, stockpiles of food. Over three consecutive nights he spent in their large run-down house, and which sealed their friendship, Solomon Wiese said, he listened for hours to Amalia Albers and Christian Buch as they began to educate him more thoroughly about their *operation*, and trained him in the art of data theft. They lent him one of their miniature cameras and showed him how to manufacture identification documents to create false library accounts. The couple had accessed local library records and set up a relay so they could observe if the records of certain accounts had been recently changed, possibly because of a flag being placed on the account by the library monitoring services (LMS), an organisation that didn't officially exist, Amalia Albers added, when she and Christian Buch first explained all this to Solomon Wiese on the first night he spent in their dingy, plant-filled living room, drinking scalding hot black coffee, Amalia Albers teasing one of their cats on the narrow leatherette sofa, Christian Buch sitting cross-legged on the floor with his cigarette papers, his specially modded laptop leaking low-frequency drones that he claimed deepened his sleep cycle. Once, Solomon Wiese had glimpsed their bedroom and had seen a pyramid structure, like a small tent, set up on the bed. The couple had been looking for someone to join their *operation*, as they called it, Amalia Albers told him during the first of these evenings, because of Christian Buch's difficulties completing their work due to a recurrent disorder, a kind of undiagnosable condition they called *reading sickness*. He had experienced it before, Christian Buch said, when they were involved in an earlier version of the operation, but at that time instead of simply reproducing stolen content for dissemination through the invitation-only file-sharing site, Christian Buch had sought to modify this content prior to distribution, with the intention of putting misleading or erroneous information *into mass circulation*—this was at the height of his anarcho-idealist phase, when he saw his work as a kind of activism against what he called the *total capture* of knowledge, in other words *digital supremacy*, in other words *the infinite archive*—that was how he'd got into data piracy in the first place, he told Solomon Wiese, through hacking circles, techno-activism, with the express aim of *disrupting* the spread of information, rather than aiding it, which was what he did now, albeit illegally, since he'd completely sold out, Christian Buch said good-naturedly, through the steam pouring up from his mug of black coffee. Solomon Wiese had wondered aloud why they bothered at all with the frankly antiquated-seeming business of covert photography and library visits, when surely it would have been easier to access the library's own digital records somehow—but what he hadn't considered, as Amalia Albers pointed out, was that the digital records were *much more securely protected* than the physical materials, and the virtual paper trail a security breach of that kind would leave behind was far more incriminating than evidence of their physical presence—their fuzzy images on the library's outdated CCTV system, for example. Their three-dimensional bodies, gliding through space, were much harder to pin down, much harder to record, than the glaring and indelible traces produced by digital interference, Amalia Albers said, as she rubbed the ears of one of the cats, a large tortoiseshell who had lost an eye. Their disguises were only intended to widen the zone of uncertainty around them—she was pretty sure the library monitoring services knew they were up to something, Amalia Albers said—but the status of most people in the visible world was really of *indecipherable blurring*, this was the true condition, and it was only when these speculative sightings were plotted alongside the concrete evidence of secure log-ins and personal transactions that they had any real value. But she also had to admit that it was possible their plan had succeeded so far mainly due to its backwardness, or counter-intuitiveness—there had been a couple of close calls a few months ago when Christian Buch had almost been caught with his camera, while in a state of semi-consciousness, brought on by his *reading sickness*, which had prompted them to temporarily relocate from the central Senate Library to the more discreet but much less extensively stocked Borough Library, where they had encountered Solomon Wiese. Christian Buch's disorder, when it was at its most debilitating, meant that he couldn't parse more than a few lines before he fell into a semi-conscious state that took him two or three hours to recover from. The return of his condition had made Christian Buch extremely nervous, he said, as he recognised the escalation of symptoms that on one occasion had led to a full-scale breakdown, and to his being institutionalised for several months. At that time Christian Buch and Amalia Albers had lived in a squat and were immersed in a lifestyle of hard-line political dissent and deep web sabotage, Christian Buch said. If he had exhibited the fervour of a recent convert in those days, it was because for a long time Christian Buch had resisted immersing himself in the techno-anarchist lifestyle, though he was powerfully drawn to it—he had a profound fear of authority, basically, he said, a belief that any infraction of the law however minor would be observed by an official organisation, and most acutely, his fear was that he had *already* committed some serious legal infringement without his being aware of it. This paranoid outlook constituted a relatively normal state of mind for Christian Buch, and his hypervigilance actually made him well-suited to the way of life he had orbited for several years. This had all changed when he had met Amalia Albers, and realised that the only way out of this impasse, that is, of being broadly sympathetic to the techno-anarchist cause, as well as a potentially invaluable asset in terms of his skill-set, but unable to commit himself, was actually to invest in it to an extreme degree, knowingly and excessively, to effectively *overplay* his commitment, and so retain some distance from his activities—or this is how he described it to Solomon Wiese, with Amalia Albers nodding in agreement on the narrow leatherette sofa. He had transformed himself practically overnight, adopting the speech mannerisms and style of dress of his soon-to-be peers—white baseball caps and outsize black sportswear, in those days, exclusively East Asian brands, and moving in with Amalia Albers in the room she'd constructed from stolen pallets on the large empty office floor, which they occupied with seven or eight others sympathetic to the cause. Some of them, recalling his long-term marginal presence, had viewed Christian Buch's wholesale conversion with suspicion, and while his excessive enthusiasm was in no way feigned, and was really a way for him to access his *genuine* enthusiasm, and eventually he won them around with his technical aptitude, in some senses they were right to be suspicious of him, and events bore this out, sadly, Amalia Albers explained. They looked very different now, of course, Amalia Albers and Christian Buch, their old friends would never have recognised them, their change in direction had required them to become more or less invisible, Amalia Albers said. Christian Buch's *reading sickness* had come on for the first time while he was manipulating files for re-dispersion—a procedure that required sustained concentration, and involved the editing of documents just enough to alter their message and functionality, changes too subtle to be noticed by lay readers, with the intention of disturbing the agreement of facts in the public domain by creating as many logic conflicts, anachronisms, tonal inconsistencies and internal contradictions as possible. Those in the emptied office building who worked on the *misinformation desk* described entering something akin to a trance state as they tweaked these files: legal documents, celebrity biographies, academic papers, public reports, textbooks, instruction manuals, exam questions, historical speeches, even cookbooks. At the height of their operations they were leaking several hundred treated documents a week, released strategically to enter the wider currents of online circulation. A certain visual disturbance had warned Christian Buch of the first onset of his so-called reading sickness—he called this symptom the *duplicate object*, he said to Solomon Wiese. The first time it happened he had been altering a scientific paper about holograms, he remembered. On his desk, as always, he had had his favourite red mug, for the incredible quantities of very hot black coffee that he drank throughout the day—he had gone through to the small office kitchen, he remembered, where he had noticed the same mug upside down on the draining board—the large, logoless red mug, whose interior was dulled from use. He went back to his desk, slowing as he saw *the mug was there too*, with some cold coffee dregs in the bottom. He paced back to the kitchen—there it was again, upside down on the draining board. He inspected it. It was his red mug. It had the same tiny chip on the rim that he had to turn slightly as he drank to prevent it brushing his lower lip. He picked up the red mug and returned to his desk, where, of course, there was no longer a red mug. Christian Buch had been disquieted, he said, but by the evening had been able to dismiss the whole episode as a hallucination brought on by caffeine and lack of sleep. But when it had happened again, a week or two later, in exactly the same way, the sight of the red mug on the draining board was accompanied by an immediate sense of recognition and dread—he had known that it had really happened, he had been waiting for it to happen again, and when he saw the mug he instantly felt sick with certainty. He assumed for a while he was the victim of a convoluted practical joke. It was the only possible explanation, he thought, though the other techno-anarchists on the abandoned office floor were hardly the practical-joking type, as Amalia Albers pointed out to him when he told her about it back in their bedroom, which although constructed from wooden pallets they had made very cosy and snug. This business with the mugs was only the beginning, Amalia Albers had told Solomon Wiese, taking over the story on the second evening—they had gone for a quiet drink at the pub on the corner of the estate, without Christian Buch, as he preferred not to revisit this series of events. Christian Buch's episode had caused concern among the group, but they had only taken it half-seriously, until things had come to a head during a protest in support of net neutrality they'd all attended, where Christian Buch had disappeared. Amalia Albers wouldn't see him again for months, she said, rocking her two-thirds-full pint of dishwater-colour ale in her hand—he turned out to have been arrested, then transferred to a mental health facility an hour outside London, informing the police about the set-up on the deserted floor of the office building in the process, they all assumed, when they were raided and shut down a few hours before learning his whereabouts. The group dispersed, and only Amalia Albers remained in contact, she said, waiting for Christian Buch's condition to improve. She had lost sight of him early on in the protest, Amalia Albers said, and by the time the crowds were gone he had been missing for several hours. Christian Buch had claimed—and here he had to be careful, she said, as part of the conditions of his release were that he recognised what he remembered happening as more or less pure delusion or fantasy—that he had seen a person that he took to be Amalia Albers at the fringes of the protest, and when she had moved into a side street, signalling to him, he had followed her. This person looked exactly like Amalia Albers, but had been dressed differently, and they had subsequently established she *couldn't* have been Amalia Albers, Amalia Albers said. Once he was out of sight of the protest Christian Buch had been cornered and attacked by three boys—three children actually, he estimated that they were aged ten or eleven, but nonetheless they had beaten him half-unconscious—Christian Buch remembered their small fists pummelling his arms and back, the soles of their children's trainers finding his head as he huddled on the ground. Not long after, Amalia Albers presumed, he was picked up by the police, whose report had described him as in the grip of a full psychotic episode, raving, partially clothed, trying to get into private buildings he had no business entering. He had spent a night in the cells, Amalia Albers presumed, before the extent of his delusions became apparent and he was relocated to a *sanatorium* near the south coast—Christian Buch didn't know what he'd said to the police, he had to admit it was possible he'd told them about the abandoned office building, which was raided soon after, but he couldn't remember. Neither could he remember travelling to or arriving at the *sanatorium*, but as the days passed and his condition began to stabilise, he gradually became aware of his surroundings. By this point Christian Buch's memory was in ruins, Amalia Albers said. During his first week in the so-called sanatorium he could recall very little of the last few years of his life. Or it was more the case that he did recall this period of time, but the content of his experience was different to the general outline that his carers were able to construct. When he slowly came back to himself in the sanatorium, so-called, he had no memory of having lived with Amalia Albers on the abandoned floor of the office building with six or seven other techno-activists, and the idea seemed completely outlandish to him. In fact he had no memory of Amalia Albers at all, other than as a girl he had gone to school with, whom he had daydreamed about, he later confessed to Amalia Albers, but not as someone he had met and got together with later in life, and he was convinced that the Amalia Albers *he* remembered had died several years previously, in some kind of electrical fire. That someone called Amalia Albers was calling him repeatedly and trying to arrange a visit, as his carers informed him, was not something he could easily accept. Even now, Christian Buch remembered having these memories, Amalia Albers said, memories that he had been told were completely imaginary—that he had to assume were completely imaginary—it had given him a strange feeling of being between lives, or even of being in the wrong life, that he had never completely lost, although his so-called real memories had eventually returned in full. Exactly how Christian Buch had ended up in the surrounds of this unusual mental health institution, or *sanatorium* as it was referred to by its staff—a large country house set in acres of woodland, more like a health spa or exclusive rehab centre than the state facility it claimed to be—was a mystery he and Amalia Albers had never got to the bottom of. They had only questioned it sometime later, when their enquiries were met with polite yet firm obfuscations, the equivalent of knowing smiles, it now seemed to Amalia Albers. Christian Buch's time in the sanatorium, which Amalia Albers had been discouraged from visiting, being kept unaware during his sequestering of its exact location, was defined by two presences, two poles by which he oriented himself—that of his doctor, Dr. Foley, and that of the man he shared his room with, who was also named Christian, Christian Buch told Solomon Wiese, when he resumed the story later that evening, back at the house. This other Christian had been an inventor of some renown before a career-ending psychotic episode, and there were questions over the criminality of his past that Christian Buch, more lucid by the day, was never able to resolve, despite several conversations, or rather the one long, fragmented conversation that they conducted over the entirety of his stay in the so-called sanatorium, during which time he was in more or less constant contact with the other Christian, confined to the plainly furnished room they shared, much like a room in an inexpensive hotel, with twin beds and a view of the garden, and beyond that the woods. For the first few days, during which Christian Buch recovered his sense of time and place, the other Christian didn't speak at all. He only began to speak one morning when Christian Buch was feeling strong enough to initiate a conversation; in fact, it was never the other Christian who initiated the conversation, Christian Buch recalled, it was always Christian Buch, although once Christian Buch had opened the door to a conversation, the other Christian was happy to oblige him—he had quickly gathered that the other Christian would talk all day and probably all night as well, if given the opportunity, and that to cut off this flow of words, consisting mainly of anecdotes that deteriorated before long into associative nonsense, he actually had to get up and physically leave the room. The other Christian would usually run on for half a minute or so—Christian Buch established this by waiting outside the door, as in reality he had no urge to enter the shared spaces of the sanatorium and so have to participate in some group activity in progress there—before winding down to his familiar silence, which he would only emerge from again if prompted by Christian Buch. Over the days, this pattern of interaction came to feel like a kind of game, Christian Buch said. He was acutely aware of the proximity of deadly boredom, which would always descend by the early afternoon—and with it came the prospect of initiating conversation with the other Christian. The only respite he could hope for, once he *activated* the other Christian, as he came to think of it, was a visit from Dr. Foley, supposedly a daily occurrence, but in reality much less frequent, and often no more than twenty seconds in duration. Dr. Foley would enter the room unannounced, flitting once or twice between the beds, hovering motionlessly for a moment or two and gazing inscrutably into Christian Buch's eyes, before he was gone again, a retinue of sleek nurses in his wake. Repeating this now made Christian Buch painfully aware, he said in the plant-filled living room, that far from relaying an accurate version of events, he was actually providing Solomon Wiese with evidence of his complete disconnect from reality over the entire period. But these details also raised the question, Christian Buch pointed out, that if what he remembered *hadn't* happened, that is, if he *hadn't* spent several weeks convalescing in a so-called sanatorium, in the company of the other Christian, watched over by Dr. Foley—then what had he been doing? It had taken Christian Buch some time to work out that he didn't know if he was staying in the sanatorium voluntarily or not, and his enquiries to this end, which he seemed to fumble when confronted with the expectant face of an orderly, were gracefully sidestepped. Over the weeks that followed he fell into the sanatorium's routines, but his thoughts increasingly came to circle the moment every day when he was forced to *activate* the other Christian. As the weather was improving they were able to conduct their exchanges on the back lawn, in front of the twin rose beds, and it was primarily in this setting that the other Christian enlightened Christian Buch about his career as an inventor of specialist objects, always working on commission, he said, for the same anonymous client. His first project, he claimed, for which he was given an effectively *limitless budget*, was the design and manufacture of a portable machine for the purpose of short-term hypnosis. The prototype was a handheld device that emitted a series of tones and clicks that had the effect of casting the listener, or about three-quarters of listeners, into a state of semi-consciousness and hyper-receptivity within seconds, the other Christian claimed. It had taken him nine months to build it, the other Christian said, and Christian Buch was able to detect a trace of former arrogance in the way he announced this, even through his mangled diction—whether a side effect of his medication or fallout from his breakdown it was difficult to say, but the other Christian always spoke as if his tongue had swelled to the point of completely filling his mouth, which introduced a further element of endurance into these exchanges, for Christian Buch. The device worked superbly well, and he had never enquired what it was intended for, the other Christian continued, although in muffled, heavily slurred speech that was barely comprehensible, nor would he have enquired if he'd been given the opportunity. He had been required to hand over the plans for the project and all related research materials to the anonymous client, destroying evidence of it on his computers, and this he had done unquestioningly, the other Christian said. There had been several other commissions of this sort that he couldn't go into detail about, the other Christian revealed to Christian Buch, as they reclined on deckchairs on the back lawn of the sanatorium, watching the bees at work among the roses, and enjoying the greenhouse smell of the garden, where the tomatoes and peaches were beginning to ripen. His current project was what had landed him here, the other Christian went on: it was a pet project, a home paper-making kit that he believed would become an indispensible tool over the next decade, as paper reserves diminished—in only a few years, paper would become a luxury available to only the very few, he believed, and his patented paper-making kit would begin making him a lot of money. The main body of the device was a clear canister, into which the user loaded any scrap paper they were able to find, then organic household waste could be added, which was slowly mulched and bleached, by an ecologically sound method, resulting in a uniform pulp that a second attachment wove and quick-dried into perfectly usable strips of paper. The quality wasn't as good as it could be, the other Christian said, the paper was still too brittle and split about fifty per cent of the time, but he believed a solution was reachable. A companion device, still in pre-production, would be used to generate good-quality permanent ink from bodily fluids. He had been discovered by a colleague in the lab space he co-rented testing an early model, which still relied on the siphoning of his own blood to produce readable results, and this colleague had of course misinterpreted what she had seen. The resulting emergency meeting of the small but tight-knit community of freelance lab users had forced him to agree to a prolonged stay here, in the sanatorium, the other Christian said to Christian Buch, who had managed to prevent his face from betraying his thoughts, which were that this person, the other Christian, was a total, irredeemable lunatic. Once, the other Christian had leaned his head towards Christian Buch, and said that he had just received word—of a new commission. An orderly had passed him a letter with the initial spec the previous night, he said, in a loud whisper impeded by the size of his tongue, and it was true that Christian Buch had noticed that the other Christian sometimes disappeared from the room during the night, for unspecified nocturnal excursions, during which he claimed he left the sanatorium grounds and wandered the surrounding countryside, where he had seen marshlights in the wood, or unmarked aircraft in the clouds—breaking out of the sanatorium grounds in the dead of night was a simple matter, according to the other Christian, if you knew where to look. This new commission should be very interesting work, the other Christian nodded, his speech slowing further as his afternoon medication took hold—all completely classified, he added. Christian Buch never asked, as he didn't wish to encourage the other Christian's delusional fantasies, but he was able to infer that this new commission was a kind of home-assembly euthanasia device, which the other Christian had predicted would become a commonplace household appliance within a decade. He was investigating patents on behalf of his client, who as ever was anonymous, he had said on one occasion, dozily, from the depths of his deckchair. Except that this hadn't actually happened, Christian Buch had to remind himself to emphasise, he said, in accordance with his agreement with the public services who monitored his mental health. He hadn't stayed at a so-called sanatorium, about which he and Amalia Albers could discover no information whatsoever, and so he hadn't met another man called Christian while staying there; nor had he heard about this other Christian's range of inventions, which he had to assume were the products of his own inflamed mind. After another week or two in the sanatorium Christian Buch had begun to despair, he said. He still refused to speak to Amalia Albers on the single landline available to patients, as, as far as he was concerned, she would be calling from beyond the grave; in the meantime, with the help of sessions with psychiatric staff he was attempting to process his recent memories, but these he found difficult to integrate with his current situation. More and more, during his stay in the sanatorium, in the grip of a deadly boredom in the early afternoon, he felt as if he had awoken from a dream to find there was no life to return to, that the dimensions of life had failed to snap into shape around him—it was as if he were still occupying the bleary second or two before the furnishings of the room solidified, and the past, with its appalling, reassuring load, was lowered onto his shoulders. And like a dream, it seemed that the life he had woken up remembering was receding ever more quickly from view—every time he went back to it, the details were sparser and sparser. He had woken with a certain atmosphere within him, when he had first come to in the sanatorium, a kind of background noise, a sense of rooms often entered, of worn thresholds, of wallpaper, even, there had been a family, perhaps, he thought, but nothing remained of these ideas now but faint outlines. Still, he didn't feel ready to confront the specifics of the new life that waited for him beyond the sanatorium, a life with unfamiliar currents, a desperate life in some kind of subcultural underclass, it sounded like, from the reports he was given by the psychiatric staff—residing in an abandoned office building with a woman he remembered as having died, years previously, in an electrical fire. In short, it was too much for him,

Christian Buch told Solomon Wiese, in the plant-filled living room, after Amalia Albers had gone to bed. He let the days fill with the digressions of the other Christian, who became increasingly unhinged as the summer progressed, and the garden doubled then quadrupled its foliage, filling itself with an almost unbelievable abundance of fruit and flowers, which the patients of the sanatorium were not permitted to pick. It was a kind of peace, and prevented him from visiting again the disquieting store of images and faces that vied for his attention whenever silence took over. One morning, sitting in a wicker chair at the window of the room he shared with the other Christian, who was lying on his bed, reading a magazine that he held very close to his face, Christian Buch had glimpsed a flash of colour in the deepening foliage towards the back of the sanatorium garden—a flash of colour that he assumed at first must have been a tropical bird. There were green or gold parakeets that had gone native in this part of the country, Dr. Foley had told him during one of his flying visits, and occasionally they could be seen in the garden, so a tropical bird was Christian Buch's first thought. He stayed in the wicker chair and stared, and soon enough he saw it again, a flash of colour, a piece of coloured material, in fact, being flourished down between the trees. As he watched, a man had passed an opening in the branches. The man was wearing brightly coloured clothes, a red jerkin of some kind, striped trousers, a yellow shirt open at his neck, which was hung with an assortment of necklaces and beads. His long hair curled from a floppy brown hat, and his tanned forearms were covered in green tattoos.

Moments later, as Christian Buch continued to watch, two or three others, similarly attired, including a young woman in a patterned headscarf holding an infant, passed the same opening in the branches, all in complete silence. Then they were gone. That night, in his bed, Christian Buch had thought he heard snatches of music, he said to Solomon Wiese, as they continued to talk in low voices in the dingy plant-filled living room and drink coffee late into the night—a flute or pipe, and perhaps a fiddle. Once again he was obliged to mention that all of this was fantasy, that none of it had actually happened, or not in the way that he remembered—that real events surely lay below the spectacular surface of these half-imagined events, perhaps only vaguely resembling them, which his inflamed mind had filled with colourful detail, no doubt, Christian Buch said. The next morning, picking a moment when the back garden was empty, he had walked past the rose beds, down to where a steel mesh fence, partially concealed by trees and bushes, marked the border of the sanatorium grounds. There was a narrow pond back there he hadn't seen before, surrounded by hordes of tiny black frogs. As he stood facing the high steel mesh fence he had smelled woodsmoke, and it suddenly became a matter of urgency to him, Christian Buch said, that he got out of there—he had to get out of the sanatorium as soon as possible, at whatever cost, though he had no idea what it would take for him to actually leave—and as the layers of his confinement were revealed to him, he experienced for the first time his presence in the sanatorium as an incarceration. It was a physical sensation he had, inside his stomach, as he stood at the border of the sanatorium grounds, smelling the inexplicable odour of woodsmoke. He realised at that moment it was intolerable, Christian Buch said, the situation he was in. Exactly as he thought this, Christian Buch said, a grubby child had appeared on the other side of the steel mesh fence, dressed in coloured blankets, with one nostril streaming clear snot straight into his mouth. Christian Buch took a step towards the fence, but panic surfaced immediately in the eyes of the infant, who was joined by an older child, a girl of five or six. The children must be connected with the people he'd seen the previous morning, Christian Buch had thought, the brightly dressed *band of travellers*, for want of a better expression, who he had spotted from the window, and who he imagined were camped, in their embroidered tents, out of sight, a little further into the woods. Hence the woodsmoke, he thought. Hence infants in old-fashioned patterned clothing. That this spectacle of a *brightly dressed band of travellers* had failed to alarm him or even stretch his credulity no doubt gave some indication of his state of mind, Christian Buch said to Solomon Wiese. Because in all likelihood he had not glimpsed a brightly dressed band of travellers through the branches, nor had he smelled woodsmoke, nor had he seen hundreds of tiny black frogs swarming around his feet. Nonetheless this was what he remembered of his time at the sanatorium, which he and Amalia Albers had never been able to locate, despite a sustained effort. Staring at the brightly dressed children through the steel mesh, Christian Buch began speaking to them in a low voice, miming with his hands, trying to communicate to the children that he needed to *get through the fence*—he made cutting motions with his arms, he pulled at the steel mesh, which made a metallic rustling sound—the children looked at him wonderingly, mutely, it was hopeless, he had thought, but then the elder one, the girl, pointed to the sky and drew her hand back with a deft motion towards her, the fingers spread. Christian Buch understood the gesture at once, he said, although he had never seen it before. Without thinking, he had bowed to the children, from the waist—he had bowed to the grubby children and watched them scurry away through the trees. My life is in the hands of grubby children, he had thought to himself, Christian Buch said to Solomon Wiese, but tonight we'll see. Because that's what the girl's gesture meant, Christian Buch had said to himself. *Night*, Christian Buch said to Solomon Wiese, in his and Amalia Albers's plant-filled living room, very late one evening. *Night*, Solomon Wiese said to me in the Travelodge bar, where it was past two o'clock in the morning. He knew it with absolute certainty—there was nothing else the child's gesture could have communicated. Towards three o'clock he had padded down the garden, wearing his sanatorium slippers and as many extra layers of clothing as he could find; it was cold now despite the day's heat, the grass looked grey in the moonlight, there were some bread rolls from the kitchen in his pockets, and at the place where he had met the children he found the mesh had been cut and prised aside enough for him to clamber through. The smell of woodsmoke was faint in the air, and further back into the trees he discovered the remains of a fire, but no other signs of a camp.

He kept walking until he hit a road, then a larger road, then a motorway, and in this manner he had returned to London, Christian Buch said—in short, he had escaped, he had fled the sanatorium. It took him several days, Christian Buch explained to Solomon Wiese, and no doubt he didn't take the most direct or the easiest route, he was proceeding largely by instinct, he said, sometimes passing along back roads, sometimes along main roads, finally along dual carriageways and motorways, trudging the hard shoulder for hour after hour, Christian Buch said, in the blue-and-yellow haze of pollen and pollution, at the height of the English summer. As he walked he was barely aware of his surroundings, but he knew that something was occurring inside him, he said, he knew that events were rearranging themselves, that his brain was trying out different sequences until it found one that seemed to hold together. The figure of Amalia Albers appeared at the forefront of his thoughts as he walked, Christian Buch said, but this was an Amalia Albers made up of two Amalia Alberses, whose images swum around each other as he walked and then began to coalesce—there was the Amalia Albers who was dead, no more than a schoolgirl in his recollection, an early infatuation, he remembered, then there was the Amalia Albers that he knew, he had been told, who he had lived with in a bedroom made of wooden pallets on the floor of an abandoned office building for almost a year—but she was only an idea at this point, a kind of repeated visual phrase that he was unable to connect to anything. Apart from the bread rolls, he barely ate or drank at all during his walk from the sanatorium back to London; a few times he chewed grass from the verge, he remembered, he drank some silty water from puddles, and he slept once or twice behind a hedge. At one stage he abandoned the roads altogether and walked alongside the hedgerows in open fields, which were high with green wheat, and where he was completely hidden from view. He had walked down the earthy avenues between the crops, in the dusty heat, and after a while he became aware that there was someone else walking with him, Christian Buch said, *someone else* was walking in a parallel furrow through the wheat, to his side, and when he stopped walking he could hear their soft footsteps on the dry, crumbling earth. It was exactly the same when he walked next to the hedgerows in the open fields; he became aware that there was someone walking on the other side of the dense, dark green foliage, buzzing with horseflies, he said, but he never caught sight of them. He called out once or twice but no one answered. Another indication, if one was needed, that Christian Buch was not in touch with reality, faintly or at all, over this entire period, he added. The only other people he encountered while he was walking were children, he remembered, and only on a couple of occasions. He remembered he met a boy and a girl at the side of a back road, who were walking their dog. Won't you be seen, out here, one of them had asked, pointing to his slippers, which by that time were in a sorry condition. But for the most part he was preoccupied with the thought of Amalia Albers—he had kept her number on a piece of paper they had given him at the sanatorium. The piece of paper bore a logo, a tree with an apple and a single leaf, and apart from the slippers it was the only evidence he had of the sanatorium's existence, he later realised. He had called her from a station on the outskirts of London, and when she had arrived, stepping out of a train carriage back into his life, it was as if he had imagined her into existence, Christian Buch said, it was as if someone he had only dreamed about had been deposited in the real world. Solomon Wiese paused as I slid him a new bottle of beer, along with a short G&T for Phoebe Glass, who for some time had had her back to us, and was conversing with three other young women, who expressly hadn't acknowledged either me or Solomon Wiese. As soon as he had the bottle in front of him, Solomon Wiese began tearing strips off the label, screwing two or three into little balls and flicking them onto the floor before continuing. Although Christian Buch had recognised Amalia Albers at the moment of their reunion, he went on, and they were together again from that moment, much of their previous life had remained closed off from Christian Buch, until an encounter a month or so later, at a riverside pub outside London. They had travelled to the riverside pub in an attempt to reawaken Christian Buch's dormant or repressed memories, Amalia Albers had explained to Solomon Wiese, when she resumed the account of Christian Buch's institutionalisation and escape the following evening in their cramped kitchen, over a vegan moussaka—it was the third night he had spent with them. By this time there had been a follow-up meeting with a mental health professional, Amalia Albers said. She had been concerned about Christian Buch's apparently fugitive status, but had received reassurances that if Christian Buch's account of events adhered to reality then they, the mental health professional said, meaning the authorities she represented, wouldn't insist on readmission. The mental health professional actually declared herself encouraged by Christian Buch's condition when they had arrived for their meeting, and she gave Amalia Albers a special emergency number in case his behaviour became erratic again. The riverside pub, in a market town a short train ride east of London, had personal significance for Amalia Albers and Christian Buch, as they had spent many afternoons and evenings drinking there in the early stages of their relationship. While they were sitting outside on a bench in the shade, the heat wave having continued into midsummer, back at their old haunt, which they had found largely unchanged, to their relief, or to Amalia Albers's relief, as Christian Buch had no recollection of the riverside pub whatsoever, Amalia Albers had spotted two men on the far side of the beer garden, which was infested that afternoon by swarms of flying ants. She pointed the men out to Christian Buch—she remembered meeting them before, Amalia Albers explained, when she and Christian Buch had been in the riverside pub one evening several years previously, during the early phases of their relationship. The two men were dressed in nondescript, scumbled clothing that appeared almost colourless, and were bowed over a large book that was laid on the table in front of them. Christian Buch couldn't recall them, Amalia Albers said, but the encounter had stuck in her mind. The men lived on a boat, and it was true, Christian Buch confirmed, speaking for the first time that evening as he put the plates in the sink and ran the tap, that they had the appearance of men who lived on a boat, not through some kind of metropolitan lifestyle choice, but because they were boat dwellers through and through—they were *boat dwellers by nature*, these two men—they ate on the boat, they slept on the boat, they washed, as far as they were able to, in a small sink on the boat, he imagined—an old narrowboat in which they travelled up and down the rivers all over the south and east of England, performing small jobs of work in the manner of latter-day itinerant labourers, or at least that was his impression. The older of the two men smoked incredibly thin roll-ups and wore a woollen hat of the same indeterminate hue as the rest of his clothing, pushed down almost to his eyes, despite the day's heat. The younger man had sparse facial hair and unsteady eyes, and he hadn't spoken much during their meeting, but had laughed often, an idiotic sort of laugh, if Amalia Albers was being honest, she said—she had the impression he was the idiot younger brother, or the idiot son of the first man. The pair were unusual, perhaps, but not really any more or less unusual than many people you might meet at a riverside pub, on a weekday summer afternoon, with the flying ants on their nuptial flight. The real reason Amalia Albers had remembered the encounter was the conversation they had, which had taken the form of a kind of sermon or lecture given by the older of the boatmen, about life and the nature of romantic love, with reference to a particular *book*—the older boatman had emphasised the word *book* in a peculiar way, Amalia Albers said, that she had always remembered, and reminded her of how holy books were spoken of by the faithful, as if the *book* was in some way definitive, as if it was the only book worth mentioning, and it was in fact the only book the older boatman had read, as he later confirmed, and it was also to his mind the only book worth reading. You wouldn't find this book in any library, he had added, drawing on a very thin cigarette rolled with brown liquorice paper, this was not the sort of book that you would be able to buy in a bookshop, the older boatman said, this was a different order of book altogether, you had to *know* people to get access to this book, and you were not free to keep the book as long as you liked, because although nobody owned this book, it had to be handed back to the person you acquired it from, after a certain amount of time. There was only one copy of this book, or only one copy that he knew of, though it was possible there were other copies, in other parts of the country or in other parts of the world, that wasn't for him to say, the older boatman said. The book was not typeset or printed or professionally bound, but had been copied out by hand, in ink, and it was added to by hand, annotated by hand, and when this copy became too weathered and dog-eared to be passed around anymore, a new copy would be made using the same method by *those-in-the-know*, the older boatman said. As to the content of this book, it was manifold, that is to say, it *ranged*, the older boatman said, gesturing outwards with both hands, it laid things out as they really were, which was something no other book could claim to do, it contained certain secrets and certain truths, and it differed again from all other books in that this information was completely practical and applicable by the reader, and had the effect of directly altering and improving their day-to-day life, if they were on the right path, that is to say, if they were in contact intuitively with *those-in-the-know*. It would change your angle on things, the older boatman said, it would give you a glimpse of the real plan, that is, of what was actually happening in the world, the plan that was hidden at all times from almost everyone, apart from *those-in-the-know*, and those *in contact with them intuitively*—those who they chose to initiate into their teachings. In this sense it was the only book that mattered, it was the only literature that was actually needed by anyone, the older boatman said. To be initiated by *those-in-the-know* was not a simple matter, and any person seeking this kind of knowledge had to have already shown their ability to find *other ways* of living, to discover *other ways* of life, that is, outside *this*, the older boatman had said, gesturing to the surroundings of the riverside pub. Keep a stale crust of bread sealed in a tin and don't eat for three days, the idiot brother or idiot son of the older boatman had said suddenly, leaning forwards, and when you open the tin and put the crust on your tongue, you won't believe how good that stale crust will taste. The bread will be almost unbearably sweet. Wisdom from the book, the idiot brother or idiot son said. And as it encompasses everything worth knowing or thinking about, the older boatman continued, naturally some of its teachings are about romantic love—as he had said this the older boatman had eyed Amalia Albers and Christian Buch in turn, from across the table, and his idiot brother or idiot son had giggled in an idiotic manner, Amalia Albers said. For example, the older boatman said, don't spend too much time as *just you and me*—he spat these words softly, his thin cigarette hanging from his lower lip—when you're with other people, the ball gets thrown deeper, if you know what I mean. That's something for nothing, for you both, some wisdom from the book, he said, drawing hard on the cigarette, so that the tip glowed. The idiot brother or idiot son had looked back and forth between Amalia Albers and Christian Buch then, Amalia Albers said, as if picking up on something for the first time. They don't know each other that well, the idiot brother or idiot son of the older boatman had said, in a triumphant tone, Amalia Albers had thought, before laughing his idiotic laugh—but it was true, at that time Amalia Albers and Christian Buch hadn't known each other that well, their relationship was still in the early phases, and this insight that the idiotic younger boatman had arrived at had the effect of disconcerting them both, Amalia Albers said. In fact, it had almost caused them to part ways before they had begun to conceive of themselves being together. All of this would have provided good enough reason to leave the boatmen where they sat, when Amalia Albers had spotted them again, years later, after Christian Buch's pronounced break from normal reality, Amalia Albers said, but she had also reached a point of desperation, and the sight of the two boatmen presented itself as an opportunity to awaken Christian Buch from his trance state, or perhaps spark some small recollection, thereby giving her cause to hope, and making things marginally more bearable. The older boatman had watched them approach from across the beer garden, and Amalia Albers saw as they neared that he looked precisely the same as he had when they'd met him at the same pub several years previously, as did the younger boatman, to the extent that they even seemed to be wearing the same items of drab, almost colourless clothing. He invited them to join their table, where the boatmen continued to pore over the unwieldy compendium before them, its large pages tattered at the edges, with additional strips and squares of paper and card attached, all covered, Amalia Albers could see from where she sat opposite, with lines of compact handwriting—you remember the *book*, don't you, the older boatman had enquired, the thin cigarette on his lower lip bobbing up and down as he spoke, and as remarkable as it was that he not only remembered Amalia Albers and Christian Buch from their single encounter several years previously, but also remembered the details of their conversation, which he was prepared to continue more or less where it had left off, at that moment it hadn't seemed remarkable at all to Amalia Albers. One of you has a companion, the idiot brother or idiot son had said, his eyes moving from Christian Buch to Amalia Albers and back again, just as his eyes had moved between them several years previously, before he swivelled his body and pointed to an apple tree in the corner of the beer garden, or more accurately pointed to *the space below the apple tree*, the pool of shade under its branches. *There*, the older boatman had said, and they all turned their heads to watch the spot under the apple tree that he had singled out, an emptiness roughly the height of a man, filled with waverings of shade and light. And in *here*, he said turning back and leafing through the pages of the book, before rotating it and sliding it across the table to point out a certain passage to Christian Buch. It was then that the strange thing had happened, Amalia Albers said—when Christian Buch had begun to read, his eyes had started to clear, there was a kind of relaxing of his features, and the Christian Buch that she knew somehow became more recognisable in them. As far as Christian Buch could remember, the passage that he'd read was written like a kind of joke or trick—it described his act of reading the lines as he was reading them, he said, as well as somehow describing things that he, Christian Buch, could see happening around him as they were happening—he remembered the passage describing the grimy hands of the boatman as they held down the page he was reading, he said, and it also described the movement of his eyes, Christian Buch's eyes, as they moved over the words, which were written in a heavy, compact hand that at times was hard to decipher, and which the passage itself also described. No immediate change had been apparent to Christian Buch after reading the passage—at which point the older boatman had taken back the book, made a note on the page, quickly and carefully put it into his knapsack, then, draining his glass and gesturing to his idiot brother or idiot son to follow, abruptly left the beer garden—he said to Solomon Wiese. Despite Amalia Albers having observed his features clearing and settling in some hard-to-define way as he had read the passage silently at the table opposite the two boatmen, Christian Buch had felt no effects at all, but over the following days memories from the past few years had begun to return to him, or it was as if they had been in some way hidden, and now they came into view, or had been somehow unattached to him, and now were being reattached. At the same time, his memories of his time in the sanatorium became more distant, and to remember them at all began to require a concerted effort from him—he could still picture the details, but it was more like remembering the plot of a film he'd once seen, or a film he'd only half-seen, and when he heard Amalia Albers describing these events, it was almost as if he was hearing about a film he had *never* in fact seen, Christian Buch said to Solomon Wiese. After this series of late nights, during which he had simply sat and listened to Amalia Albers and Christian Buch, he was in some definitive way connected to them, Solomon Wiese said to me in the Travelodge bar. And by that time, feeling that they had made him aware of the most significant and also the most inexplicable details of their past, they felt comfortable enough, they had decided, to initiate Solomon Wiese into their *operation* in a full capacity. And so Solomon Wiese began visiting the Borough Library, and also other libraries in the vicinity, to copy documents using the special miniature camera, later cataloguing and uploading the data to the subscription site, and receiving a share of the income it generated. The layout of some of the reading rooms, he soon discovered, made the taking of photographs next to impossible, and he was forced to improvise—he had discovered a deep desire to please Amalia Albers and Christian Buch, to impress them with his first assignment—so without consulting them he began typing up the documents by hand. It was as he surreptitiously typed out whole sections from publications on the properties of powerful acids that Solomon Wiese first lost track of what he was doing—although that is an unsatisfactory way of putting it, he said to me in the Travelodge bar—it was more as if I *woke up* after an indeterminate period of thoughtlessness, he said. Having started copying out a passage on the chemical make-up of strong acids, I woke up with pages of writing on the screen in front of me, which I could see matched the material in the document I had requested from the library stacks. But I couldn't remember typing out any of it, Solomon Wiese said, it was as if I had been asleep, in a fully dreamless sleep, as I copied out the relevant passages. After this I would quite often wake up mid-sentence, I would *wake up* to see the cursor blinking, it was not as if I had finished the whole section or even the whole sentence before coming out of this *trance state* I must have entered while copying out what was admittedly extremely dry material concerning the concoction of strong acids, capable of dissolving bone, for example, and even some metals, Solomon Wiese said. Of course when I worked out what had happened, I immediately thought of Christian Buch, and the so-called trance state he had experienced while undergoing his pronounced break from normal reality. The nothingness felt very close to me at these times, in the library, as if I were somehow overlapping with it, Solomon Wiese said. These so-called trance states continued to occur quite frequently. Then one day I saw a series of people in the street, Solomon Wiese said, there is nothing very remarkable about that, a series of people such as you will certainly see every day if you live in the city—but something struck me as odd about this series of people, it was as if there were something not quite believable about them, or as if their appearance so close to one another indicated to me that I had now entered not a different *area* of the city, but rather a different *order* of the city—I had entered a city with *different rules* from the city I had occupied moments previously. When I saw this series of people I understood that I was now in a place where the rules were *very slightly different*. A difficult feeling to explain, Solomon Wiese said, caused by witnessing this series of people, none of them on their own very remarkable at all. First, an extremely tall teenager with a white cane getting off a bus, speaking into her phone, which looked peculiarly out of date. Then an elderly man dressed entirely in black, with dark glasses, walking in small shuffling steps. Then a small, very old woman with bright blue eyes, who looked straight through me as she passed. Each of these individuals seemed like less substantial versions of the people they moved among—apparitions, in other words, Solomon Wiese said in the Travelodge bar, *broad daylight ghosts*. Without thinking, he had ducked into the nearest doorway, a shop that sold greeting cards, but inside there was no one behind the counter, and what's more, all the cards on the racks were completely blank, inside and out. A man in a dog costume had walked past the window. Back on the street he had looked around; everything had appeared to be more or less normal. In the upper windows of one of the buildings opposite he could see a screen, he said—through an upstairs window there was a large screen with a projected image on it, from the perspective of a gunman—one of the countless video games where you play as a sniper or assassin, obviously, Solomon Wiese said, but there was something about seeing the in-game street from the perspective of a gunman hovering over the *actual street*, that made the actual street seem to drain of its sense of reality. He watched the crosshairs drifting in the middle of the screen, over the broken-up clouds of the in-game world, above the street where everything was continuing as normal, and it seemed quite possible that he was watching the person in the upstairs room carry out *an actual assassination*, Solomon Wiese said. It seemed to him that it would be simple, in fact, for people to carry out actual assassinations of real people while believing they were playing a game in which they assassinated fictional people, shooting them in the head with powerful rifles with telescopic sights. This kind of thing would surely be the simplest thing in the world for a so-called tech giant to come up with in collaboration with the military, and if you went high enough they were always the same organisation anyway, Solomon Wiese said. As he watched the unseen assassin dispatch several people, this had occurred to him, he said, as an obvious solution to the problem of individual culpability in modern conflict scenarios. But in fact the thought wasn't quite that direct. It was more that the possibility occurred to him, watching the rifle sight hovering over the broken-up clouds, that in *pretending* to do something, in *playing* at doing something, in this case at shooting in the head with a powerful assault rifle a seemingly innocent person, a person might *actually be doing something.* And what was it, he had asked himself, that he, Solomon Wiese, was pretending to do? It had seemed to him then, quite suddenly, looking back, that it was conspicuous how each phase of his life had happened at what seemed like precisely the most *appropriate* time, in what seemed like exactly the most *appropriate* way. He had the clear impression suddenly, looking back, that everything had arrived in his life in exactly the most *appropriate* way, at precisely the most *appropriate* time. In other words, that everything had seemingly become available to him with the *ideal* timing, in the *ideal* fashion, with a pace and logic that was neither too quick, resulting in a situation that would have produced catastrophe, nor too slow, when these developments would no longer be of ideal use or interest. That the sequence of the events of his life had seemingly been neither too easy, allowing him to become complacent, nor had they seemingly been too much of a struggle, meaning that he would have given up. That instead, each phase, each development, had occurred precisely when he could make the *best use of it*, it seemed to him now, looking back. The periods of success and the periods of hardship had been neither too fleeting, nor too sustained. The strokes of fortune and misfortune, emboldening and chastening in different measures, had seemingly been *ideally* staggered. He meant with regard to his career as a writer, with regard to his *destiny as a poet*, of course. That every stage seemed to have occurred with uncannily *appropriate* timing, looking back, almost as if according to a plan, a plan to create a kind of *ideal situation* for the composition of a *significant work*, Solomon Wiese said. He had already spoken to me about the force of his inner convictions, he had already spoken about the machinations he believed were at work, the hands that were always in motion behind the *curtain of appearances*, as he put it, he said. And he knew that I recognised this feeling, he said, however I happened to formulate it. The conviction that had come to him while standing on the street, looking up at the rifle sight hovering over the in-game clouds, was that he had stumbled upon the true nature of the experiment he was in—that is, that the environment around him simply represented a kind of ideal setting for him to produce a work of *lasting power*, that the *work of lasting power* was his version of shooting in the head with a virtual assault rifle a seemingly innocent person. That the sheer appropriateness of everything that had happened in terms of his artistic development, that is, each event in his life seemingly arriving with an exact and even *deadly appropriateness*, was not an accident. That it had been built this way for a purpose—just as the landscape on the screen above him had been built precisely for the use of a powerful assault rifle with telescopic sights, for the shooting in the head of seemingly innocent people at long range—so his environment had been created for his production of a *work of lasting power*—ultimately it was shooting people in the head *by different means*. Just as simulating the predicament of a killer armed with a powerful assault rifle as a form of entertainment would produce people capable of seamlessly becoming real killers, as long as they were provided with a similar interface for their missions, so somebody had *simulated the conditions of the artist* in the hope that they—that is, he, Solomon Wiese—would complete *his* mission, that is, the production of a work of *real art.* Even the current phase he found himself in, that is, of being exiled from the so-called creative community, was an obvious and important stage in the production of the *real artist*, and therefore in the production of *real art*, art that would still function as real *outside the conditions of the simulation.* Of course this impression, powerful though it was, hadn't lasted, and he no longer believed these were really the circumstances of his existence, he said, glancing up at me in the mirror behind the bar for a second—in other words, he no longer really believed he was living in a simulation designed for the production of real artworks—that would mean that nobody else here was a real person, Solomon Wiese said. Behind him I could make out the bodies of poets in various states of undress, some with their make-up smudged and their hair mussed, and some with bruised and bloodied faces, as there had been some fisticuffs behind us in the Travelodge bar while Solomon Wiese had been speaking. But really it didn't matter on what basis one was able to justify one's belief in oneself as essentially *chosen* in one's role as an artist, Solomon Wiese went on. In other words, it didn't matter if one laid this at the feet of genetics or circumstance, an actual deity or an engineer of virtual environments. The point was exactly the same, he said, looking down again with his small smile and resuming turning his bottle of beer on the bar. During this period—less than a month, during which anaemic cherry blossoms opened and immediately fell from the scrawny trees that lined his daily walk to the library—he didn't hear anything from Christian Buch or Amalia Albers, Solomon Wiese continued. He had interpreted it as a test—Christian Buch and Amalia Albers were seeing if he could carry out the task with a minimum level of supervision. But when he had messaged Christian Buch to tell him the duplicate documents were ready, he still heard nothing, Solomon Wiese said. He had let a day or two pass, then went directly to Christian Buch and Amalia Albers's house, as he been instructed to do, where the nothingness was waiting for him in the front yard—the nothingness was slowly circling the house, it seemed to Solomon Wiese. There was no one at home, as he was able to confirm by pressing his face up to the windows, speckled with grime, and seeing familiar items of furniture and areas of wall. He had gone back again the next day in the rain, and it was instantly clear to him, finding the house in exactly the same condition, that they had left for good, Christian Buch and Amalia Albers, that they weren't coming back, that he would probably never see them again, despite his being able to make out their belongings through the windows, now speckled with rain in addition to general dust and dirt. He had spotted the old tortoiseshell cat with one eye sheltering under a piece of corrugated iron, and decided to come back again, with food, which he did, but on that occasion he was unable to find the old tortoiseshell with one eye, despite circling the house several times and attempting to coax it out of its hiding place. There was no longer any point in his staying in London, he had decided. He was to all intents and purposes done with London for the time being, Solomon Wiese went on, scraping at the ridges of dry glue on his beer bottle. He realised that to stay in London any longer would be to perpetuate a kind of destructive fantasy that staying in London would do him any good, psychologically and emotionally speaking but also professionally and socially speaking—he knew of many people, former friends and acquaintances from the literary sector, who had continued to believe their presence in London was somehow required, or was somehow beneficial to them, when all the evidence was to the contrary, and he had recognised for a long time this position as fundamentally a delusional one, that in the end these people were only further weakened by their decision to stay in London, despite all indications that they should leave London permanently and as soon as possible. He had seen what happened to those that remained, despite the warnings that were practically being screamed in their faces, that they should leave London immediately and never return, in some cases he had seen them actually destroyed by the dangers they insisted on ignoring, being too caught up with the romance of living in London, despite the totally illusory and in fact dangerous nature of this so-called romance. Of course he wanted to avoid such a fate for himself if at all possible, having seen through the romance, however fleetingly, so before it reinstated itself, as it was inclined to do—as he had observed many times in the cases of these same people, who having eventually decided to leave London, having sworn they were leaving London, ended up remaining in London for many further years, the romantic fantasy somehow righting itself, during which time they were continuously sapped by the city's demands, and by their obvious incompatibility with it, a process culminating in their eventual destruction—before this could happen, he began making his plans to leave London. He finally made the decision as his train slid into his local station, and he saw the usual row of blanched, miserable faces on the platform, squinting into the rain. That was what finally did it. It was still far too early for him to think about staging a return to the literary scene, anyway, Solomon Wiese had realised, he said, despite his renewed determination to do exactly that; it had only been two or three months since the intervention of QACS, and he knew that it would be a fatal mistake to return too early, before anyone missed him or had begun to really question the nature of his departure; they were all still busy congratulating themselves on enforcing his expulsion from their social spaces, he was certain, and to return now would be disastrous, if he hoped somehow to effect a change in his fortunes and restore his reputation. First he needed to work out if such a thing was even possible, he thought, and this required a further withdrawal from the scene surrounding the poetry world, in other words, withdrawal from the capital itself, to somewhere a safe distance away, where he could devote himself to planning his return. *Plotting his return*, he almost said. Like many people, he had moved to London from a smaller city outside London, due to an unavoidable cultural imperative he was powerless to resist—people were powerless to resist the lure of the capital, or resisted only to their cost, because if their weakening and eventual destruction by the capital was in many cases a foregone conclusion, their weakening and eventual destruction in their hometowns was just as assured, or more assured, drained as these towns and cities were of resources and attention by the insatiable demands of the capital, which was intent on sucking all life and vitality out of these smaller so-called satellite cities—and the nearer to the capital they were, the more surely they were drained of their already pitiful resources and vitality. Like most who had moved from these depleted and moribund cities-as-suburbs, Solomon Wiese openly despised the capital on one level—its confidence in itself as a cultural spectacle, its taking for granted that the eyes of people everywhere were turned continually towards it, its relentless suction of energy and vitality for its own bloated and absurd cultural productions, which made little or no sense in any other setting, and the complete dominance of those productions as the supposed cultural vision for the whole country—so while he was not sad or upset to be leaving London, he was aware at the same time that it meant resigning himself to a less rich and less vital experience of life, as he would have far reduced access not only to those cultural productions that drew millions of visitors to the capital every year, but also, for example, to certain foodstuffs, drinking establishments and salubrious atmospheres that could be taken for granted within the capital's payzones, but could not be taken for granted beyond them. Living beyond the paywall, demarcated by the last Underground stations, Solomon Wiese knew he would struggle to stay abreast of the narratives that pertained most to his activities, as the satellite city he had selected, the town of Diss, situated about an hour and forty minutes' train ride north-east, had no cultural institutions of its own to speak of, and therefore had no access to even the most rudimentary cultural package offered to neglected regional centres in half-hearted government initiatives from the previous election cycle. Once you were outside the capital, you really were outside the so-called bubble of culture, especially since the introduction of the payzones, Solomon Wiese said—but this suited him, as he wished to even more completely withdraw himself from the literary scene, so as to make his return even more emphatically, when the time came—he required, he thought, *total* removal, in order to stage an *emphatic* return. His situation was sufficiently desperate that he was even prepared to believe this calculated withdrawal would provide him with the necessary circumstances to renew his artistic endeavours—perhaps even to inject them with a modicum of authenticity that in theory only living in culturally reduced circumstances could provide. He still believed, on some level, that the *renewal of the art form* that he would stake his return on would originate with an *earlier rendition* of the art form, a regression that in fact emerged as a progression, as this was how the culture cycle worked, he was well aware, but it was an untested strategy, as far as he knew, to actually remove oneself from the advantageous circumstances of dwelling in the capital with the intention of achieving this. These nonetheless were his thoughts when he took up residence in Diss, an hour and forty minutes north-east of London by train. Any hope he had had of finding artistic inspiration there was immediately revealed as a ridiculous daydream, Solomon Wiese said. He wondered what he had been expecting to find, some unrecorded folk poetry, for example, some undiscovered lyrical style emerging from an overdue return to nature that he could repackage as a new form, it was an insane notion, as there were no such traditions in the regional zones and there hadn't been for centuries, as everyone knew. The sole popular interest in Diss that could be in any way described as a cultural interest was buggy racing, which was livestreamed into every pub and eatery and betting shop he walked past, due to the large sums, proportionally speaking, that the residents of Diss lost and won, but of course mainly lost, gambling on it. Every shopfront he passed, those that weren't boarded up, and every pub or café he went into, those that he dared to go into, looking for a part-time job to subsidise his stay in Diss, which he was beginning to realise couldn't be anything other than extremely short-term, played non-stop buggy racing, whether on huge screens, medium-sized screens or small screens, provided in all cases by the firms that had advertising revenue tied up in buggy racing, Solomon Wiese presumed. Around and around the buggies went on their oval track, piloted remotely by buggy drivers from pods installed in their homes, the buggy drivers who were minor local celebrities, Solomon Wiese learned, the most devoted of them being so amazingly obese they could hardly be removed from their buggy-driving pods, but were installed there more or less permanently while they carried out a non-stop itinerary of buggy races, buggy race practice, and local business endorsements: lawnmowers, scratch cards and butcher's cuts. It had been a ridiculous idea, that he might discover some untapped folk tradition in the satellite city of Diss that he could repurpose for his own artistic ends, he realised as he watched the buggies go around and around on their oval track—as if he could realistically make the claim that to go *backwards* in art was ever a way of going *forwards*, that art or poetry in its folk-tinged, rusticated state could ever emerge with something approaching relevance in the rarefied salons of the capital. The culture cycle relied on change, that was true, but he had to admit the culture cycle was really most comfortable and operated at its smoothest when its products stayed in some irreducible way the *same*, having only the superficial appearance of having changed—the appearance of change was of course necessary for any new product, as novelty is always necessary for a new product, even if it's just the misleading suggestion of novelty, while the product continues to fulfil its basic functions as always, he thought as he watched the buggies going around and around on their track. The products of the culture cycle changed only on the face of things while the actual substance of these products remained identical. So one could never argue that the cultural product that denied change or that actually *regressed* was somehow more authentic—and to say this would be to deny, Solomon Wiese thought, that change was a true condition, it would be to deny that life itself changed, that it continuously changed through evolutionary and revolutionary processes; it had its seasonal cycles but below them it also *continuously* changed—it only *seemed* to stay the same, in fact, while in reality it was always changing, and at the deepest level, while the culture cycle, by contrast, only *seemed* to change, while in fact remaining exactly the same, and in this sense the mortifying processes of the culture cycle were the antithesis of the dynamic processes of life, Solomon Wiese thought, as onscreen one of the buggies spun away from the track with smoke pluming from its engine. To create poetry that advocated staying the same, without offering even the semblance of change, would be tantamount to saying that everything was fine as it was, that nothing *needed* to change, Solomon Wiese thought, it would be to argue for the acceptance and even the approval of the way things currently were, when it was clear to anyone that, to the contrary, there was a lot wrong with the way things currently were. And to create poetry that actually *regressed* would be tantamount to saying that things were better *in the past*, that there was some golden age of art and poetry that we no longer had access to, and this was a popular falsity that Solomon Wiese could in no way convince himself to swallow. Then again, he thought, to advocate *progress* in poetry was equally misguided—to imagine that poetry in the future would be better than it was now, or that poetry was better now than it had been in the past—to believe this would be to subscribe to the superficial logic of the marketeer, of the cynical production and senseless waste that plagued all modern art forms, and so really there was no escape. Even if it had been pointed out to Solomon Wiese that there were aspects of his modern existence that, he would have to admit if he looked at it soberly, were indeed better than in previous periods—general quality of life, the chance for individuals to pursue their individual lifestyles, access to technology and luxurious foodstuffs and grooming products among them—he would respond to this assertion by pointing out there were also aspects that were very much worse. Nonetheless, it was the fantasy of every era to claim that the current moment was a new nadir of human hopelessness and alienation, that these were the end times, when actually this was mere narcissism, Solomon Wiese thought. It was the seeking of a mere egotistical thrill that enabled the sayer of these obvious falsities to delight in the hopelessness of their situation, as if they were in some way a spectator of their situation and no longer a participant, Solomon Wiese thought. Things had got better *and* they had got worse, and things would only continue to get better *and* things would only continue to get worse, Solomon Wiese thought. I am living through a period in which things are continually getting better, and things are continually getting worse, Solomon Wiese thought. He had found work in a barn-sized pub in the town centre, which like everywhere else in Diss showed non-stop buggy racing on its multiple screens, and like everyone else in Diss, Solomon Wiese became well versed and to some extent invested in the narratives of the various buggy racers. He was soon on friendly terms with most of the regulars, too, in particular a large, fair-skinned old man with a lame leg that he dragged behind him without the aid of a stick or crutch, and whose otherwise bald head was covered with large black scabs. These large black scabs fascinated Solomon Wiese, as they never seemed to heal and drop off but were a permanent feature of the man's appearance, and when the man hauled himself up to the counter to order a drink and his dinner, which he ate every night at the same time at a table away from the windows of the brightly lit barn-sized pub, it took all of Solomon Wiese's self-restraint to resist observing their textured surfaces under the bar lights, and to see that the raised black scabs on the man's head bulged in such a way that made them appear extremely soft. He had a detailed daydream in which he pressed his finger into one of the scabs, which broke immediately to the touch, his finger simply carrying on into the man's brain, meeting no resistance, as thick black fluid welled around his knuckle. It was immediately obvious to Solomon Wiese, he said to me in the Travelodge bar, that this fair-skinned old man with scabs on his head was seeking to unburden himself of something, and that he was searching with his apparently casual conversation for a chance to begin this unburdening—any man of a certain age who visits the same pub every evening is sure to be harbouring some story that he wishes to unburden himself of, that much is obvious, and the tiring insistence with which the old man with scabs on his head attempted to keep the conversation at the bar going, apparently at all costs, even when he had completed his order, and all the necessities had been dealt with, and an acceptable number of pleasantries exchanged, made this even more apparent. The scabs themselves were never referenced by the old man with scabs on his head, which somehow made it even more difficult for Solomon Wiese not to examine them when the old man with scabs on his head was at the bar, taking a long time over his order, which nonetheless was always the same, hunting with his apparently casual questions and observations for a window through which to begin unburdening himself onto Solomon Wiese. It didn't take the old man with scabs on his head long to begin making allusions to a war in some distant place, the terrible heat in this distant war zone, the sand that got everywhere, the flies that lived in the sand, the eggs the flies laid in the lining of one's clothing, the maggots that hatched from the eggs and infested every crevice, as well as his own duties in this arid, infested theatre of combat. For some reason he was reluctant to identify the actual region and so the specific war he was referring to, it could have been any one of five or six separate although of course inter-related wars, Solomon Wiese thought, but that omission aside, the old man with scabs on his head didn't spare any detail in his accounts, which after his initial tentativeness he launched into with minimal warning, having gauged Solomon Wiese and found him to be a sufficiently willing listener, or at least one who offered little resistance; once emboldened by Solomon Wiese's politeness and passivity he piled detail upon detail, in fact, as he leaned on the bar, the bar lights illuminating the scabs on his head, which appeared almost like clots of dark mucosal blood, when Solomon Wiese dared to examine them closely. These details circled other unspoken details with enough regularity for Solomon Wiese to become certain that the old man with scabs on his head meant him to understand that he had returned with *spoils* of some variety from his war years, that there were *considerable spoils* that the old man with scabs on his head had returned with, considerable *undeclared spoils* of some sort, discovered in the desert, as became clear, as every time the old man with scabs on his head began detailing his war-time experiences, that is, every night Solomon Wiese worked a shift in the barn-sized pub in the centre of Diss, an hour and forty minutes' train ride north-east of London, he covered essentially the same ground but in a little more detail, revealing a little more of the terrain and sequence of events with each telling, and it was through this lengthy process of nightly retellings, spanning several weeks, of essentially the same sequence of events, that Solomon Wiese discovered that these spoils, the exact nature of which remained unclear, had been discovered in a kind of underground palace, a series of empty rooms built of marble and stone and hidden beneath the desert sands, the co-ordinates of which had been provided by an enemy prisoner that the old man with scabs on his head, as a much younger man, had been instructed to guard single-handedly or almost single-handedly for an extended period of the hostilities. Such was this prisoner's significance in the conflict that he was kept by himself in a cage in a small courtyard within the prison camp where the old man with scabs on his head had been posted for much of his tour, the old man with scabs on his head said. Spending so many hours in the company of one other person meant that they had to communicate, that much was inevitable, but their communication was hampered by the fact they didn't speak the same language, and at first their one-sided dialogue consisted only of the simple, almost musical-sounding phrases that the solitary prisoner repeated to himself day in and day out, while imprisoned in his cage, the old man with scabs on his head said. The old man with scabs on his head had realised that these phrases were not simple, reassuring statements that you could imagine making to yourself in a situation of such extreme adversity; he knew enough to recognise there was more to them, that these were phrases the prisoner had memorised before his capture, possibly many years before his capture, perhaps even as a small child, and that he was drawing on these phrases now to sustain himself through his imprisonment, he was accessing them in his cage as a secret reservoir of strength and spiritual resolve, which had the effect of replenishing the solitary prisoner's seemingly indefatigable spirit and determination. The old man with scabs on his head, who told Solomon Wiese his name was Dimitri Radic, had begun repeating the sounds of these mysterious phrases back to the solitary prisoner, at first in a way that could have seemed antagonistic, and probably would have been taken to be hostile if they had been words of prayer or words from some sacred tract, but his repeating of these sounds actually caused the solitary prisoner nothing but delight, and he had responded to Dimitri Radic's uncomprehending sounding-out of these phrases with the same phrases again, correcting or sharpening Dimitri Radic's pronunciation, and then with further phrases, and then the phrases that came next in an apparently never-ending sequence of phrases through which the solitary prisoner made his way every day he spent in the cage. This process was the basis of their entire communication, which eventually became rich and involving for Dimitri Radic, in some ways the most rich and involving dialogue of his life, leading him to memorise a long sequence of simple, almost musical-sounding phrases, which he had never been able to identify, though he had spent some years trying after returning from his military tour, and which he was now certain formed a *long poem* of some description, that the solitary prisoner had memorised or perhaps had even written in his youth, and recited daily in order to marshal his inner forces and so survive his imprisonment. It was safe to say that he had had absolutely no interest in poetry prior to his military tour, but he had become *deeply interested* in it subsequently, when it had become clear to him, guarding his solitary prisoner, that it provided him, the solitary prisoner, with an inexhaustible inner resource that enabled him to endure the extreme hardship of his imprisonment in the cage. He knew that Solomon Wiese, a barman in the barn-sized pub in Diss town centre, was also a poet, Dimitri Radic said. He followed all the little magazines and he had recognised him immediately from a picture that had appeared in one such publication. He was being direct about it because he was seriously unwell, Dimitri Radic confided to Solomon Wiese—his illness was no secret—that he was a very sick man indeed was obvious to anyone who bothered to look at him. It would be no surprise either if he told Solomon Wiese that he didn't have much time left, and probably it wouldn't be a surprise if he said he didn't have any relatives, or any friends to speak of, living in the city of Diss, in the east of England, many hundreds of miles from his place of birth, he said. His line of work after his military service hadn't exactly encouraged lasting or intimate friendships, he said, circling another detail, and so indicating to Solomon Wiese that this was a point he would be returning to in future. After he had been guarding his solitary prisoner, the *poet of the long poem*, for several months, Dimitri Radic said, after he had learned something like fifty of these simple, almost musical-sounding phrases, which he and the prisoner spent hours reciting in alternating bursts, at first as a kind of game, a way to escape the boredom and heat and the discomfort of being basically infested with flies and maggots, but then as a kind of self-hypnosis, Dimitri Radic came to believe, or a form of meditation, the prisoner had scratched with a small stone a series of numbers into the sand on the floor of his cage; each number, as he was able to convey to Dimitri Radic, corresponded to the syllabic value of one of these simple, almost musical-sounding phrases, and Dimitri Radic with his military training at once recognised the series of numbers as geographical co-ordinates, co-ordinates moreover that he had already memorised, through the repetition day after day of the prisoner's sequence of simple, almost musical-sounding phrases. Much later he had gone to the location they pinpointed and discovered the marble rooms, dark and cool under the sands, and returned home with his spoils, the spoils of war, he said. He had no idea what had happened to the solitary prisoner after his internment, or why he had decided to reveal to Dimitri Radic the location of the underground chamber, when they both understood he couldn't assist him in obtaining his freedom or anything approaching it, and neither did he have any idea what the phrases that he still knew by heart meant—he had given up trying to find out a long time ago. At one time he had approached various academics and linguistic specialists in the prisoner's native language, only to discover that none of them recognised a single phoneme among the simple, almost musical-sounding phrases when he spoke them aloud. It was as if he were speaking a completely made-up language, Dimitri Radic said, and as far as he could tell no one on earth knew what any of the simple, almost musical-sounding phrases referred to, apart from the sequence of numbers the prisoner had scratched in the sand on the floor of his cage. The so-called spoils of war had been converted by him into hard currency at the earliest opportunity, Dimitri Radic confided to Solomon Wiese, he couldn't go into any more detail than that, and over the years he had barely made a dent in the small fortune that had resulted, being by nature fairly frugal, even though he had spared himself nothing he really desired—he had discovered his desires were relatively modest, in the end, he concluded, and now more than anything he only wanted to unburden himself of his small fortune, as he had no use for it anymore, by donating it in its entirety, or almost in its entirety, to a person who might use it for one of the few things he felt had any value, in other words the poetic enterprise—that is, he was saying he would transfer the money directly to Solomon Wiese. It had started to make him feel incredibly restless, the small fortune, the old man with scabs on his head said. He had found himself replaying the days he had spent guarding the cage, and replaying too the sequence of simple, almost musical-sounding phrases that in a compulsive way had begun to trouble him, and his hope was that by bestowing the small fortune resulting from the spoils of war, stolen from the cool rooms of marble and stone hidden beneath the desert, to a kindred spirit of the solitary prisoner, that is, to another poet, he would be in some way able to assuage his conscience and finally have some peace, both from his memories of his days guarding the cage, of the terrible heat and the sand flies, and from the sequence of simple, almost musical-sounding phrases, which had begun to haunt and obsess him, depriving him of sleep and rest, replaying as they did endlessly in his head, day and night, with no sign of abating. And that is what happened soon after, Solomon Wiese said, he actually did receive by bank transfer a *small fortune*, as promised, from the old man with scabs on his head, who asked for nothing in return, just as the solitary prisoner, the unidentified poet of the long poem, had asked for nothing in return, the old man with scabs on his head said—he didn't even expect Solomon Wiese to thank him or to keep him informed of his activities, the knowledge that he had unburdened himself of his small fortune was enough for him. Solomon Wiese had seen the old man with scabs on his head, Dimitri Radic, less and less often after this at the barn-sized pub in Diss town centre, where in any case he only worked a few more shifts, and when he did see him, the old man with scabs on his head had barely said a word, simply ordering his meal at the bar and quickly retreating to a small table away from the windows. So in the end Solomon Wiese hadn't discovered the nature of the old man with scabs on his head's activities since his military tours, nor had he heard if his bestowing of the small fortune on Solomon Wiese—which he had apparently begun to feel psychologically oppressed by, to the point of saying he thought he had been *cursed* by the small fortune—had relieved him of his symptoms to any degree, that is, the sequence of simple, almost musical-sounding phrases repeating endlessly in his mind, that was driving him slowly insane. When Solomon Wiese said that he had selected the city of Diss more or less at random as the destination of his strategic retreat from the capital, he hadn't been completely truthful, he went on. So far he had avoided talking about his background, as he didn't regard this information as having any significance, beyond the few things he had been obliged to include; there was nothing unique or remarkable about his background, nothing in other words that I couldn't deduce for myself, but it was necessary at this point to mention that the choice of Diss hadn't been altogether random, as he had suggested, and that actually he had selected Diss as he had grown up not very far from it, he was familiar with it, he knew people there, and while his parents would not be playing any further part in what he had to relate, they still lived in the countryside outside the city, and they were aware of his presence in Diss, though not of all the factors involved. When he had moved back to Diss, his parents, trying to be helpful, Solomon Wiese supposed, had put him in touch with another poet, a young man called Max Mikkaels, who resided in a seaside town two train rides from Diss, where he lived alone with his father, leading an otherwise isolated existence, Solomon Wiese's parents had said, on an otherwise typical phone call, during which they had repeated the name Max Mikkaels ten or fifteen times, as if trying to impress it into Solomon Wiese's memory. He was mentioning his parents now so as to not have to mention them again, not even once, Solomon Wiese said. He regarded them as completely irrelevant, as he had already said, for the purposes of his account—he had nothing against his parents, of course, he had got past all that in early adolescence, he had nothing but largely positive feelings towards them, towards both of them; he still spoke to them regularly, and they had supported him during his time in the capital and his time, latterly, away from the capital, without pretending to understand their son's sudden relocation and without troubling him with too many questions about it. Like many people who had moved to London in early adulthood he had only managed it with his parents' support, both financial and moral—in fact his efforts to install himself and make a success of his artistic career there, so-called, had been one hundred per cent bankrolled by his parents, and obviously he was grateful for this, as went without saying. Both he and I knew this state of affairs was far from remarkable—it was totally pervasive among the young would-be cultural contributors who moved to the capital in early adulthood, that is, to be totally dependent on their parents for financial not to say moral support, yet it was also a state of affairs that remained largely undisclosed in social situations, for understandable reasons, Solomon Wiese said. The discussion of parental support was in fact mutually and silently agreed to be *off limits* for normal conversation, by the aspiring creatives of the capital—it was a weapon that was recognised by unspoken agreement as too shameful and too devastating to wield publicly, to ever be brought into the open, although sometimes it might be alluded to—if one of the conversants felt reasonably assured of their comparative *lack* of support, in that particular context—but most of the time the *mutually assured destruction* of the topic guaranteed a kind of truce on this front, between the vying young creatives of the capital, who had been sent out to *do battle* at the behest of their parents, having been armed by their parents with their respective advantages, and whose unobtrusive designer label wear was noted without comment, despite the conspicuous logic conflicts it created with whatever artistic origin story they were currently promoting. It was possible, when he reflected on it, that Solomon Wiese's parents could have expected to see some evidence of his progress by this point, given that they had been supporting his artistic activities for years, which remained entirely mysterious to them—they had never seen any evidence whatsoever of these so-called artistic activities, Solomon Wiese said, as he had kept his growing publication record carefully hidden from them, which also meant, mercifully, that they were unaware of the reasons for his retreat from London, that is, his sudden fall from favour due to his works being penalised by the newly operational quantitative analysis and comparison system (QACS). They might have expected something more definite by now than the emphatic zero he had provided them with, and even if they didn't express their disappointment in his unexplained flight from the capital back to the comparative safety of Diss directly, he was able to sense it, he said. He was able to sense it in their confused yet careful questions—he could barely stomach the sequence of polite and delicately phrased questions presented to him by his parents without fail whenever he saw them, almost as if they were interviewers for a cultural highlights programme and he was some respected yet highly secretive artist or writer—their questions that always refrained from offering a judgement or opinion on his actions, and yet did so anyway, in a covert or even underhand way, his parents' questions' apparent total lack of judgement *belying* the real judgement that lay behind them, so that Solomon Wiese often wished his parents would just express their disappointment and bemusement to him directly. He could recall without effort many occasions when his actions, or lack of them, had been met with this covert or unexpressed disappointment and bemusement—the sense that the considerable investment of time and energy his parents had put into his upbringing and his early orientation with regard to the arts had *gone to waste*—in fact Solomon Wiese suddenly remembered his mother had once asked him, with uncharacteristic tactlessness or recklessness, as if momentarily forgetting the parental policy of non-judgement with regard to his artistic activities, or lack of them—she had actually asked if he wanted all the time and effort she and his father had put into his upbringing to *go to waste*—all those hours reading you stories, his mother had said, all those books we bought for you, do you want them to go to waste?—making it clear in this moment of uncharacteristic honesty that she regarded her reading of stories to Solomon Wiese as an infant as basically an investment, put away as into a bank or building society, for the recoup of some future reward, a future source of cultural esteem and parental pride, in other words, rather than as a simple expression of affection and a means of nourishing his infant brain, stirring in it curiosity about the world. His parents had been unable to make any entrance into the cultural arena themselves, despite one or two doomed attempts, Solomon Wiese went on, and with her question his mother had made it clear that they regarded it as his duty in his familial role to confer some much-needed cultural esteem upon the Wiese family name—a family name that decades or centuries ago, as his father would sometimes remind him, had been connected with cultural esteem and recognition of the highest order, but this cultural esteem and recognition had since dwindled and sunk from view completely, and been replaced by the thoroughly average bourgeois set-up that Solomon Wiese knew well from his childhood, and which like all thoroughly average bourgeois set-ups desired nothing more than that cultural esteem and recognition be somehow conferred upon it. His family was eager to branch out, in other words, in its uncomprehending way, from the typical occupations of its social bracket into the venerated reaches of the arts, and it aimed to accomplish this through its offspring, Solomon Wiese said, in whom they had instilled a reverence of music, literature and painting—a child in this instance being understood as nothing but a more or less eerie reiteration of its parents, down to its innermost dreams and desires, desires that had merely been put to one side for a generation, while more urgent matters were attended to, only to transmigrate and emerge with uncannily renewed vigour in the following generation, in other words *in me*, Solomon Wiese said. And no doubt I am worse still, Solomon Wiese said, I am worse than my parents with their uncomprehending and narcissistic art aspirations, in my taking this expectation of a *career in the arts* as my birthright and natural destiny, in shamelessly carrying out my parents' all but openly declared vicarious ambition for me, and in basically following their plans to the letter. But as I've already pointed out, I seem to be unable to shake these convictions, Solomon Wiese said. Knowing about the origins of my convictions doesn't seem to make them any less certain, in fact it only seems to make them all the more incontrovertible, Solomon Wiese said—he had been unable to even imagine shaking himself of these convictions until recently, and it would be impossible now, he thought, for him to do so, unless he was confronted by someone else who displayed *exactly this same set of convictions*, which would allow his own to appear in all their true, truly disgusting reality, and make it psychologically necessary for him to detach himself from those convictions, to the extent he would perhaps even deny that such convictions had ever lurked inside him, as a source of private pleasure and imagined wealth. He had been frolicking on a mountain of gold coins, in his head, for years and years, he had been playing among unimaginable riches—to abandon his convictions now would be to wake up and discover the ocean of coins was nothing but an ocean of common shale and shingle, stones and sand. That is the only way

I could imagine anything changing, Solomon Wiese said, casting a penetrating look my way as he said it. Anyway, it was his parents who had put him in touch with Max Mikkaels, during a phone call in which they had mentioned the name Max Mikkaels between ten and fifteen times, at which point he realised he was doomed to make contact with Max Mikkaels, just as he was doomed to pursue a career in the arts, Solomon Wiese said. Solomon Wiese was in a sufficiently desperate social position, as he had already explained, to consider any option he came across—not to mention that the receiving of the small fortune from the old man with scabs on his head had made him considerably bolder in planning his return to the capital, sometime in the next year, he now thought. Soon after the conversation with his parents, and this was to be the full extent of his parents' involvement in the proceedings, it was the last time he would be mentioning them, Solomon Wiese said, he had gone to visit Max Mikkaels in the small seaside town an hour or two from Diss by train. He had alighted at the small seaside town's train station and walked along the seafront, which was completely deserted, its arcades shut, their windows facing a dull grey sea with distant banks of wind farms, before cutting inland, deeper and deeper into the town's outskirts, the same outskirts he'd passed through on the train, a mandelbrot of culs-de-sac and crescents, unpeopled on a weekday afternoon, the residents at work or at school, their cars absent from the forecourts and garages, until he came to a bungalow that matched the address Max Mikkaels had given him, where the young poet lived alone with his father, who was elderly and infirm, Solomon Wiese's parents had said. It took a long time for Max Mikkaels to answer the door. Solomon Wiese heard the chimes from the doorbell resounding inside the bungalow, followed by footsteps hurrying back and forth behind the blurry glass. Inside there was no sign of the elderly father, but Solomon Wiese noticed that Max Mikkaels, who greeted him enthusiastically as he invited him in, had removed several photographs from their places on mantelpieces and windowsills and walls, where their shapes were clearly outlined in dust or indicated by bare hooks. Solomon Wiese assumed that the Mikkaels family portraits had been hanging there until a few moments ago, when Max Mikkaels heard the doorbell announcing Solomon Wiese's arrival and had rushed through the bungalow, seizing these items and depositing them in some hiding place on a sudden impulse. These Mikkaels family portraits must contain images of the young Max Mikkaels, Solomon Wiese thought, and were presumably a source of embarrassment for Max Mikkaels, at least in Solomon Wiese's presence, perhaps because he was Max Mikkaels's senior in the loose hierarchy that had brought them into connection. His exile from the capital had probably demoted him to a level around the same as Max Mikkaels's, in fact, but this was a situation Max Mikkaels couldn't be expected to appreciate, given his rural location and limited access to the most recent developments in the literary scene. All the signs were that Max Mikkaels regarded Solomon Wiese with a measure of awe, probably resulting from Solomon Wiese's recent stint in the capital and his appearance in some of the more popular journals there that Max Mikkaels would surely have known by reputation, even here, far beyond the payzones, with the region's built-in comms delay of two to three weeks. Sharing a creatively minded outlook and a regional background, they might very well be able to assist or advise each other, they might even *befriend* each other, as Solomon Wiese's parents had put it, despite Solomon Wiese's inner resistance to this idea, and his vague plan to sever all contact with Max Mikkaels if it transpired from their meeting that he was likely to become a burdensome acquaintance. Once they were inside the Mikkaels family home, Max Mikkaels wasted no time in leading Solomon Wiese through to his bedroom, where empty packets of food were strewn all over the floor, with clothes strewn below the empty packets of food, and newspapers strewn below the clothes, so that the floor itself was completely hidden from view, and where Max Mikkaels immediately launched into a lengthy explanation of a particular media platform he had begun using, and that he regarded as an indispensable tool for the emerging poet, especially an emerging poet with the innate disadvantages of living in one of the regional areas, and therefore beyond the capital's payzones and their premium-level access to events and publications of cultural significance. The application was called Locket, Max Mikkaels said. He had used it to connect with other young poets around the country—actually poets of all ages, as some of the most avid Locket users were older poets who were nonetheless stuck at the *emerging* stage, as defined by the culture cycle. But the useful thing about Locket as an application was its regional emphasis, Max Mikkaels went on, meaning you could easily connect with other creatives in your immediate vicinity; in this way the app sought to stand in for the now-vanished regional hubs where aspirational and creatively minded people had once met one another, face-to-face, before these hubs were effectively purged of cultural activity by the introduction of the payzones, and the irresistible lure of the capital, for all those who could afford to make the upgrade. The Locket app went some way to remedying this situation, Max Mikkaels said, providing a means for the average regionally located yet creatively minded person to steel themselves against the isolation and antagonism they were sure to encounter in their communities. In Max Mikkaels's estimation, any poet worth knowing about, indeed any cultural contributor worth knowing about, would be using the Locket app daily in a matter of months; many poets of notoriety were already prolific on the platform, he said, and soon there would be no poet however established who wouldn't be using it. Poets would come to be known *mainly* through their engagement with the Locket app, in Max Mikkaels's estimation, and those poets who for whatever reasons did not or could not engage with it would be at a profound disadvantage, in fact they would soon be forgotten altogether, they would join the ranks of dead and forgotten poets who were of interest only to a scattering of scholars and historical enthusiasts, as everyone today recognised that poetry was a *living* art form, thanks to the drastic reappraisals resulting from the recent industry-wide adjustments—the only true poets were *living poets*, and if you couldn't see a poet recite their work, if you couldn't hear a poet's voice, he doubted whether the material in question was really poetry in the way it was popularly understood, Max Mikkaels said. In his estimation it was not putting it too strongly to say that poets who were not listed on the Locket app would effectively *cease to exist*, and this would happen in a matter of months, however secure their reputations seemed now. The special feature of the Locket app, even if it seemed gimmicky and superficial at first, was actually the real source of its growing appeal, in Max Mikkaels's estimation—namely the ability to add other creative users to your "locket," the platform's unique point of attraction, visualised as a pendant-shaped window next to the user's profile picture. The locket was "unlocked" to casual viewers only when they were approved as active Locket participants, necessitating proof of some level of cultural output, however perfunctory—and the user who appeared in your locket window was the individual whose creative output you were at that time *most engaged with*, Max Mikkaels said. The special thing about this feature, Max Mikkaels said, was that you couldn't simply select whoever you liked to appear in your locket window—it wasn't a simple popularity contest—instead, whoever appeared in your locket window was determined by your *actual engagement* with that user, as calculated by the platform. In other words, you couldn't mislead the general viewer by putting whoever you chose into your locket window, rather, your locket window would only show the image of the user whose work you had *genuinely engaged with*, in the most sustained and concerted way, whether that meant reading, listening, viewing, sharing or providing commentary on their output, and whether that output was in the written, audio or audio-visual categories. In this way, it being difficult though not impossible to contrive a particular result for your locket window, Locket aimed to provide users with a more authentic picture of their patterns of interest, and therefore to provide a more trustworthy basis for communication, collaboration and exchange, Max Mikkaels explained. If it *were* a popularity contest, then Solomon Wiese had to concede it wasn't a *simple* popularity contest, it was a fairly *complicated* popularity contest. It remained true you couldn't be sure how many users sought to mislead those viewing their profile by attempting to contrive a particular result for their locket window, Max Mikkaels said. But to use the Locket app in this calculating and cynical way would be to go against the whole ethos of the Locket app community, and such instances were treated severely if they were discovered, with the user generally banned for six weeks—a harsh penalty, but one that reflected the seriousness with which the Locket users regarded proper use of the platform. He himself had never been tempted to exploit the Locket app's special feature in this way, he added, especially as he had been involved for a short time with its development, a fantastic experience, in Max Mikkaels's estimation, but an unfortunately short-lived one, as the developers had inadequate funds at present to expand their team, so currently he contributed on a voluntary basis, fundraising for the soft launch, mainly, and the more funds he raised, the more likely it was that the developers would take him on again, this time in a permanent role. Or that was his hope, Max Mikkaels said. All of this meant he had to admit he was probably more emotionally invested in the Locket app than the average user, more concerned that it was used in the correct spirit, as outlined in the Locket app's community guidelines, a document every user had to sign before receiving their approval certificate. An idea had started to form in Solomon Wiese's mind as he listened to Max Mikkaels speak, he said to me in the Travelodge bar, where it was past four o'clock in the morning. He was aware even as this idea was taking shape that it represented a kind of personal disaster for him—in fact as Max Mikkaels spoke part of him was actively *preventing* the idea from taking shape—but it already had its own energy, its own mass, and all he could do was try to slow its formation. He realised that his attempts were hopeless, and that once the idea had formed and become completely clear he would be doomed to carry it out, to bring it into reality; it was in this sense that the idea was actually a personal disaster in the guise of an idea, Solomon Wiese said. He was aware of this, even as the idea was yet to completely assemble itself—he already realised at that stage that once it formed it would begin its sequence, and he would experience its full disaster, because he saw that once he had *had* the idea he would have to act on it, and there was nothing he could do about it. The miraculous thing about the idea was that with its formation, as if in one movement, it extended seamlessly into the world, so that its appearance in the world seemed to coincide almost exactly with its appearance in Solomon Wiese's head, in that almost before he knew it, he had managed to let it be known to Max Mikkaels that he had come into possession of a *small fortune*, the provenance of which he couldn't divulge; he managed to let it be known, too, that he had recently been informally exiled from the capital and its literary communities; and, finally, he managed to let it be known that he was keen to rectify this situation, and was considering all available options. Once his idea had extended into the world, through these pieces of information, he didn't have to do anything else, he simply watched as Max Mikkaels took hold of these pieces and the reality of Solomon Wiese's personal disaster materialised before him. The solution was provided in a matter of seconds by Max Mikkaels, at which point a *sly expression* appeared in his eyes that there had been no sign of before—it was as if an oleaginous liquid had been added to a container that previously contained only water—it made his gaze mobile and his movements more fluid, it took control immediately, altering his mannerisms, and the speed with which he worked at his terminal, and after this moment Solomon Wiese never saw Max Mikkaels *without* this sly ingredient added to his eyes—it was visible whenever he needed it as evidence of the inevitability of his idea, and all its disastrous consequences. For the rest of the afternoon Max Mikkaels's fingers, their nails bitten down to the quick, hurried over the grubby keyboard as he constructed Solomon Wiese's Locket profile, embellished Solomon Wiese's publishing history, connected Solomon Wiese to all the relevant regional and national literary bodies, those who were represented on the Locket app, and then, having agreed with Solomon Wiese a sum for his services, and insisting that Solomon Wiese deposit the amount by instant bank transfer into his account before he went any further, he began the more delicate and demanding process of recruiting a host of artificially generated profiles to the platform to form Solomon Wiese's new legion of followers and fans. Max Mikkaels used his developer's access codes, which were still valid, to populate these profiles from existing user templates created in an alpha version of the platform, finessing and refurbishing them as he went, a process he called a *migration of souls*. What he was attempting went against all the codes of use he as an assistant developer had helped to implement, something he intended to make amends for by anonymously investing in the Locket app with the payment he had just received from Solomon Wiese, Max Mikkaels said, and thereby regaining employment at the tech start-up. His plan was unprecedented in terms of the sheer quantity of fake users he was bringing into existence, he went on, his fingers darting around the grubby keyboard, of all ages and nationalities. The destiny of this virtual crowd, among their randomly sourced companion interests, was their enthusiastic, widely shared fandom of Solomon Wiese, so that soon Solomon Wiese saw his avatar adorning each of their locket windows. The more locket windows Solomon Wiese's image appeared in, as Max Mikkaels worked, the more surely his profile rose in prominence throughout the platform's literary and artistic networks, so that soon *genuine* users were signing up to receive access to his personal newsfeed, and later that same afternoon his image was appearing in the lockets of these self-same *genuine* users, among them several prominent literary influencers who, carried away by the sudden wave of support for this publicly discredited poet, were soon adding their voices to the revivifying chorus of praise surrounding his name. Solomon Wiese had watched in awed silence as Max Mikkaels spent the next five or six hours parsing and editing code in something akin to a trance state. During this time he perched on various narrow ledges around Max Mikkaels's bedroom, these ledges being the only places free from piles of clothes, newspapers and empty packets of food, apart from the large gamer's chair facing the terminal that Max Mikkaels occupied, none proving comfortable enough for Solomon Wiese to settle on for more than a few minutes, as Max Mikkaels immersed himself in the fabrication of Solomon Wiese's legion of followers—so when evening eventually came and Max Mikkaels suggested they have a break, perhaps to head down to Max Mikkaels's caravan, which was parked in some woodland near the beach a ten-minute walk away, Solomon Wiese agreed readily. A minute or two later they were walking out of the Mikkaels bungalow. They passed at the door a person on his way in, his headphones leaking music, and dressed from head to foot in sheaths of glossy streetwear, layers of bright webbing and shiny synthetic fabrics that hung off him like cloaks or priestly vestments. My brother, Max Mikkaels informed Solomon Wiese, who had glimpsed a dome-like white baseball cap with an abbreviated peak, tattooed wrists and a pair of enormous orange trainers with various panels and inlays, some of which showed animated characters engaged in anarchic activities. As well as moving within an aura of trilling hi-hats, Max Mikkaels's brother was enwreathed in a cloud of cherry-scented vapour that poured from a flashing inhalation device he held at his lips, lips that were framed by an immaculately shaped and incongruously dark beard; his eyes, too, were fringed by solid and well-shaped brows, aiming downwards into the screen of his palm-reader, from which the deep whine of buggy engines could be heard over his music. In his other hand he cradled a deep, metallic canister of something sweet-smelling and effervescent. Solomon Wiese would have described Max Mikkaels's brother's appearance as completely alarming, if he hadn't remembered that this choice of attire and conjoining apparatus was regulation wear for the youths of Diss and the surrounding areas. It was hard to imagine, Max Mikkaels said, as his brother passed them without stopping and entered the bungalow, followed by a contrail of fluttering snares, mood-altering vapour, odours of energy brew and the non-stop whine of buggy engines, a person more alienated from his environment and more in thrall to modern consumption than his brother—it was especially strange when you considered that half a century ago both he and his brother would have been employed on the land, as in fact their father had been, although even their father had worked at a significant remove from the land itself, operating a range of programmable farming machinery, their *grandfather*, on the other hand, would have had an intimate acquaintance with the land, Max Mikkaels said. But even Mikkaels the elder had been one of only a handful of farmworkers required to run an enterprise that spanned hectare after hectare of arable land in this region, and Max Mikkaels thought that today there were perhaps only one or two agricultural managers who oversaw all crop production in the parish, an expanse of fields that stretched for miles around them, production that was of course fully automated, meaning that for his generation alienation from the land that had sustained their family for centuries was now complete. It was actually hard to picture a way of life that was *more* remote from its physical surroundings if you tried, Max Mikkaels went on; he doubted if his brother had ever pressed a finger into the moderately fertile clay-heavy soil that lay beneath them, and if he had, he would have immediately disinfected his hands, having a powerful aversion to dirt that was typical of youths of the region, who also harboured a host of newly identified allergies, allergies that no one had ever been heard to suffer from before, probably caused by the so-called smart pesticides now used on all farming land, the long-term effects of which were unknown and uncontemplated. Detachment from the natural environment was now so pronounced that even the most basic principles of rural living had passed into obscurity, no one remembered them and no one used them, Max Mikkaels said, least of all his brother, but he had to admit he was hardly any better himself. His father had been able to identify hundreds of trees, plants, flowers and insects by sight alone. His father had been able to identify all the local species of bird and fish, whereas Max Mikkaels could identify only a handful of the most common and easily recognisable trees and plants, and a handful of the most common and easily recognisable animals and fish, which in any case he seldom had reason to notice, as they had almost completely disappeared from the vast, featureless landscape of automated crop farming that reached all the way to Diss from the coast, so they were not common and easily recognisable any longer. The worst part of it was that nothing had mitigated this remoteness from the land for those like his brother who would have once had a thorough knowledge of it and its creatures, who would have been happiest when heaving hay into a cart with a pitchfork, and who, if Max Mikkaels was being completely honest, would *still be happiest heaving hay into a cart with a pitchfork.* Instead, Max Mikkaels said, his brother spent his days occupied by fantasies—his brother's life was filled with nothing but fantasies of the most cheap and hollow kind. He was utterly in thrall to a culture that churned out the material of his cheap and hollow fantasies, and that he imagined existed in full beyond the immediate region of the seaside town and the regional hub of Diss, but in reality did not exist anywhere *apart* from the seaside town and regional hub, and others like it. This fantastical vision of so-called luxury brands, synthetic stimulation and neuro-affective competitive entertainment that Max Mikkaels's brother believed constituted life beyond the village boundaries and the outer limits of Diss, in reality *evaporated* at precisely those thresholds, it ceased to exist as soon as one passed beyond them, and the sad truth was that if Max Mikkaels's brother ever visited the capital or any other population centre, his reference points, as outwardly displayed in his mode of dress, and his worldview, as broadcast by his consumer choices, would seem completely outlandish and at the same time completely provincial to those cultural influencers in the capital to whom he imagined he was appealing, with his array of contemporary presentations. That his brother had been sold an egregious and blatant lie, an outright fiction, would be obvious to anyone who hadn't spent their life in a small town at the end of a train line, Max Mikkaels said, but the tragedy was that this lie had been devised exactly *for* people like his brother who lived in a small town at the end of a train line, and would never leave, and so would never find out that their understanding of life beyond their immediate environs was a vulgar caricature, concocted and sold to them in the interests of keeping them content in their state of detachment and alienation. Max Mikkaels's brother's foundational idea of the world did not exist in any real sense, apart from as a shallow and cynical marketing ploy—it was, in other words, a specialised, lucrative, front-facing industry targeted solely at the culturally and, for want of a better expression, spiritually directionless people that remained in the regional areas. The separation of people like his brother from the land they lived on was now total, just as the separation of people like his brother from the true cultural life of the city was total, and the natural and historical connections that had once existed were damaged beyond any hope of repair, Max Mikkaels said, as they turned onto a narrow lane lined with hedgerows signposted "Next-the-sea." If these digressions had been of more interest to Solomon Wiese, that is, if Max Mikkaels's revelations about his brother had not been a matter of indifference to him, he would have made a counter-argument at this point, Solomon Wiese said, in the Travelodge bar—had he thought it worthwhile he would have put forward the argument that Max Mikkaels's brother's predicament was not anywhere near as bad as it appeared, and although Max Mikkaels's brother's lifestyle and set of priorities might appear superficial and disconnected from the outside, from the *inside* the experience was hardly an unhappy one, and he would have asked Max Mikkaels if in fact it wasn't *Max Mikkaels's* way of living, with its highly tuned cultural anxiety and morbid ethical neurosis, that wasn't the unhappier way of living. Max Mikkaels's brother's way of living, which Max Mikkaels regarded as inferior and in some important way *untruthful*, was in fact more in tune with the age, Solomon Wiese could have said. He could have argued, had he not realised that it would have been a waste of his breath to make this argument to Max Mikkaels, that in some ways it was their *education* that was to blame for the predicament of people like Solomon Wiese and Max Mikkaels, their so-called liberal education, in that once they had been educated they came to understand their predicament as fundamentally compromised and basically irredeemable, that is, as tied to complex processes of exploitation in which they were of course personally complicit. And just as people like Max Mikkaels and Solomon Wiese profited from the exploitation of others, in the maintenance of their educated and enlightened way of living—they profited from the exploitation of people such as Max Mikkaels's brother, in fact, who for his serf's wage was probably grinding out figures in a data mine, or filling forms in content management—so they *themselves* were exploited for the profit of others living in a higher socio-economic tier, who probably regarded *their* activities, that is, Max Mikkaels's and Solomon Wiese's activities in the aesthetic domain, as equally stupid and pointless as the way in which they regarded Max Mikkaels's brother's doubtlessly stupid and pointless activities. The difference is that we understand ourselves *only* within this pattern of exploitation, Solomon Wiese could have said to Max Mikkaels, had he thought there was any point in doing so, whereas Max Mikkaels's brother understood no such thing, on the contrary, he probably regarded himself as relatively fortunate—and once we have understood ourselves fundamentally as exploited *and* as exploiters, as essentially compromised in our reliance on the exploitation *of* others, and as essentially demeaned in our exploitation *by* others, that is, once we have been *educated*, we are done for, we begin living in the afterlife, that is, a basically purgatorial existence emptied of meaning. Once we have been *educated* it is all over for us, Solomon Wiese resisted saying to Max Mikkaels. But that definition in no way described the life of Max Mikkaels's brother, which was rich in meanings and possibilities, of the kind that were meaningful and possible for him, Solomon Wiese could have said, but didn't. For us, however, the purpose of life is always occurring on some other plane, we understand our lives only in terms of other people's lives, and in terms of the chains of exploitation that connect us. We realise that we are unable to change anything, we have arrived after the fact, it is too late, and all we can do is tolerate this state of affairs, and *endlessly interpret* this state of affairs, in a perverse deepening of our exploitation—not only must we be exploited, but we must constantly analyse and *attempt to interpret* the terms of our exploitation. This is our principal leisure activity, in fact. Once we have understood our situation as one inextricably bound up with multiple types of nefarious exploitation, we are done for, Solomon Wiese could have argued, but he couldn't be bothered to make this argument to Max Mikkaels, instead he had decided that Max Mikkaels should be allowed to enjoy the feeling of superiority that his critique allowed him, which was really only another layer of alienation, another *distancing mechanism* between him and his immediate situation, Solomon Wiese said in the Travelodge bar—he would spare him this argument, he decided, so that rather than be inducted into yet another gradation of awareness regarding his exploitation, Max Mikkaels could live a bit longer without having to consider adding it to his current analysis apparatus, which he was basically the prisoner of. Let him enjoy not knowing for a little while longer, Solomon Wiese had thought, as Max Mikkaels continued to speak about his brother's existence, which he was now comparing to sleepwalking—Max Mikkaels's brother's existence was akin to that of a sleepwalker, according to Max Mikkaels. By now they were walking through sandy woodland, almost within sight of the sea. Tall silver pines grew from a carpet of sand and dry pine needles, threaded with wooden gangways, but as they neared Max Mikkaels's caravan Solomon Wiese stopped paying attention to him altogether, because the sight of these silver pines had caused him to remember something, he said to me in the Travelodge bar, where in the windows the pallor of dawn was starting to become discernible. Sitting on the floor of Mrs. Hewitt's classroom at storytime, listening to a story about a boy made out of bark, Solomon Wiese said—that is what I remembered, looking at the pines, the story of a boy made of silver bark. Vulnerable to such elemental forces as air and fire, yet still intrepid and brave, this so-called bark boy, Solomon Wiese said. And when I graduated from Mrs. Hewitt's class, and joined Mrs. Rayner's class, I remember I reproduced this bark boy story almost verbatim, for a class storytelling project, it was probably the first piece of writing I did, Solomon Wiese said, it was the first piece of writing I did and yet it was nothing but a word-for-word replication of the story of the bark boy I had heard while sitting on the floor in Mrs. Hewitt's classroom, Solomon Wiese went on. I didn't see anything wrong with this fact, I remember. I remember that I changed the name of the protagonist of the story, the little boy who encounters the boy made out of bark—I called him Nicholas, which was the name of one of the other boys at my table in Mrs. Rayner's class, Solomon Wiese said. I used his name in my version of the bark boy story, and I didn't see anything wrong with it, although the fact that I changed the name of the principal character perhaps shows I understood in some intuitive way that a transformation like this was necessary, if I was going to call the story my own, Solomon Wiese said. In the story, the bark boy is nothing but a few markings on a tree that somewhat resemble a face. The markings start out on a branch near the ground, but as over time the tree grows, the markings on the branch change to *more and more* resemble a face, and the branch gets *closer and closer* to the window of the little boy's bedroom, that is, Nicholas's bedroom, in my version of the story, Solomon Wiese said. Until one day the bark boy's face is level with the window, and a twig attached to the branch with the bark boy's face on it begins to tap on the glass, like a thin little arm, it taps on the window *over and over again*, until the little boy, Nicholas, gets out of bed and opens the curtains, and there he sees the silvery face of the bark boy looking in at him. And that is the start of their adventures, Solomon Wiese said, as chronicled in the bark boy book series, about which I can now remember absolutely nothing. Of course Mrs. Rayner recognised the story at once, my changing the boy's name had not been enough to disguise it, and my theft was paraded in front of the class, I was publicly disgraced for my theft of the bark boy story—this was the only time I felt I had done anything wrong, Solomon Wiese said, before that, the story of the bark boy was simply a story that I knew, and so I felt entitled to tell it. It was, in fact, my story, Solomon Wiese said, I would go as far as to say that it is *still* my story, and the fact that someone else wrote and published the story of the bark boy twenty or thirty years before I was born is nothing but an accident of attribution. A coincidence that is basically irrelevant, in terms of my connection to the story of the bark boy, which I regard entirely as *my own story.* The strange thing is that when I tried to locate this story years later, I could find no trace of it, Solomon Wiese said. There was seemingly no record anywhere of the story of the bark boy, or any version of that story, or any story that seemed even vaguely comparable, or not that I could locate. I was always a little bit afraid of the bark boy, I think, Solomon Wiese went on, afraid that I might hear tapping on *my own window* at night, that I might open the curtains of *my own bedroom* and find the bark boy's silvery, strangely old face looking in at me, Solomon Wiese said, I don't think I would enjoy that at all. As Solomon Wiese said this, I found myself thinking again of Christian Wort, of his ashen complexion when I had encountered him in the Southbank Centre the previous evening, and I remembered, as I had successfully prevented myself from doing up until that moment, the request he'd made before we'd parted company, that I sign one or two documents that required a witness. I had been reluctant to return to this detail until now, I thought as Solomon Wiese continued to talk, as he had been doing more or less uninterruptedly for the past five or six hours, I'd been reluctant to revisit the moment I had agreed to sign the documents that Christian Wort had shown me on his tablet, hardly bothering to glance at them, accepting Christian Wort's explanation that my witnessing the forms would allow him to complete the purchase of some materials that, when ordered together in the quantities he needed, for some kind of new commission, he said, required the signature of an identifiable witness. I had not had a good feeling about it but had simply swiped my thumb in the box as indicated, at which point Christian Wort had immediately turned away from me, already muttering his excuses, gazing out of the windows to where a delivery drone had detached itself from its orbit around a charge point and set a path for our position, its printer arms working. I hadn't hung around to see what it was that Christian Wort had sent for, via drone delivery, the moment I'd signed the form, and he hadn't offered any explanation, but I presumed it was connected to one of the business interests he had mentioned during our brief conversation, all of which, he had told me, received significant investment from anonymous foreign clients. Christian Wort's face hung in my mind for a moment, a face drained of life, almost the colour and texture of paper. The problem now was content, Solomon Wiese was saying—according to Max Mikkaels everything had gone to plan, but it would be hard to proceed any further without *content*—raw material, in other words, with which to furnish Solomon Wiese's newly activated Locket profile. His previous poems had been administered out of existence by QACS, and he could hardly re-emerge as a poet so soon without any actual poems to his name, Max Mikkaels said, as he and Solomon Wiese sat beside the fire he'd made outside his caravan, sharing a two-litre bottle of cider. Although a poet without any poems was perhaps an intriguing proposition, now he mentioned it—all of the romance and allure with none of the tiresome obligation, Max Mikkaels said. It was strange no one had thought of it before, the *poet without poems*. Or even the poet without poetry—but that sounded like a step too far, to Max Mikkaels. Poetry surrounded the poet, whether or not there were any actual poems, poetry was simply the poet's aura, it was the element they moved in, without poetry there could be no poet, that much was obvious. But a *poet without poems*, that was actually conceivable, Max Mikkaels went on, taking a swig from the cider and staring into the flames. The poems would be like promises that were never delivered on, but never reneged on either—the poems remained a continual possibility, for the poet without poems, even if they never materialised. The poet could still do all of the things that poets did, apart from the writing and publishing of poems—the poet without poems would *participate in poetry*, obviously—and in fact there were many of these individuals already in existence, if one admitted that the things they called their poems were nothing of the sort, that they were actually word-approximations; they were arrangements of words that resembled poems when you looked at them, but turned out on further examination not to be poems at all; they turned out to be nothing like a poem, at best they were simulations of poems, if he was going to be honest, Max Mikkaels said. They disintegrated as soon as they were touched, these word-approximations, Max Mikkaels said. The poet without poems was simply the next logical step on this journey into falseness and duplicity, Max Mikkaels went on, and if one accepted that, there was no shame in being the first to take that step. But were people ready for it, would they accept it? Max Mikkaels wondered, pausing as the flames cast their patterns onto his face, and threw larger, blurrier shapes behind him onto the trunks and branches of the pines. His instincts told him not, he said. His instincts told him people *might* get it, but that they wouldn't *want* to get it, and so they wouldn't *allow* themselves to get it, at least not yet. Still, it was an idea to hold on to, for a future date, the *poet without poems*, Max Mikkaels said. In that moment Max Mikkaels reminded me of myself, Solomon Wiese said to me in the Travelodge bar, it was like listening to myself talk as I sat there listening to Max Mikkaels talk, watching the flames tap at the logs. I used to talk that way too, at the fireside, I remembered, Solomon Wiese said, there was a time when it only took a fire and something to drink and I could talk endlessly. I had hardly talked at all since I'd left London, I had listened to other people as they talked, but hearing Max Mikkaels talk it was as if I remembered how to talk myself, it was as if I saw myself talking as a teenager, talking endlessly by the fire, as the soles of my trainers melted in the embers, Solomon Wiese said. When I was a teenager and I used to talk by the light of the fire I would always talk about the same thing, Solomon Wiese said. I would talk about how we should allow ourselves one full-hearted attempt at life, and if it didn't work we should back out of the whole idea, in other words we should cross ourselves out, if by the age of thirty, which seemed to me an unreal age, we hadn't done what we wanted, or perhaps even if we had, we should simply get out of the way, we should *take ourselves out of the equation*, Solomon Wiese said. His verbal onslaughts had always had the effect of slowly alienating everyone who was gathered around the fire, yet somehow he was unable to resist the subject, and he returned to it every time there was a fire in front of him and someone to listen, Solomon Wiese said. The fire reminded him of the nothingness, without his knowing it, he now thought, Solomon Wiese said. Every time he sat around a fire with his friends he would launch into one of his onslaughts about *taking oneself out of the equation*, Solomon Wiese said, so that his friends came to dread these onslaughts, and were able to recognise the signs of their impending arrival. *Once you have sucked as much from life as you can, you should really think about taking yourself out of the equation*—an onslaught would typically begin like that, Solomon Wiese said. These onslaughts would always have the effect of alienating everyone who was listening, Solomon Wiese repeated. Initially they would feel alienated from Solomon Wiese, but soon they would begin to feel alienated from one another, too, and gradually the group would begin to doubt itself, as its members retreated into the uncomfortable and isolated mental state produced by his verbal onslaught, Solomon Wiese said. The group would disband, if not physically then mentally and emotionally, there would no longer be any social cohesion or *group spirit* at the fireside. It was a guaranteed way of ruining an otherwise enjoyable evening, Solomon Wiese said, and despite realising this he was unable to stop himself from launching into one of his onslaughts whenever the opportunity occurred, whenever the conditions were right. Sometimes his listeners would form alliances—they would attempt to unite against him and interrupt the flow of words that seemed to well up from inside without any effort, Solomon Wiese said, but usually they were not powerful enough, and they soon fell silent again under its torrent, which although not fast-moving was relentless. Once his friends had become wise to the warning signs it was harder for him to begin, they were on the alert and would interrupt him before he could really get going, so eventually he was forced to change tactics, Solomon Wiese said. He would start by talking about something else entirely, and when the predominance of his voice had been established he would suddenly switch topic, so before his audience knew it they would be listening to him talk about the need to *take oneself out of the equation* again—in other words they would be helpless in the currents of his onslaught. He would begin by talking about a certain charity event they were all aware of, for example, a high-profile charity concert that they had all watched segments of on TV that day; of course, it's run by fascists, Solomon Wiese would say. You do realise that this charitable organisation is in reality a fascistic organisation run by out-and-out fascists, and if you think a penny of any money you're stupid enough to donate to them ends up benefitting the poor and needy, you are sadly deluded. All charitable organisations are actually run by out-and-out fascists, who have taken it upon themselves to bring about ever-more repressive and punitive governments, the more repressive and punitive the better, as only the presence of a highly repressive and punitive government *can ensure that the work of their charitable organisation continues to receive maximum public attention*. The more hostile the government is towards their charity's mission, the better, for these fascist charity workers. Because the less supportive the government, the more essential their charitable efforts appear, and so the greater the status of their so-called charitable organisation, and so the greater its assets, and so, inevitably, the greater their salaries. The presence of a repressive and punitive government regime is, these people realise, indispensible to the successful running of their charitable organisation, it is the only way they can continue amping up their fundraising efforts through the eye-catching public events and advertising campaigns that are the sole reason for their organisation's existence, Solomon Wiese would say. The owners of these charitable organisations are actually out-and-out fascists who strive to bring about the most adverse circumstances imaginable *precisely for those people they purport to be helping*, and they do this solely in order to improve the stature of their charitable organisation, which is the only thing they care about, after lining their own pockets, of course, Solomon Wiese would continue, before switching his theme with no change in his tone or delivery, so the next thing his listeners heard would be the sentence: We may as well dispose of ourselves, after the first flush of excitement as teenagers, once we reach the age of thirty we should admit it's the only plan that makes sense, *to take oneself out of the equation*. On some level it had dawned on him by the fireside with Max Mikkaels that this was his way back to poetry, Solomon Wiese said—in other words that he would become the *poet without poems*; as he listened to Max Mikkaels talk he had become aware again of the presence of the nothingness, and he understood that anything could be added—the nothingness would take it—whatever you wanted to delete could be deleted by directing it towards its non-shape, a watery outline that seemed to shiver above the fire, where it appeared to be processing the flow of Max Mikkaels's speech. This is how he would arrive at his famous technique, Solomon Wiese said to me in the Travelodge bar, this is how it was revealed to him, and how he would be able to stand up before an audience only a couple of weeks from that night by the fire and simply begin speaking, and in doing so create for want of a better expression *genuine poetry*. It was like being in a nightmare, when he stood up on stage, having returned to London a fortnight or so later, Solomon Wiese said—try to imagine standing onstage with no notes, with nothing prepared, and being expected to deliver quote unquote *genuine poetry*. He had actually had dreams about this, he remembered, years earlier, when he had first started to perform at poetry recitals, Solomon Wiese said, dreams in which his poems reverted under the stage lights to indecipherable symbols, and he had to improvise his way towards a *genuine poem* through these rudimentary markings, or perhaps it was a shopping list or an old email he found himself staring at, as he was picked out by the spotlights, which in that moment he was required to elevate spontaneously into an example of the highest literary art. It was barely worth relating the next part of his account, Solomon Wiese said, of what happened before his return to the capital, that is, the logistics of tracking down suitable local poets through the Locket app, with Max Mikkaels's help, and of approaching them with an offer—basically of finding a way of taking their all-but-unknown poems off their hands, and of doing this without arousing their suspicions, so he could procure sufficient material to publicly regurgitate at a later date. These poets had to be at the appropriate level of obscurity, in other words not so well known that their works would be recognised, and not so inexperienced that their works would be completely lacking in literary merit; therefore the poets he and Max Mikkaels targeted had tended to be older, all-but-unknown poets, poets who had abandoned hope of recognition but perhaps continued to publish regionally, practicing their art alone in semi-isolated rural locations. The Locket app, as it was designed to, had provided a lifeline for such poets—older poets thought to be at the *emerging* level especially were among its most prolific users—they had found hope in this application, where for more than a generation there had been no hope for the regional poet, no route to an informed, appreciative readership. This part of his account couldn't realistically be of any value, Solomon Wiese said, but in the interests of transparency he would give me a sense of what had occurred, even though they were hardly worth bothering with, these episodes, writers always being in person fundamentally uninteresting. To meet a writer was always a crushing disappointment, as they were basically non-functioning people who had systematically destroyed their friendships and mercilessly strip-mined their families for material, which was the only thing they cared about, Solomon Wiese said, so they had by middle age usually managed to isolate themselves completely, and any relationships that had survived this ruthless treatment were probably inherently bad relationships. Any relationship that had survived years of exploitation at the hands of a writer was transparently a subservient relationship of the most demeaning kind, in which the writer was permitted to heartlessly dominate their unfortunate friend or family member, simply because there was no one else around to question it. The writer in middle age was a solitary character, but only because one by one they had alienated all their friends. If their friends were ordinary people rather than writers, the writer had most likely neglected them in the callous and cold-hearted way we have come to expect of all writers, except of course to make some unrealistic, completely selfish demand out of the blue from time to time, Solomon Wiese went on, but if these friends were *other writers*, the friendship would have soured dramatically at some stage, and become instead a vitriolic and mutually toxic adversary-ship, usually because the writer had stolen or copied some idea or expression from their writer friend, and been caught doing so, or because they had accused their writer friend of copying from them some probably worthless idea or expression. These adversary-ships were the only thing that sustained the writer into old age, either completely obsessing them or simply providing a stimulating source of drama which of course they fed off in a typically unhealthy manner. In all cases these relationships infected the writer's day-to-day existence with a low-key toxic atmosphere. Their family, on the other hand, had normally been dispatched years or decades previously with a single gesture—*one move* had normally accounted for their entire family, Solomon Wiese said, one monumental act of betrayal and bad faith, usually. After this their family had woken up to the threat the writer presented to them, and if they had any sense at all they had cut the writer off, severed all contact, in order to prevent the writer from further infecting the family with their bad faith and toxicity, and in the end dismantling the family entirely, Solomon Wiese said. It's even worse if you harbour some form of respect for the writer, and then you meet them, Solomon Wiese said, the worst thing you can do is to meet a writer you in some way respect, because you will leave the meeting having lost all respect for that person, and you will be unable to re-capture or reconstitute that respect by returning to the work, which you will find has been contaminated by the writer's tedious and egomaniacal private persona. The value of the work will be irretrievable in light of what you now know, having encountered the real-life writer, and having seen in cold daylight that they were serious precisely where you had thought they were joking, and that they were joking precisely where you had assumed they were serious, making the writer appear in person as a kind of cartoonish travesty of their once dignified writer profile, which never again recovers its nobility and esteem. This was precisely the case with the writers he had sought out with Max Mikkaels, Solomon Wiese went on, some of whom at first glance he had had a certain amount of respect for. These were writers who now probably considered themselves to have been robbed by Solomon Wiese, the situation no doubt having been presented to them in that way, following news of his second encounter with QACS, Solomon Wiese said. Soon we would be hearing from these wronged and isolated rural poets as they expressed exactly this sentiment, once they had been tracked down by those with enough patience and determination to do so, in other words those with enough material greed and thirst for attention to do so. From a legal angle, these poets didn't have a leg to stand on, Solomon Wiese said, as they had signed away to him their rights to assert themselves as the authors of their poems, for which they had received more than generous financial compensation, although that would hardly matter now that the commentariat had succeeded in portraying them as the victims of Solomon Wiese's manipulations. But at the time these poets could hardly wait to foist their poems onto him; they had practically thrown their poems at him the second he had walked through their doors, it was more important to them that their poems find a readership than anything else, they had said, they would have happily given him their poems even if he had offered no financial incentive, Solomon Wiese said, he was completely serious. They had blithely signed away their poems without a care in the world, on the flimsiest of pretexts. The only assurance they had required from Solomon Wiese was the statement that he was editing an anthology of contemporary poetry, the poetry anthology still being an unparalleled lure for the aging and unappreciated poet. The poetry anthology remained the last hope of the dying and forgotten poet—if sensitively compiled and edited, the poetry anthology was a redeemer of reputations, collecting in its pages works long since out of print, and restoring to the public record works that were deserving of a second look—or more than likely a *first* look, if we were being honest, as most of the poems collected in these poetry anthologies, which were usually little more than ineffectual marketing devices for the poetry publisher short on ideas and resources, hadn't been remembered by anyone for more than a minute or two after their initial appearance, however many decades ago. These hopeful poets, coaxed out of their cottages and manors, their terraces and first-floor flats, were of course wilfully oblivious to the fact that ninety-nine out of a hundred poetry anthologies were read by precisely no one, that they simply travelled from shelf to shelf, unopened and unread, eventually reuniting with their unopened and unread siblings in charity shops and secondhand bookshops, and, when further years had passed and their obscurity was assured, they were quietly disposed of, that is, pulped or burned, as the sheer quantity of these unwanted and near-identical poetry anthologies had finally become intolerable to the typical secondhand bookshop owner, who had long ago abandoned all hope of selling even a single copy of one of these poetry anthologies, and who had been unable even to *give away* copies of these poetry anthologies to customers buying novels or biographies, anything instead of poetry anthologies. These customers always came up with some desperate excuse, rather than take a copy of the poetry anthology off the secondhand bookshop owner's hands—their bags were too heavy, they said, gesturing to the poetry anthology's uninviting bulk, or they were sure they already had it at home—no matter how cunning the secondhand bookshop owner was in his attempts to redistribute copies of the poetry anthology, he always ended up with the same copies of the poetry anthology back in his possession. Sometimes he would actually manage to palm off a copy of the poetry anthology onto some seemingly obliging member of the public, only for the poetry anthology to be returned the following day, sometimes in the company of *another copy of the same poetry anthology*, left on the doorstep of the secondhand bookshop in a plastic bag, presumably in the middle of the night, where the secondhand bookshop owner couldn't fail to notice it. Nor could he bring himself to throw both copies of the poetry anthology straight into the bin where they belonged, so he was obliged instead to take them back inside his shop, where they joined the multiple other copies of the same poetry anthology that were waiting there—and the more copies of the poetry anthology he had, *the more he was certain to acquire*, there was a pattern to it that he had become familiar with over decades of handling, or rather failing to avoid handling, poetry anthologies; poetry anthologies with their cheap, too-white paper and unattractive, incompetently set type, poetry anthologies with their hysterical and deceiving blurbs, poetry anthologies with their deranged forewords, often produced under duress, with their pointless biographies, and their even more pointless indexes and contents pages, never to be perused by anyone apart from the poets who were themselves included in the pages of the poetry anthology, who would scan the column of names, and alight as if at random on their own name, and then turn as if at random to the page number where their own poems were displayed. Eventually the secondhand bookshop owner steeled himself and actually *burned* these poetry anthologies in their tens and twenties, at night, when he hoped the sacrilegious act wouldn't be observed—only the poetry anthology brought a lover of books like the secondhand bookshop owner so low as to *burn the bound and printed word* like a common extremist, only the poetry anthology made extremists out of otherwise entirely reasonable people, only the poetry anthology was capable of blighting the conscience to this extent, and making extremism appear justified to such mild and moderate characters as the secondhand bookshop owner. Nonetheless the appeal of the poetry anthology held firm, and from the perspective of the emerging poet it was an honour that couldn't be declined. Solomon Wiese would describe for me two or three of the poets he had visited and enticed with inclusion in his *one hundred per cent fictional* poetry anthology, thereby procuring their thoroughly unremarkable poems, which were exactly suited to his purposes—if I insisted, he said. For example, there was the poet who lived in a small town house in Diss, who had welcomed Solomon Wiese and Max Mikkaels with a spread of carrots, hummus and Indian tea, handing her pages over while the uneasy creak of her husband's footsteps was audible overhead, from the upstairs room where he had presumably been banished during their visit. This fortunate poet was one of several to receive remuneration for her poems, which, once they were back in Max Mikkaels's rust heap of a car, Solomon Wiese had examined cursorily and then, without fully understanding what he was doing, folded into his mouth and begun to chew. It seemed to him, as he chewed on the poems of the fifty-eight-year-old classroom assistant from Diss, that there was some kernel inside them that he needed to get at, some mineral deposit he could access only through ingestion. Once the poems were reduced to cud he had gradually stopped chewing, gobbed them back into his hand, looked at the ball of wet pulp for a moment, then wound down the window and thrown it into a passing hedge. Max Mikkaels watched all this from the corner of his eye as he drove, Solomon Wiese said, but he didn't react. Or, another example—he remembered how the abode of a poet on their list had reared into view as they turned the tight country bends, who knows where this poet came in the sequence and frankly it didn't matter, Solomon Wiese said, but he remembered how the poet's *massive pile* had hoved into view above the fields, to his astonishment and that of Max Mikkaels. The countryside that spread out around the isolated stately home was depopulated, exposed, bared to the sky, a terrain entirely without mysteries, it had seemed a moment before, attended to with mechanical scrupulousness, interrupted only by the tinselly arm of a sprinkler system, by the occasional pillbox or dying oak, but here reddish walls climbed and windows flashed from a copse of old woods. The poet, who strode to meet them across the wide, unkempt lawn, which was sunken and bulging in places due to an ongoing sewage problem—as he informed them—had lived in the near-ruined house alone for more than twenty years. He made beetroot salad for lunch and served a bottle of white wine before giving a tour of the rooms, which were deathly silent, some taken over by ferns and creepers, others partially destroyed by flooding, their floors swollen and their ceilings burst. He seemed to be living in the aftermath of a natural catastrophe of some magnitude, and his poems were as quietly despairing and middling as you'd expect—in other words they were perfect. Solomon Wiese had chewed those up too, once they were back in the car. Having chewed up the poems of the classroom assistant from Diss, and the poems of a childless heir from the decrepit manor house, as well as a few others, he felt he had somehow *stored* their material inside him, Solomon Wiese said. Of course it sounded absurd. Having reduced their material to mulch it was all indistinguishable anyway, he said, each chewed-up poem was the same as the next. This seemed not to matter, Solomon Wiese said, and in fact it revealed the basic truth of the situation—in some ways the poetry of all these poets *was* one indistinguishable mass of more or less inert language and feeling, the more of it he saw the clearer this became, the more of it he chewed in the car the more readily available it was to him—he felt more and more as if he could simply open his mouth and the poetry he'd semi-ingested would simply begin to pour out, just as the words had welled up whenever he had sat in front of the fire as a teenager and subjected his friends to his endless verbal onslaughts. When, weeks later, during his performances he opened his mouth and the words instantly began to follow each other out, he didn't feel that he was sending poetry out into the world, not at all, Solomon Wiese said, it was completely the opposite, he felt he was releasing these words *back into the nothingness they had come from*, the nothingness he still had with him at all times, hovering at his shoulder—it was just as it had been when he first came to write poems, he was expelling this unnecessary mulch of words from the world, getting rid of it, converting it back into the non-material state it longed for. But at the time, he was unable to explain his chewing-up of poems to Max Mikkaels, who continued to drive Solomon Wiese around the country roads in his barely functioning car; for almost a week they bombed along the country roads, morning and night, ticking off names on the list of poets they had compiled from the Locket app, watching rabbits scatter in their headlights. One poet on the list had stayed with him, Solomon Wiese said, after a pause during which he checked on Phoebe Glass, who was slumped on the bar stool next to him, her face pressed to the Travelodge bartop, fast asleep. A poet they'd visited in a small village not far from the sea, a poet now sadly deceased, only three months or so later, he was sure, Solomon Wiese said. The old poet had been more or less on his deathbed when they'd seen him, in the small cottage where he lived with his wife, who had invited them into their cosy flagstoned kitchen, full of watercolours and cookbooks. Solomon Wiese and Max Mikkaels had introduced themselves to the old poet's wife as aspiring young poets, who had only recently become aware that the old poet was living here—as aspiring young poets they were keen to meet him, so as tradition dictated the *aspiring young poets were visiting the home of the old poet*, to pay tribute. It was a nice thing to happen, the old poet's wife had said, the old poet was quite weak but she was sure the visit would cheer him up enormously, especially because the old poet, as they probably knew, had attracted to his work no younger readers since his books had gone out of print ten or fifteen years previously. The old poet had sunk into a deep despondency about his art, though he had continued to write—she could show them some of his poems, if they were interested, the old poet's wife said, in the cluttered kitchen that was fragrant with frying onions. *The young aspiring poets were visiting the old poet* in his home, as tradition dictated, and she understood the importance of this—they were here to pay tribute to his achievements, and they were hoping as well, she thought, to glean some lasting wisdom or insight from him, they were hoping, weren't they, that the old poet would offer them something in return for their time, the old poet's wife suspected, some *nugget of gold*, she said with a look of humorous mischief, a *nugget of gold from the old poet*, a clue to some otherwise inaccessible experience, the secret of the poet's journey, perhaps, from one who'd lived it almost all the way through—they were hoping to have this knowledge reflected upon them by his presence, to be handed the proverbial *nugget of gold*. At least this was what Solomon Wiese and Max Mikkaels admitted to the old poet's wife, as she quizzed them with a mischievous expression, clearly delighted by the visit—but if those were their actual hopes as they traipsed by themselves up the narrow staircase to the poet's chamber, they were to be sorely disappointed, Solomon Wiese said. The room had clearly been converted for the purpose of easing the old poet through his last weeks—pieces of medical equipment stood around the raised bed, where the old poet was lying, facing a window that looked out onto the garden; it was a bright afternoon and the sun made an unfocused square on the wall behind his head. No sooner had they entered the room than the old poet had begun to speak to them in a dry whisper, his voice made even more indistinct by his dirty grey beard, and from above his purple cheeks his yellow eyes locked first onto Solomon Wiese and then onto Max Mikkaels—he didn't even wait for them to find some place to settle themselves, but started to talk while they were still squashed by the door in the corner of the room, and that is where they remained for the duration. So the young poets have arrived, the old poet said in a dry, barely audible whisper, they have come at last, but I'm afraid it is too late, it is a wasted journey, because I only have one thing to say to you, young poets, and I doubt very much that it's what you're hoping to hear. You can see the state I am in. Probably you think you know why I am in this terrible condition, the old poet rasped, or you imagine you can guess what has reduced me to lying here in bed for weeks at a time, anticipating the end—you might think you already have a good idea of what has brought about my rapid decline. Most likely it's a combination of old age, you imagine, and the sedentary, addled life that all poets lead, or should lead, a life of sitting down and reading, and pursuing all kinds of intoxications of the senses, the old poet said. I have no tolerance at all for these poets who seem to spend every day in the gym, these *poets who jog*—have you ever heard of anything as ridiculous as a jogging poet, the old poet said. And I don't deny that this is part of it, the fact is I have spent most of my life sitting in a chair staring at books, and another large part of it indulging in pleasures known to ruin the body and mind, but that isn't the main reason you find me here, in this condition, the old poet said. It's all my wife's fault, the old poet said. She means well of course, but a few months ago, though it seems a lot longer than that—I could still stand by myself then, even a few months ago I was happily digging the garden—a few months ago my wife signed me up for a kind of service, on the computer, supposedly to help publish my poems. As you know, I haven't been able to publish any of my poetry for over a decade, the old poet said, for more than a decade no magazine has accepted my poems and no publisher has agreed to publish them. I've been reduced to self-publishing my poetry, the old poet said, this is something I normally wouldn't admit to, that I have suffered the indignity of self-publishing my poetry, but I am past caring, and the only person who has seen my self-published poetry is, undoubtedly, the archivist at the British Library, which is obliged to acquire all collections of poetry, self-published or otherwise. Imagine, the old poet wheezed, the catalogue of horrors that the archivist at the British Library has been exposed to! But the archivist at the British Library aside, I've been resoundingly ignored by every poetry reader and poetry editor in the country. So it wasn't a bad idea, my wife's idea, I thought at the time, as I've written hundreds of poems in the intervening years, perhaps thousands of poems, hundreds or perhaps thousands of poems which no one has ever read—not a soul has so much as glanced at them. They are in no kind of order, of course, they're all on scraps of paper or scrawled in notebooks, as that is how poems should be written, in my opinion, not on a machine that tells you where to put the line breaks in. Many of my poems are written in the margins of other books of poems, in fact, the old poet said, and it would be difficult to locate all of them. While I have been writing my poems in total obscurity, a long sequence of poems that comprises my best work, by the way, and that no one has paid the slightest bit of attention to—while the magazine editors and publishers have been throwing my poems straight into the bin without even glancing at them, many of my acquaintances in the poetry world continue to publish their poems with no difficulty whatsoever, the old poet went on. Many substandard and mediocre poets whose works I am well acquainted with are publishing their poems by the dozen in all of the magazines and periodicals, many of them are publishing books, and some of them are actually publishing *a book a year*, the old poet said, while I have published no books at all for almost twenty years, despite having written thousands of pages of poetry. Why do you think this is, the old poet said, peering intently at Solomon Wiese and then at Max Mikkaels. Perhaps you know the answer—it is because I live out here, in the arse end of nowhere, and all of my esteemed acquaintances live in the capital, where they enjoy regular lunches with each other and with the editors of the best-known magazines and publishing houses, and in fact many of my esteemed poet acquaintances are *one and the same* as the editors of the most significant magazines and publishing houses, the old poet said, that is, in many instances they are *one and the same person*. All of them have addresses in the same one or two London postcodes, and all of them meet up on a weekly basis to massage each other's poetry egos, they don't shy away even from *publishing their own books* at the publishing houses where they work, the old poet said, even though it would be a simple matter for them to persuade one of their esteemed friends who works at an adjacent publishing house to publish their books for them. You want to know how I can be sure, the old poet said, how I can be so certain that that's the reason? It is because it's not an isolated incident, the old poet continued without pausing, that's how I can be so sure, because I know of other poets in precisely the same situation, a fine poet who lives not far from here, for example, who lives like all of us beyond the so-called paywall, this is a poet who has had exactly the same difficulties that I have had. No one will publish her work or even look at her work seriously, despite the fact that she is one of the finest poets of my generation, the old poet said, she suffers in exactly the same manner as me. A few years ago one of my old poetry world acquaintances came to visit me, the old poet said, one of my London literary acquaintances actually got on a train and came up here to meet with me—this kind of thing is unheard of. It was probably closer to ten years ago, now I think of it, but time seems to contract when you spend as long as I have living here, by the sea, far beyond the paywalls, important information simply doesn't reach you, and so time moves faster, the old poet said. It's like scenery in a train window that seems to hardly be changing but actually the miles are rattling past, and before you know it another three or four years have gone by, putting us at another disadvantage, the old poet said. I told this editor, once a good friend of mine, now merely an esteemed acquaintance, that I had noticed he had published a book by a total nonentity of a poet who we both knew reasonably well, let's call him G., the old poet said—my editor acquaintance had published another book by G. that year, the old poet said, despite the fact that we had often discussed G.'s work and agreed we found it to be substandard, derivative, cold-hearted, cold-handed, tin-eared, the work of a dilettante and mercenary, in other words, the old poet said. A *cold-blooded poet* can quite easily be both a dilettante and a mercenary, the old poet went on, despite the apparent contradiction, that is what classes them as a *cold-blooded poet*—they seek to take on the warmth of hot-blooded poets by replicating the style of a genuine hot-blooded poet, with invariably dismal results, and they do this with the sole intention of furthering their own poetry profile—this is not part of an apprenticeship or a form of homage, it is a quite deliberate parasitical process. Despite this, my editor acquaintance had chosen to publish a collection of poems by G., and not only had he acquiesced to G.'s no doubt zealous campaign for publication, he had published G.'s book in the same year he had *turned down* a book of poems by C., the poet who I just mentioned, who lives not far from here, and is clearly the finest poet of my generation. This news was completely inexplicable to me when I first heard it, as I said to my esteemed editor acquaintance, the old poet said, and I demanded to know how had he arrived at his decision, knowing full well that my manner of speaking would mean he never returned to this part of the country and never solicited my poems again—I knew this, and yet I still demanded to know. It had to be some kind of sick joke, the old poet had said to his esteemed editor acquaintance.

What could it be, other than some kind of sick joke, to publish the work of G., a poet not worth the admittedly large volumes of paper his name was written on, and to disregard the work of C., a finer poet than all the other poets on his list added together. It could only be a sick joke of some kind, the old poet had said to his esteemed editor acquaintance, that was the phrase he had used repeatingly. It was nothing but a sick joke to have neglected C. in this way, it defied belief, the old poet said. And what's more, to do it in the same breath with which he *rewarded* G.—to have *neglected* C. and *rewarded* G.—the opposite of what any sane or creditable person would do—could only be a sick joke, concocted by the old poet's esteemed editor acquaintance, for reasons known only to him and his incestuous London clique, the old poet said. This outburst sealed not only my fate but the fate of C. as well, the old poet went on in a terrible whisper, struggling weakly on his pillows, as no doubt my esteemed editor acquaintance wasted no time in spreading news of my behaviour to his friends in their nooks at cosy London restaurants, and as a result neither C. nor myself received any correspondence regarding our poems from that day on. I *condemned myself to obscurity* and also *reconciled myself with obscurity* on that day, the old poet said, at the moment I accused my editor acquaintance of making C. the subject and G. the beneficiary of his sick joke. I no longer entertained the thought that anyone would publish my poems. I was exiled from the poetry world due to my unacceptable conduct, with immediate effect, and denied access to its audiences, or to its *customers*, as the drones at the Poetry Centre probably phrase it. All of that changed a few months ago, thanks to my dear wife, the old poet said. For all the years we've lived here, no one in the village has had any idea whatsoever that I write poems, and that was how I liked it, the old poet said. Poetry is a secretive affair, and the fewer people who know you do it the better—the more people who know you write poems, the more thinly your energy will be spread, the more dispersed your resources, as you'll find you have to talk to people constantly about your poems, or to talk about poetry in general; people will actually ask what it is you're writing, what it's about, how long it is, and if you want to dry a poem out completely, to transform it into the husk of a poem, that is precisely what you should do—you should go around talking to people about it, the old poet said. The poem will turn into onionskin under this treatment, then it will simply disintegrate. A few months ago *word got out* in the village, through this scheme that my wife, meaning well, signed me up for, *word got out* that I was a poet, and soon everybody in the village knew that I wrote poems, and what's more they knew I hadn't been able to publish my poems for more than a decade. From that moment on it was all they could talk about, in a village this size nothing happens, the old poet said. For them, the villagers, it became a juicy subject for gossip; for me, the poet, it was complete disaster, the old poet said. Only two months ago I was happily digging the garden, I was walking to the pub once a week, I was birdwatching, I was getting the bus, but now I am confined to this room, and it is likely that quite soon I will be dead—all because *word got out* that I am a poet. As soon as people in the village got wind of it they wouldn't leave me alone, the old poet said. Not only was it the only thing that they talked about in the village—they talked about it in the post office, on the green, in the pub, at the bus stop, because like all villagers they have a deadly curiosity about their neighbours, and so they committed themselves immediately to this new opportunity for invasive gossip—not only this, but the villagers themselves began to *come to the house*—here the old poet suffered a short coughing fit, Solomon Wiese said—they began to come to the house, the old poet continued when he had recovered, they would walk into the kitchen without even knocking, they would sit down at the table and ask me, flat-out, to *write them a poem*. The main theme of discussion in the village had become how the villagers were going to help me, how they were going to help their *local poet*, a role they had developed a sudden and inordinate pride in, completely misconstruing what it is I am seeking to accomplish with my poetry, of course, none of them having bothered to seek out any of my books, or read a single word of one of my poems, obviously, the old poet said, but that didn't stop them coming one at a time into the house without knocking and trying to *commission* a poem from me. That was their big idea—to *commission* me to write poetry for any reason that came into their dozy village heads—to commemorate the village fete, that was one, or to commemorate their daughter's wedding, or to commemorate their nephew's christening, or commemorate the Christmas lights being turned on, or commemorate the war memorial on the appropriate commemoration day—to commemorate an already existing commemoration, in other words, the old poet said. There are still simple village people in this part of the world, and their obsession with commemoration became linked immediately and indissolubly with the knowledge that I was their village poet, the old poet said, and so naturally they demanded that I *commemorate* anything that happened in the village that seemed to anyone worth commemorating. A fever of commemoration activity ensued. I was expected to commemorate with poetry not only weddings and funerals, but the size of a particularly impressive cauliflower or cabbage, or the fact that the farmer's favourite cow had won a medal at the country fair, or the arrival of the Easter holidays, or the village shop coming under new management. Pretty soon the old superstitions returned to the surface too, the old poet said. The real village beliefs were never far away, and soon the old poet was having to write poems protecting the village girls against unwanted pregnancies, or poems blessing the crops, or poems to ward off bad weather on the dates of certain sporting events, the old poet explained. The villagers assumed that they were helping the old poet, but in reality they were *fatally weakening* the already old poet with their endless requests for poems; they had quickly drained him of his powers, the old poet said, in a matter of weeks he was a shade of himself, and they were now very close to actually killing him, yet still they continued to visit, they continued to demand that his barely functioning mind compose poems at their convenience. One of them will come in at any minute to finish me off, the old poet whispered, they'll come right up the stairs in muddy boots and stand where you're standing now and demand I write a poem, on the spot, because the butter's gone bad in the churn, or the baby's got mumps. The way of life here hasn't really changed for generations, the old poet went on—his wife wouldn't admit that this constant production of poems was making him ill, and he was too weak now to refuse them. I should have refused the first time, the old poet said, but they appealed to my vanity, of course like all poets I am an incorrigible narcissist, the old poet said, and once I had fulfilled one village commission I couldn't very well refuse the next—on what basis? All poets are dangerous narcissists, intent only on securing their own legacies, the old poet said after a short pause, and you two are no exception, I can see that from here, just as I am no exception, and look where it has led me. Poets are the most dangerous and megalomaniacal of all types of writer, and writers are the most dangerous and megalomaniacal of all types of people, the old poet said. Behind every genocide or dictatorship there is always a poet somewhere, and it is a mercy that we have mostly been spared the consequences of the insane plans of megalomaniacal poets. These dangerous and megalomaniacal poets, given the opportunity, always take it upon themselves to spy inordinately on their colleagues and peers, the old poet went on, their dangerous megalomania makes them consider it their natural right to know the innermost thoughts and fears of their colleagues and peers. If they could get away with it they would set about actually founding a secret police force with which to spy on their peers and colleagues properly—that would be their first order of business, given the opportunity, the old poet said. Given the opportunity, any typically dangerous and megalomaniacal poet would quickly found a violent and secretive organisation for the enforcement of their own values and opinions. I wouldn't trust a poet to efficiently and humanely run a *day-care centre*, for very small children—in fact, I would absolutely expect a poet placed in charge of a *day-care centre* to persecute the very small children in their care, with a brutal, bizarre and inhumane regime of their own devising, goading the children to inform on one another, no doubt, or to turn against one another in private, while performing sentimental songs of the poet's own composition extolling the values of community and solidarity. The worst part of it is the pittance the villagers are paying me for these poems, which are admittedly pieces of doggerel of the worst kind imaginable, the old poet said. Some of them give me supermarket vouchers, or stamps, or else they give me *nothing at all*, assuming the joy for me is in the making, that the penning of these dreadful excuses for poems, which I have to force out like I'm literally shitting stones, is *its own reward*, but usually they value one of my poems at about the price of a loaf of bread—not even a good-quality loaf of bread, the old poet said. If I refused them now I would run the real risk of offending one of the village families, on the occasion of their niece's first word or their son passing his driving test, when many other village families of similar standing have already been given the honour of having similar events commemorated in verse. The consequences of such a slight in a village this size would be dramatic, the old poet said, pausing for a second or two, his eyelids fluttering. If I refuse a commission now, it could drive a wedge between two of the village families, families that have always been close, or have been close for so many years that the feuds some of them still remember are in no danger of resurfacing and disturbing the village's tranquility, the old poet said. Representatives of these families had gathered at his bedside the day before yesterday, with a new set of commissions, and as he had looked up into their rude, healthy faces he had known with absolute certainty that they were draining him of the last of his lifeblood, the old poet said—he had realised then that the village faces looking down at him were the faces of well-meaning, ruddy-cheeked vampires, who were finally on the verge of wiping him out for good. But at least no poem will be written to commemorate me, the old poet said, and as the old poet spoke these words a church bell began to chime in the distance, Solomon Wiese said. My advice, the old poet wheezed, as the bell of the village church continued to toll, its chimes increasing in volume until they seemed to fill the room, is to give up now. You must stop. Detach yourself at once from this terrible pastime that will lead only to ruin. It will never please you or anyone you care about, it will never make you happy, it will simply become the basis and means of recording *your own unhappiness*, the old poet had said, lurching into an almost upright position and stabbing the air with his finger, before slumping back onto his pillows, completely exhausted, at which moment the machines surrounding the bed had started to flash and bleep in concert, Solomon Wiese said, and he and Max Mikkaels had rushed out to fetch the poet's wife. A bundle of papers was waiting for them on the kitchen table, which Max Mikkaels was able to seize in the confusion as they made their way from the house, containing upwards of thirty poems, they discovered in the car, as they sped away at once from the seaside village. The old poet's poems had tasted familiar, Solomon Wiese said, as he began to break them down with the enzymes in his saliva, but who could say if they really were as remarkable as he claimed. If no one read them and no one promoted them, that remained incontestably the case, Solomon Wiese said. The poems of the old poet remained without discernible qualities, they were quite characterless, and all that could really be said of them is that they were poems, or even that at a glance they appeared to be poems—presumably they were not shopping lists or instructions for feeding fish, or other arrangements that outwardly resembled poems but were nothing of the sort. He hoped this would suffice, he said, as an account of how he came by the material for the performances that would bring him notoriety only a few weeks later in the bars and salons of the capital. He had at least given me a sketch of his activities with Max Mikkaels before his return to London, a few months after he had fled it. He had attempted to coax Max Mikkaels into accompanying him, but Max Mikkaels had flatly refused, saying he had no desire to visit London; he had never been to London, he had no wish to go there now, and there was nothing Solomon Wiese could do to change his mind. On the eve of his return, sleeping on a bunk in Max Mikkaels's caravan, he had dreamed about Amalia Albers, Solomon Wiese said. She had climbed out of a black pond in the woodland by the caravan and chased him towards the sea. As she ran after him she kept saying that she wasn't a wallflower—I'm not a wallflower anymore, Solomon, she said as she emerged from the black pond, she was completely naked in his dream, and as she rose from the pond he saw her skin had a silver shine to it, the colour of silver pines. Her skin had turned to silver bark, her hair was full of wet leaves, and she told him she wasn't a wallflower as she rose from the black pond and started across the sand towards him. She would be sleeping in the pond again when he woke up, he remembered thinking, as she ran naked onto the beach after him, her skin all silver in the dream. The next day it was summer and London smelled of high-grade marijuana; he'd forgotten, Solomon Wiese said, but everywhere it was wafting in strong, citrussy clouds along the streets. His mood had transformed the instant he arrived back in the capital, Solomon Wiese said. He remembered that London had always had the effect of *resetting* his mood, and now he remembered his London mood, as it returned in full. His overriding impression was of the *closeness* of everything, and therefore the *surface quality* of everything—the sounds of the vehicles as they passed, their almost wet-seeming reflective surfaces, their avid revving noises and the sleek curves of their carapaces; strange as it might seem to a city dweller, he had forgotten about the proximity of things to other things in the city, but this didn't provoke his usual feelings of irritation and unease; for some reason this time it was precisely the opposite, Solomon Wiese said, and he found himself strangely *aroused* by the proximity of things to other things in the city, which itself seemed to be in a state of abandon and intoxication brought about by the prolonged heatwave. As the cars cruised past over the sparkling black tarmac with their windows open, trailing citrussy clouds of marijuana smoke, their contours seemed erotically charged to Solomon Wiese, he was startled by the way the cars almost but not quite bumped up against one another, playing pulsing rhythms through their open windows, the way they almost but not quite touched one another as they fitted their bulging forms into the tight spaces on the sides of the roads. He became aware for the first time of the skin of passers-by, the skin shining through the stubble on men's heads and faces, and the flushed skin of women's cheeks as they walked the city streets in sportswear and summer dresses, some pressing frosted water bottles to their brows. In short, he perceived for the first time the truly *libidinous condition* of the city, like a seething ant heap he wasn't repulsed by, but that to the contrary he was *aroused* by—the tense, salacious city, the glorying, soliciting city—this was the city that revealed itself to Solomon Wiese, on his return from the regional areas, which quickly became a dreary memory. Not for the first time Solomon Wiese lamented his lack of female friends and acquaintances, in these first days back in the capital. His newly awoken interest, which had remained entirely dormant since his expulsion from the city's literary communities, made him long for the company of female friends, but it was also a stern reminder of why it was that he had never managed to sustain a close female friendship, Solomon Wiese said. Solomon

Wiese had always gravitated towards predominantly male friendship groups, he said, he had always had predominantly male friends, and predominantly male influences, to his endless disappointment—this gravitation towards predominantly male friendship groups and predominantly male influences was completely unconscious, on his part, he thought. It was true he had had female friends in the past, for periods of time, but he had always sabotaged these friendships sooner or later, with a more or less disastrous seduction attempt, Solomon Wiese said. Even if the friendship had lasted for several years and become indispensible to him, he had always sabotaged it sooner or later by attempting to seduce his female friend, Solomon Wiese said. All might have been going well with the mutually rewarding friendship, but, unbeknownst to his female friend, a countdown had begun at the moment the friendship formed, and at the end of the countdown Solomon Wiese would make an ill-judged seduction attempt. At that moment, at the end of the countdown, the friendship would be destroyed forever, no matter how mutually rewarding and patiently built it had been; it would be destroyed in an instant by a seduction attempt that was guaranteed to backfire, leaving him among the sad ruins of the friendship, without even the short-term gratification of having carried out a successful seduction attempt, Solomon Wiese said. *Seduction attempt* was in reality too refined a phrase for what ordinarily took place, Solomon Wiese had to acknowledge, it would be more accurately described as a *lunge*, or even a *reckless lunge*, that without fail backfired and resulted in the destruction of the friendship. It was this inevitability that accounted for the predominance of male friendship groups and male influences in his adult life, Solomon Wiese said—as his recently reawakened interest had reminded him. What he really wanted was a shopgirl with a fat bum, he realised, Solomon Wiese said. A shopgirl with a lovely big tush. A shopgirl with a large behind, Solomon Wiese said, that swayed as she walked, in her summer dress. A round bum encased in black jeans. A behind that was round like a peach, or a plum, or an apricot, or round like two apples rubbing together. A big bum that rolled as she walked: that was all he wanted to see. A girl who worked in a bar or a shop, with a fat bum that was plainly displayed, in tracksuit bottoms, or a loose skirt that displayed the contours of what was beneath. This strength of feeling surprised him, Solomon Wiese said, this desire for a girl with a fat bum, who worked in a shop. The other details didn't seem to matter, but there was no arguing with the crude announcement of the desire, the way it controlled his gaze while walking the city streets, in all its embarrassing urgency. But he would have to wait, that much was obvious. He had no avenue towards a shopgirl with a fat bum, for now, unfortunately—he would have to wait until he was able to announce a recital of his poetry to his new audience, via the Locket app, some of whom were actual people, and therefore able to attend, the others being fake profiles concocted by Max Mikkaels, in exchange for a proportion of the small fortune bequeathed to Solomon Wiese by the old man with scabs on his head, Dimitri Radic, in Diss, Solomon Wiese reminded me. He ardently hoped to meet a shopgirl with a fat bum at such an event—who knows why, Solomon Wiese said. It hardly seemed likely, when he considered it now. The easiest way to meet such a girl, that is, a girl with a fat bum who worked in a shop, would presumably be in her place of work, that is, in a shop or a bar or even a café, not at some kind of rarefied poetry salon, but he didn't allow this consideration to interfere with his plans. Perhaps this image, of a shopgirl with a fat bum, in black jeans or loose-fitting trousers that tightened towards the waist, was a way of covertly motivating himself, of making himself do what he was about to do—that is, attempt a poetry recital with zero preparation in terms of written material, instead simply trusting the recital of poetry *to the nothingness*, where the poetry of the regional areas was stored, and to which he would return it. The poetry would *take care of itself*—somehow he felt able to make this statement, Solomon Wiese said. When he had considered it, the nothingness had changed in character since his return to the city, Solomon Wiese said. The nothingness had been replaced in some sense by an *abundance*, in a strange reversal—the vague outline that accompanied him everywhere, rather than being emptied and void, was now filled with an *abundance* of thoughts and images, culled from scores of unsung regional poets, and waiting to spill out of his mouth, at what would be his first poetry recital for over a year. This image of abundance only seemed to enhance his urgent, almost dizzying desire, that is, his desire for a shopgirl with a fat bum, a desire that he could barely contain when out on the streets of London, in the carnival heat, walking around with his eyes practically popping out of his head. On arriving, Solomon Wiese had arranged to stay with one of the few non-literary friends who he hadn't severed contact with, using his *termination of friendship notices*. If some part of Solomon Wiese had been hoping for a renewal of their old, easy-going rapport during his stay, he understood that this wouldn't be possible once he had spent twenty minutes in the company of his old friend and discovered that they had grown apart irrevocably. It was clear his interests had diverged completely from those of his old friend, just as everyone's interests in the end diverged completely from the interests of all the people they knew, Solomon Wiese said. Every person alive becomes increasingly individual and particularised as they grow older, and therefore increasingly lonely and isolated. It was impossible *not* to be friends with certain people at certain times, under certain conditions, Solomon Wiese had reflected, listening to his old friend, and there was no doubt that his friendship with his old friend had been that kind of friendship, that is, a friendship born of necessity. It had been inevitable that they became friends, for a period, to alleviate their shared boredom and loneliness—this boredom and loneliness had been the sole basis and *subject* of their friendship, Solomon Wiese realised. The friendship had simply been a means of alleviating their intense feelings of boredom and loneliness, as younger men. During the twenty-minute conversation, which was in reality a twenty-minute monologue delivered by his old friend, he could barely follow what his old friend was saying, Solomon Wiese said. He did not ask his old friend to explain the specialist terms he used frequently, and that Solomon Wiese was unable to grasp, so that once twenty minutes had gone by, as they walked along a canal in east London near his old friend's home, Solomon Wiese didn't respond by explaining his own interests in return, as they would have bored his friend in precisely the same way his friend had been boring him. It seemed that although they were both still as lonely and bored as they had been when they were younger, they no longer shared this loneliness and boredom, Solomon Wiese said—each was occupied by *a different and separate loneliness and boredom*. They had simply let the conversation draw to a close, and the walk passed in a silence that was neither comfortable nor uncomfortable—it was as if each were walking alone. Over the following days, making plans as he reacquainted himself with the streets of east London, he had wondered who his new fans were, as they doubled and then tripled in number on the Locket app, Solomon Wiese said. He had looked into the faces of the people as they passed, but the faces of the beautiful young people of east London seemed blank and inscrutable. After a few days of this, walking the streets, he determined that the unending series of beautiful and expressionless young people who passed him were in possession of a new attitude, Solomon Wiese said. It had become clear to him that there was a studied element to their uninterest or expressionlessness—in other words, that there was a determination to it. The series of beautiful and expressionless young people who walked past him seemed *carefully uninterested*, Solomon Wiese said, as if, in a sense, their uninterest was not genuine, but was born out of a fear of seeming *unduly interested* in anything about their surroundings, and therefore it was actually a fear of *seeming unfamiliar* with their surroundings. That the sequence of beautiful and expressionless young people were determined not to seem unfamiliar with their surroundings of course revealed the exact opposite, Solomon Wiese said, it revealed that they were in fact newcomers to the city who were desperate not to betray this fact, and were therefore careful to wear their expressions of studied uninterest whenever they stepped out of their front doors. In all likelihood they wore these non-expressions inside their flats and houses as well, Solomon Wiese said, they probably continued to wear these non-expressions when they looked at themselves in the mirror, the beautiful and expressionless young people; they didn't allow themselves to imagine life without their carefully maintained non-expressions. This of course prevented them from becoming in any way *truly familiar* with their surroundings, meaning these beautiful and expressionless young people were doomed to a sheltered, tertiary existence, behind their carefully maintained non-expressions, a life of *seeming* rather than being, Solomon Wiese said. While this information was resolutely hidden in their non-expressions, or by their expressionlessness, the young people were eager to volunteer *other* kinds of information about themselves. They were heartbreakingly eager to communicate some pieces of information, Solomon Wiese said, and heartlessly determined to conceal other pieces of information, but it would have been preferable, in his opinion, if the situation were reversed, and the information they were desperate to conceal took the place of the information they were desperate to communicate. These pieces of information usually volunteered their allegiance to a specific cultural product or cause, Solomon Wiese said. Seemingly as a by-product, these public statements also of course communicated loudly and clearly the young person's economic bracket or social status; the typical young person assumed they were communicating only or mainly their cultural allegiances, and secondarily or inadvertently their economic bracket or social status, but in reality, of course, the recipients of these statements saw only the communication of the young person's economic bracket or social status, while their so-called cultural allegiances remained strange ciphers that were devoid of meaning. This was the reason it would have been preferable if the young people had *hidden* their tokens of cultural allegiance, and had *communicated* instead their suppressed interest in their surroundings, Solomon Wiese said. These tokens of cultural allegiance belonged properly in the private realm, where they could be *finessed* and *interrogated*, to use the parlance of the beautiful and expressionless young person, and their private or repressed interest in the people and buildings that surrounded them belonged properly in the public realm—the beautiful and expressionless young people had it the wrong way around, in this regard, Solomon Wiese said, which accounted for their expressionlessness, of course, but also, and equally, he speculated, accounted for their beauty. It was interesting that many of these so-called cultural messages were literary in origin, Solomon Wiese said, when a few months ago, prior to his period of informal exile, they would have referred to bands and performers—now they referred to literary magazines and publishers. Where once the young people had worn the name of a band or rap artist, they now wore the name of a publisher or magazine, where once they would have proclaimed their commitment to music as the foremost artistic venture of their time, they now advocated literature. What had happened to these young people, Solomon Wiese wondered, to have made them retreat into the silent, static world of reading and writing, away from the dynamic and spontaneous spaces of musical performance? Rather than T-shirts, the chosen vehicle to express their cultural allegiances was now the tote bag, he had noticed, Solomon Wiese said. The bookshop tote bag had replaced the band T-shirt, who knows how it had happened. As the sequence of beautiful and expressionless young people had processed past him on the streets of east London, he had taken note of the names that adorned their so-called tote bags, Solomon Wiese said, he had taken note of the *names they were toting*, and a range of literary enterprises was advertised, including but not limited to *Zorb*, You Can See the Stars Books, *Xenith*, White Rhino, *Vile Love*, untapped-untuned, Triste Tropiques, Serious Books, *Remit*, *Queue Journal*, *Purview*, *OrgAn*, *The Newer Review*, Mathews's, *Let Me In*, Korean Bodega, the Jello Fund, the Institute for Concrete Poetry, Hana Hewitt's Horoscope, *Gestural Forms*, *Formal Gestures*, *Entrapment*, Disincentive of Praise, *Curse Charter*, Books of Shade, and, of course, the indispensable *Albion Poetry*. These names turned out to be useful when

Solomon Wiese was planning his return to the arena of poetry recitals, he said in the Travelodge bar, which was at last beginning to empty, and where the first breakfasts were being served. His return to the poetry recital's *gladiatorial arena*, Solomon Wiese said, as a full English breakfast glided past, trailing steam. But instead of swords and spears and other adversarial tools of death, the weapons available at the poetry recital were *deadly words of praise*, Solomon Wiese went on. These words of praise were brandished like the swords and spears of the gladiatorial arena, and like the swords and spears of the gladiatorial arena they were plunged into the hearts of the poetry recital competitors. No one escaped the deadly words of praise that everyone arrived at the poetry recital armed to the teeth with, and in a certain sense all perished at the hands of those who wielded deadly words of praise. After the recital, the words of praise were guaranteed to come thick and fast from every direction at once, turning every poet into a virtual pincushion of words of praise, riddling every poet with words of praise—and eventually every poet at the poetry recital fell under this unending hail of words of praise, when they realised at last the monstrous insincerity that powered these words of praise, targeted as they were at every poet regardless of their so-called talent, whereupon the words of praise detonated, destroying the poet instantly. Solomon Wiese planned to evade these deadly words of praise by a very simple method, he said. He would leave the poetry recital as soon as he finished reciting, or rather as soon as he had finished *spontaneously inventing* his poetry—he would walk off stage and he wouldn't stop walking until he was out of the door of the venue and safely inside the taxi that he had ordered to wait at the curb outside. He spoke his spontaneously improvised poetry to rooms of near darkness and silence, and then he immediately left, Solomon Wiese said, thereby avoiding the deadly words of praise that the audience was no doubt bristling with. So began a new season of his life, Solomon Wiese said, as the London summer waned. He had immediately conquered the salons and cabarets on his return to the arena of the poetry recital, he said, that wasn't an overstatement, and in doing so he had rediscovered his appreciation of *life seasons*—a renewed sense that in life things happen *all at once*, or else they fail to happen at all. Now, for him, a new season of activity, of people and events tumbling over one another, had begun. There was momentum and synchronicity to it, there was almost a *theme*, Solomon Wiese said, that went far beyond his usual understanding. He felt for the first time that he trusted absolutely in the forces that were carrying him along. This state coincided with a series of dreams, Solomon Wiese said, in which he was led through the city by a young woman with prematurely grey hair, grey hair that was really preternaturally silver when you looked at it properly—in his dreams the young woman with silver hair would simply walk next to him, and the awareness of her small frame next to his larger frame gave him an extraordinary sense of peace and tranquility. The comforting proximity of this young woman, in his dreams, night after night, endowed everything with a sense of calm, he said, which translated into an untroubled confidence in the *forces that were carrying him along.* He regarded the city with a new hunger, Solomon Wiese said, and during the late summer days he began to stalk the city; he became a daylong *city stalker*, and when he tired of the city streets he went into the cafés and pubs, where he became an authentic *café creeper.* When he tired of the cafés and pubs he went into the art galleries and museums, where he became a *bona fide museum lurker.* When he had exhausted the art galleries and museums, he went to the numerous city parks and became a *persistent park lingerer.* He quickly realised that parks were the ideal lingering spaces, that they were spaces where people could appear and disappear without warning—he had seen an old man in an old-fashioned suit disappear as he walked behind a tree, Solomon Wiese said, like a ghost in broad daylight. He had seen a woman from the city's past appear from behind some bushes, in the middle of the lunch hour, another *broad daylight ghost.* It was on one of these excursions that he had first encountered Phoebe Glass, two or so months ago now, though it felt like much longer, Solomon Wiese said. In fact, these sightings of *broad daylight ghosts*, in retrospect, only seemed to herald her appearance, clutching a large signpost with a flashing arrow on it, which was her primary means of income—she was paid to hold a sign showing a flashing arrow and to walk with it around the centre of London. She had answered an anonymous advertisement—that was how she'd got the job of anonymous sign carrier, and she had never met her anonymous employer. She simply picked the sign up from a pre-arranged anonymous location, deposited it there anonymously again at night, and her wages were sent anonymously into her bank account. So she had no idea who was paying her to carry the sign around central London, a sign that showed only a flashing arrow that sometimes pointed up, sometimes pointed left, sometimes pointed right; she had no idea how the flashing light was powered, and she had no idea why they were paying her—not that it mattered, she told Solomon Wiese when he stopped to ask her about it, during one of his regular park-lingering sessions. Prior to approaching Phoebe Glass, his city-stalking, museum-lurking, café-creeping state of arousal and yearning had reached an almost unbearable pitch, Solomon Wiese said, otherwise he doubted he ever would have dared talk to her. He had been sitting on a bench in the park, before he first caught sight of her. It was the last really warm day of the year and the dusty grass was scattered with sunbathers, with most people confined to splashes of shade under the elm and beech at the park's edges—only one woman lay alone, far out in the middle of the green, in a tremor of heat haze, as if seeking the sun's focal point. Almost naked, completely still, she had looked like a shard of shapely bone, Solomon Wiese said, bleached out, desiccated to the point of weightlessness. Solomon Wiese had stared at her for almost half an hour, hypnotised, her form becoming abstract, and then, it seemed to him, becoming the shape of his longing itself. That was when Phoebe Glass had made her appearance, holding her arrow sign, like a stage direction aimed only at him, Solomon Wiese said. There was a kind of café in this part of London he always looked for: overpriced, with dated décor, never busy, sometimes with a mysterious abundance of fresh flowers, cool and dim—he took Phoebe Glass to one of these places, as she was talkative, it turned out, and keen to escape the heat. She leaned the sign on the street outside—it never occurred to anyone to steal it, Phoebe Glass said. Phoebe Glass wouldn't usually allow him to go into any detail about this, Solomon Wiese said, but she was still asleep, face down on the Travelodge bar. It was in this overdecorated and overpriced café, with its morbid scent of lilies, that Solomon Wiese had said after a only couple of minutes the words *you're very beautiful*—leaning back in his chair, having spoken them, he had felt astonished, he said, because he had said them almost without intending to, without the expectation of a response. He had simply been relaying a piece of information, in an almost neutral manner—it had been entirely involuntary, he said in the Travelodge bar, but it had roused the scorn of Phoebe Glass, who immediately launched into an all-out attack on Solomon Wiese's statement and the series of assumptions it promoted. The strange thing was how enjoyable he found it, being on the receiving end of this withering critique, Solomon Wiese said. The other thing that became apparent was how much Phoebe Glass herself was enjoying the chance to mount this withering critique, directly to the face of her target, and once her enjoyment had become noticeable to Solomon Wiese, she immediately noticed that he'd noticed, and her amusement became obvious for a moment or two—but, as if denying herself this distraction, she deepened her all-out attack on Solomon Wiese, pushing it to a new intensity, which in turn deepened her amusement, and his amusement, so that he even began to offer the occasional phrase in response to Phoebe Glass's onslaught; he countered her withering critique with deliberately obtuse phrases, it had to be said, that necessitated an increased dose of withering critique, inspiring Phoebe Glass to further rhetorical heights. They spent much of the afternoon in this way, having left the cool of the café with its huge shadowy lilies, walking the hot streets of central London together, under Phoebe Glass's flashing sign. Eventually, she tired of her all-out attack on Solomon Wiese's presumptuousness and insensitivity, Solomon Wiese said, and they were able to move on to other topics; but it transpired that there were few things that *weren't* able to stir an impassioned denunciation from Phoebe Glass, especially when it came to the field of the arts, which in her view were riven with a bare-faced hypocrisy and self-serving mendacity so firmly entrenched as to make the whole industry obsolete and deserving of being razed to the ground—the arts themselves should be *razed to the ground*, in Phoebe Glass's opinion. The true artist was incapable of surviving in an environment so determined by careerism and nepotism that it had become a kind of open sewer, Phoebe Glass said, where the imagination was entirely in thrall to the routine contractions and expulsions of professionalism—the outputs of these so-called artistic processes being identical to the outputs of the bowels, in Phoebe Glass's analysis. The contemporary artist was a charlatan of the most pedestrian and self-serving variety, Phoebe Glass said, contemporary artists weren't artists at all, rather they were cold-blooded charlatans who had identified the arts as the easiest place to make cold-blooded money, if you were in possession of no artistic inspiration or serviceable talent, but you *were* in possession of a spirit of self-serving opportunism, and a quantity of industry connections. With the right equipment it was now easier to make money from a so-called arts career than it was to make money from a traditional profession, meaning that artists were now the true professionals, that no one was more professional than the professional artist, in other words, no one was more calculating or self-serving than the professional artist. The arts at this point were a kind of self-defeating joke that everyone involved in them was aware of, but for some reason having a bad joke as an occupation was accepted, it was not even an effective deterrent—people continued to work in the arts despite or more likely because of this obvious fact, Phoebe Glass said. People enjoyed having a bad joke as an occupation, this was the only conclusion she could draw from her many years of observing the art world, seeing it stripped of its dignity and otherwise demeaned by the charlatans of the business world, until the art world had become the new base of the business world—in fact, it was the best example of the ruthlessness that the business world prided itself on, and it made other areas of the business world seem folksy and tame by comparison, Phoebe Glass went on. For this reason the arts as they stood should be *razed to the ground*, Phoebe Glass said, only the true artist would survive, by *returning underground*, which was the only environment for the genuine artist. The artist could not exist for long above ground, without becoming a basically fraudulent imitation of an artist, producing counterfeit artworks appealing only to the incentives of the business interests that ran the arts above ground, Phoebe Glass said. But these business interests had built the foundations of above-ground art so deeply and solidly that there was actually *no underground* any longer, Phoebe Glass went on—the so-called underground arts were simply the supply pipe of the above-ground arts. It was inevitable that the output of so-called underground art was spewed up above ground, like so much waste, Phoebe Glass went on, because in reality the so-called underground was the squalid breeding pen for the *abattoir of above-ground arts*. The underground artist was simply *prime above-ground art fillet*, in its earlier organic state, Phoebe Glass said, before it had been given the necessary value-adding treatment in one of the nation's countless *art abattoirs*, in other words, in one of our world-class arts institutions. Phoebe Glass was talking about the visual arts, but she could have been talking about practically any other facet of contemporary culture, according to her, Solomon Wiese said, mainly because in every cultural field, not least the visual arts, men were still dominating the conversation, while doing their utmost to ensure no woman was allowed to speak—the men implicitly used their so-called physical advantages to ensure that the women didn't interrupt them and provide another perspective, which would have completely disrupted and completely exposed the men's perspective, as women were privy to *another reality* that men were not privy to; that is, they observed and in some cases recorded the conduct of men in public spaces and institutional spaces and work places, they noted the stares and the words of men, which formed the hard edges of a reality that the men dominating the conversation had no conception of, either because they were one of the extreme minority of men who did not help to form with their words and stares the hard edges of a social reality implicitly hostile to women, or else because they assumed they were the only men who displayed what they saw as a certain kind of roguish irreverence toward women in public spaces or institutional spaces or work places, that is, through their stares and words, which they regarded as completely harmless, without realising that practically all men in this situation displayed this same so-called roguish irreverence, thinking they were the only ones who did so, but in fact each was one of a countless multitude, and so the roguish irreverence, it was clear to the women, was not roguish irreverence at all, but unasked-for boorish harassment of the most tedious kind. Everywhere you went in the cultural sphere men were talking over one another and over women particularly, they were basically attempting to talk one another into the ground; they regarded being able to talk over a woman as a sign of strength aimed at the other men present, or else if they were more cunning about it they simply repeated the same statement that a woman had recently made, of course ignored by all the men present, word for word, as if they had just thought of it themselves, before congratulating themselves on their originality, and thereby silencing the woman by other means. This non-stop talking was nothing more than a blatant attempt to overpower, with statistics or ratings or some other breed of so-called accurate measurement, the other men and women present, this vaunted ideal of *objective accuracy* itself being an absurd concept that made sense only in the realms of mechanical production and cold transaction—failing that, the men sought to overpower purely with the bass notes of their voices, so it was no surprise that everywhere these bassy voices were droning on endlessly, droning themselves into positions of dominance simply by virtue of being able to drone longer and more loudly than their rivals—everywhere there were bassy, droning voices comparing the ages or prices of art objects or the relative merits and demerits of particular art-world destinations, bassy voices staging extravagant disagreements over insignificant divergences of opinion—disagreements about which was the best museum in a given European capital, disagreements about how long a certain gallery had been open or closed, disagreements about how far this or that museum or gallery was from another museum or gallery in the same European capital, how long the journey took on foot versus how long it took by taxi, how regular or irregular or reliable or unreliable were the other available modes of transport—they disagreed on these and many other points, and debated them endlessly, irritably, without good grace, until one of the bassy voices became so irritated they simply strode away from the conversation without warning, still droning away under their breath, leaving their companion to their own droning reflections. More recently, the men who had achieved dominance in these cultural scenarios, those who were paying a minimum of attention to cultural developments outside their own immediate interests, for nothing more than strategic purposes, evidently, had begun incorporating a commentary *on* the dominance of men *into* their own endless monologues, Phoebe Glass said—as if by granting this concession, the man speaking could bargain his way more surely into his indefinitely continuing dominance, that is, his indefinitely continuing droning monologue. This noting of the tendency of men to bore on at every opportunity *by* a man who was himself droning on in his bassy voice, had become an extremely common cultural deflection in recent years, meaning that now almost all men who sought to dominate these situations themselves were obliged to acknowledge it, as a commentary on and an additional part of their constant boring on, but she wanted to emphasise that this changed nothing, that the men acknowledging their own boring dominance as part of the content of that dominance did nothing to affect or soften that dominance, in fact this acknowledgement had become another of their weapons in their hostile, hard-edged effort to fully dominate the proceedings, as they always had done. There was only one exception to Phoebe Glass's blanket disapproval of contemporary life as she saw it, as Solomon Wiese learned over the days and then weeks they ended up spending together, and this exception was an old friend of hers, who she had lived with for several years after graduating, in the market town of Bury in the east of England, called Jessica Lake. When it came to Jessica Lake, Phoebe Glass had only the softest and sweetest things to say, and the softness and sweetness of these statements were made all the more striking and unexpected by Phoebe Glass's otherwise unremittingly bleak analysis of the contemporary scene, particularly in its cultural manifestations, Solomon Wiese said. Jessica Lake, in Phoebe Glass's analysis, was a genuine artist and extraordinarily gentle person who had been treated monstrously, in the scope of her short life, and the true reason for Phoebe Glass's pessimism and refusal to accept what she perceived as the irredeemable mendacity of the modern world and its inhabitants could be traced directly back to Jessica Lake, Solomon Wiese said. I showed no reaction to this mention of Jessica Lake. I continued leaning on the bar as I had been for the previous six or seven hours, and although in the back of my mind the thought that I should leave resurfaced, as it had throughout the night, it quickly submerged again, and I remained where I was, I stood at the bar and made no attempt to leave. His relationship with Phoebe Glass, because that's what it was, there was no point denying it, had allowed him to retain a lofty presence at his poetry recitals, Solomon Wiese continued, mainly because he was no longer desperately pursuing his urgent desire for a girl with a fat bum, which had begun to seem as creepy and absurd to him as it had probably sounded to me. His performances in the capital were becoming notorious, Solomon Wiese said. He was in high demand and by this point was receiving a stream of booking requests via the Locket app—the generated fans were now outnumbered two to one by genuine fans, and his feed was a river of dreamy adulation. During his performances he had continued to quote unquote *channel* the material harboured by the nothingness, and even though this material, harvested as I knew from the unsung poets of the regional areas, was in his judgement completely middling in every respect, it was somehow transformed in its improvisatory fragments and amalgamations into something bright and mysterious, that had lit up the dark rooms of the capital's poetry recitals. As Solomon Wiese streamed this material back into the nothingness where it belonged, basically *regurgitating* it for his admiring audiences, he said, he had sometimes had the suspicion that, while it had never been his choice what exactly emerged from his mouth, when he stood up to recite his *spontaneous poetry*, there was in fact an order behind it that he couldn't quite discern. The feeling he had on stage once or twice was more accurately that he was *delivering information* of some kind to the audience, information that he himself didn't understand, in other words that he was *delivering encrypted information* to the audience in the form of a poetry recital, that the lines he spoke perhaps had some numerical or otherwise coded value he was unaware of, more than likely for the reception of one person in the audience, who was able to decode this information and so discover its true purpose and application. On these one or two occasions, when the conviction arose that he was announcing *encrypted information* rather than poetry to the darkened room, he had thought he had seen someone in the audience he recognised, Solomon Wiese said—he thought he had seen Christian Buch at the back of the room, in fact, on both occasions, but when he had looked more intently, still mid-spate, he hadn't been able to make him out clearly, nor had he been able to find him in the heaving room following the recital. He also found that the impulse to announce his *spontaneous poetry* began to occur not only when it was appropriate to do so, that is, in the environment of a poetry recital, but at other moments too, when it would have been insane to start reciting poetry—one night he almost started reciting poetry on the London Underground, Solomon Wiese said, he almost recited a poem to a busy tube carriage, he even opened his mouth to begin reciting, but something held him back. He had opened his mouth and was on the brink of actually reciting a poem on the London Underground, at half past twelve at night, but fortunately something had prevented him from doing so. Just as he had begun to form the first word with his mouth, he managed to stop himself, to his relief. It could have been dizziness in the wake of my high approval ratings in the poetry recital arena, Solomon Wiese said, or it could have been something else, this impulse to spontaneously recite poetry on public transport. Nonetheless it's strange how quickly I became accustomed to success, Solomon Wiese said. I felt that I had been recognised in the appropriate way, of course, that a state of affairs I had long been convinced of was simply being acknowledged more widely. I had seen the treasures behind the *curtain of appearances*, I had always known they were there, so I settled quickly into a feeling of comfortable superiority, in a position high above my fellow poets. Once I had been rewarded with a series of successes in the poetry recital arena, it became a source of delight for me to look down on the poets I had formerly shared the stage with, who hadn't enjoyed the same series of successes. It was as if I had never been in their situation,

Solomon Wiese said, but had always been above it, and when I quickly graduated over the summer to larger venues and more prestigious line-ups it was simply evidence that I had been destined for something better all along. It was part of the natural progression of events, and as far as I was concerned it could scarcely have been any other way. I wish I had some nice things to say about the poets I shared a stage with, my peers, Solomon Wiese said, but the truth is I have nothing nice to say about them—the line-ups I participated in were line-ups precisely of nonentities and hopelessly grasping frauds. But at around this time he had noticed a new class of attendees at his spontaneous poetry recitals, so-called, Solomon Wiese went on. He recognised these new attendees as poets whose reputations preceded them—they formed a clique of high-profile poets who seldom entered the vulgar arena of the poetry recital, preferring to hold themselves some distance above it. It was a mark of his impact on the scene, he decided, that they were stooping so low as to attend these events, with their garbling crowds and beer-slicked tables, which this clique of high-profile yet elusive poets no doubt regarded as a populist debasement of the worst kind—in the estimation of this clique of high-profile yet elusive poets, as Solomon Wiese would discover, the poetry recital was where the art of poetry was sullied and trodden into the mud, it was where the art of poetry was *brought into disrepute*. Like all aspiring poets, he had been instructed to read these elite poets at various stages of his apprenticeship, Solomon Wiese said—he had been instructed by an assortment of his superiors, as no doubt I had been as well, to study the work of this elusive and inaccessible *poetry clique*, to deepen his appreciation of the craft—and that was why he had never read a single line written by any of them. He had refused outright to read a book by any member of this select group, he had refused outright to even flick through one of their intimidatingly dense and exquisitely produced publications. He had gone out of his way *not* to encounter, even passingly, or to so much as glimpse a single one of their poems, at any time, and so form preconceptions about its subject matter and formal arrangement, which would inevitably have gone on to influence him, consciously or unconsciously, positively or negatively. He had intended to remain completely untouched by this select group of poets, and, having never set eyes on any of their poems, he had ensured he remained free of their influence. He had no basis on which to *imitate* their example, just as he had no basis on which to *avoid* their example. Advocates of the work of this *exclusive poetry clique* claimed that it transcended altogether the limits traditionally ascribed to poetry, Solomon Wiese went on; they claimed this was a poetry that had transcended everyday meanings, that had risen to a plane of *transcendental meanings*, which suggested of course that nobody understood what the poems meant, perhaps even the poets themselves, but that at the same time, in a sense, *everyone* understood them—their transcendental meaning was *equally unavailable to everyone*, and therefore it was *equally available to everyone*. The members of this select group of poets were able to glide and somersault on their higher plane of transcendental meaning, and they seemed to exude a kind of satisfaction as they did so, a satisfaction that their devoted readers claimed to share, but in reality inclusion in this mutual sense of satisfaction was strictly limited, as when faced with the general populace, and specifically the earthbound poets restricted to the concrete plane of the everyday, the select group of poets invariably showed a contemptuous and austere countenance. Very occasionally, representatives of this elite order of poets would descend from their plane of transcendental meaning *en masse*, for mysterious reasons; they would gather at an otherwise unremarkable poetry recital, and only later would the purpose behind their appearance become clear, when a certain poet was abruptly elevated to join their ranks, or when a certain poet, selected apparently at random, was judged to have committed a specific offence against poetry, becoming the target of sustained attacks, on multiple fronts, resulting in the unlucky poet's total withdrawal from poetry and public life. Because of this, their sudden appearance at a poetry recital was regarded with anxiety and apprehension, or even muted, superstitious terror. This exclusive clique of poets was the only clique of poets that properly warranted being called a *school of poets*, Solomon Wiese went on, as they were by and large products of elite educational institutions, and had become known by those who aspired to join their ranks as the *scholastici*. An atmosphere of esotericism and arcane knowledge enclosed their so-called school, an effect that was enhanced, as I knew, by their disconcertingly formal bearing and style of speech. Solomon Wiese had found them *very crisp* when he had spoken to them, as he was clearly expected to, when they had descended on an otherwise unremarkable poetry recital, one rainy Wednesday evening. It was fair to say he had found them altogether *too crisp*, Solomon Wiese went on, altogether *too dry*—with their parched voices and archaic dress sense, their crisp facial expressions and dry verbal expressions, their succinctness, their precision, and, there were no other words for it, their unrelenting *crispness and dryness*. They had obviously spent some time assessing his output, in their crisp and dry style, however it had been reported to them, prior to descending on the poetry recital *en masse*. And although he thought now they had only wanted to profit by association—that they had spotted an opportunity in his sudden ascent to reassert themselves within the poetry community at large—it had been impossible not to feel flattered by the attention. He hadn't understood, at the time, that it was fundamentally a base and mercantile transaction—he hadn't understood that they were only speaking to him on the understanding they could collect some of his social currency, and siphon it off for their own use. The scholastici gave the impression that these concerns were far beneath them, as poetical practitioners of the highest order, but in reality all members of this *exclusive poetry clique* were grimly obsessed with popularity and relevance—they were unhealthily fixated on the reactions of the poetry community, and in private spoke of nothing else—and in fact they were much more thoroughly corrupted by the social economy's intoxicating powers than the most outwardly aspirational and ambitious poets Solomon Wiese had encountered in the conventional poetry recital arena. But he had been completely disarmed,

Solomon Wiese went on, as soon as he was exposed to the crisp, dry style of speech employed by the scholastici, which had the effect, when aimed straight at you, of making you feel you were being treated with a kind of uniquely intimate consideration. It was a brutal seduction technique, he now recognised, pure and simple: it was a brutal seduction technique that far surpassed any he had previously encountered, and of course he had fallen for it the instant he was exposed to it. Any negative preconceptions he may have had about the nature of this exclusive poetry clique, the scholastici, were immediately neutralised by a series of *fluent disclaimers*, Solomon Wiese went on, issued in their typically crisp, dry style of speech, early in the conversation. These *fluent disclaimers* concerned the general backgrounds and educational histories of the scholastici—it was the first time he had been exposed to these *fluent disclaimers*, Solomon Wiese said, and the effect was devastating. The *fluent disclaimer* took the form of a disarming statement that anticipated the effect of, and in a sense demanded *forgiveness* for, a blatant fact that the utterer of the *fluent disclaimer* had just acknowledged, making the fact appear regrettable, of course, but ultimately understandable as *the fault of no one*, and so the fact remained in some obscure way *in play*, rather than being addressed directly or responded to by the listener—the *fluent disclaimer* actively guarded against the *direct response*, he now recognised, and emerged as its more powerful opposite number. A direct response would appear unforgivably crass, it was obvious, in the face of the calm and sophisticated *fluent disclaimer*. Within their atmosphere of calmness and sophistication, the *fluent disclaimer* seemed to allow the members of the scholastici to simultaneously acknowledge and ignore their status as products of their backgrounds and educations—the obvious fact that it was an inevitability, pure and simple, given their backgrounds and educations, that they would end up in the elite orders of their scholastic poetry circle, was simply shrugged off; they saw themselves instead as self-determined agents, individuals whose innate critical faculties had led them, naturally, into the elite ranks where they were currently stationed. Still, they did not regard this as an inevitability of circumstance, but rather as a situation they had willed into existence with nothing but their powers of imagination. For example, it seemed not to have occurred to them, Solomon Wiese said, despite their calmness and sophistication, that the rival group of poets they defined themselves against in all ways, the so-called *grammatici*, who haunted the scholastici's debates and symposia, and determined their every move by counter-example, were their rivals only due to the observance of tradition, a tradition that was followed with equally unerring loyalty by the grammatici. This tradition determined that the students of universities *w* and *x* would follow one pathway in their pursuit of artistic greatness, and the students of universities *y* and *z* would follow a separate and parallel pathway, in search of the same goal. So, naturally, the students of universities *w* and *x* admired poetry by the poets *a* and *c*, while the students of universities *y* and *z* admired the poetry of poets *b* and *d*, going out of their way to openly disdain the poetry of poets *a* and *c*. None of those involved questioned this division; all accepted it as completely natural, and reaffirmed the dividing line at every opportunity, wherever possible propelling the ancient rivalry to further extremes of adversity and ill feeling. Nonetheless, the actors in this drama considered themselves autonomous agents, rather than simply the pawns of these traditions, Solomon Wiese said—so it had been for many years, and so it would continue, if the members of these elite orders of poets had anything to do with it. But, Solomon Wiese went on, the obviously contrived nature of this long-running poetry conflict made him suspect that it was conducted largely in a spirit of *nostalgia*—the main actors in this ongoing poetry drama were *deeply nostalgic* for a time when these aesthetic distinctions really meant something, he thought, and their theatrical poetic rivalry was in reality a *reliving of bygone days*—when people's lives were actually staked on these issues—by people for whom nothing whatsoever was at stake, Solomon Wiese said, so in reality this distinguished and long-running poetry conflict was conducted in the spirit of a *historical re-enactment*. In other words, it was as unbearably stale and tired as a *long-running soap opera*, this long-running poetry conflict. It no longer mattered to anyone, for example, that the grammatici believed in explaining the circumstances of their poetic inspiration, at length, before delivering aphoristic poetry in a clipped and rapid style of speech, while the scholastici never explained the circumstances of their poetic inspiration, and read their discursive, dense poetry in a crisp and dry style of speech. It no longer mattered to anyone that the scholastici wrote their poems in a sloping cursive hand, evoking the monastic scribe, while the grammatici wrote in perfect roman script, evoking the impersonal typeface. It was far more obvious what these rival groups shared, to the outside observer, and a novice could easily mistake a grammatici poem for a scholastici poem, or vice versa—one was clipped and rapid, one was crisp and dry, but a surer means of distinction, and it was a generalisation approved of by neither the scholastici or the grammatici, was that the scholastici by and large produced *long poems*, while the grammatici by and large produced *short poems*. Beyond this, even the informed commentator would concede that they shared many stylistic tendencies and artistic convictions—they shared, in fact, precisely the same set of stylistic tendencies and artistic convictions, bar the one he had just mentioned, as I no doubt already knew, Solomon Wiese said. He had been forced to acknowledge, having spent some time among the scholastici, which was the only group he could comment on with any authority, that they had an understanding of the quote unquote *poet's calling* that closely mirrored his own, Solomon Wiese said, and which he had described at the beginning of our conversation. Observing these convictions about the poet's destiny in the scholastici had forced him to review his *own* convictions about the poet's destiny, and, for the first time, he had seen their grotesque proportions, Solomon Wiese said. He was still unable to relinquish these convictions completely—it would most likely take some kind of final push, Solomon Wiese said. These convictions appeared to be situated very close to the centre of who he was, as a person, and to abnegate his convictions now would require a complete restructuring of his personality, it seemed to him, Solomon Wiese said—in fact it would entail the wholesale destruction of his personality, most likely. Once the ranks of the scholastici had closed around him, in apparent friendship, he had quickly become revolted by everything the scholastici represented, Solomon Wiese said. As abruptly as his new *life-season* of abundance and activity had begun, it had ended, and a different season was ushered in to replace it—a darker, more changeable season, in Solomon Wiese's estimation. Soon he was looking for some way to extricate himself from the clutches of the so-called scholastici, Solomon Wiese went on, but the situation was made more complex by the fact that the ranks of the scholastici had closed around Phoebe Glass as well, in apparent friendship, and the effect of their crisp, dry style and *fluent disclaimers* on Phoebe Glass was even more dramatic than they'd been on Solomon Wiese—in short, Phoebe Glass was swiftly and totally indoctrinated by the scholastici, Solomon Wiese said. She aligned herself with them on all matters, viewing them as the ultimate authority, meaning that Solomon Wiese had to disguise his newfound suspicions of the scholastici from Phoebe Glass, as he was no longer certain that Phoebe Glass would be loyal to him before serving the scholastici, Solomon Wiese said. She is loyal only to them, even now, he went on, lowering his voice and gesturing to Phoebe Glass, who was still sound asleep with her head on the Travelodge bar, wrapped in a green scarf. Phoebe Glass had begun to write poetry at this point, Solomon Wiese said—*to his despair*, he had to confess. He had never imagined Phoebe Glass as a poet, he had thought her all-out attacks on arts establishments and general contemporary mendacity were expressions that were best confined to and enjoyed in the social sphere, if not entirely suppressed—but the fact was that once she became attuned to the stylistic convictions of the scholastici, her effortless and seemingly endless withering critiques were smoothly converted into works of poetry that were deeply appreciated by her new peer group. She began producing long poems in a crisp, dry style that held various state apparatus and commercial interests to account, according to her vigorous ethical sensibility. That her inexhaustible and merciless critiques, which Solomon Wiese had enjoyed for a month or two now, were fully formed and always to hand, meant Phoebe Glass was able to compose her poetry rapidly and fluently, once the floodgates had opened. Her private withering critiques, meanwhile, had begun to circle the inexplicable fact, as far as Phoebe Glass was concerned, of Solomon Wiese's lack of meaningful employment and significant-seeming private wealth, as he had so far avoided telling her about the origin of his quote unquote *small fortune*, for some reason, Solomon Wiese said. That was probably an indication of something, he thought. That Phoebe Glass's poems, which were suddenly abundant, had at their source the genuine and unextinguished sweetness and seriousness of the memory of her old friend, Jessica Lake, gave them a force that was striking, even to the elder members of the exclusive *poetry clique* she and Solomon Wiese had found themselves absorbed by, Solomon Wiese thought. Although his initial response, as he had already admitted, was despair, it didn't take Solomon Wiese long to see Phoebe Glass's poetry for what it really was—Phoebe Glass had emerged, he realised, as a legitimately wonderful poet. He was unable to resent the fact of her writing poetry when her poetry was so obviously wonderful, he said. We can never resent this kind of poet, the legitimately wonderful poet, whatever success they have, Solomon Wiese said, we can only resent the overrated or fraudulent poet. We cannot even *dislike* the legitimately wonderful poet, as this kind of poet, however egotistical and self-centred, ultimately seems to be correct in their self-assessment; we can only resent and begrudge the overrated and fraudulent poet, who has deluded themselves with egomaniacal self-belief. Both the legitimately wonderful poet and the overrated, fraudulent poet adopt exactly the same attitude, but there is no mistaking the legitimately wonderful poet, when we encounter their poetry, Solomon Wiese said—that was the experience he had had when he read Phoebe Glass's poems. He was unable to resent the fact that she had begun writing poetry, or her newfound success, which quickly threatened to eclipse his own, by virtue of her poetry, which was wonderful, he said. But while Phoebe Glass's public profile was gaining prominence by the day, her relationship with Solomon Wiese was deteriorating, Solomon Wiese said—as her reputation in the poetry world was climbing its steep curve, so their relationship was declining along an opposite gradient, of equal steepness. He started to notice an element of performance in their conversations, Solomon Wiese said, particularly in public, but also at home; he had been living with Phoebe

Glass for a month or so at this point, having moved into her one-bed flat in south-east London. In public, perhaps, it was understandable, he went on, as every couple is aware of performing their relationship to some extent, for those around them who might overhear their conversations, but this *performance element* had also begun to creep into their conversations when there was no one around to overhear them, and therefore no one for whom to perform their relationship, apart from themselves, Solomon Wiese said. At times Solomon Wiese almost felt as if he were *interviewing* Phoebe Glass, while eating dinner in her flat this feeling had come over him, that he was *interviewing* Phoebe Glass at some kind of literary event, and his awareness of it only exaggerated his behaviour, so he felt obliged to ask question after question about her newfound success as a poet, questions that Phoebe Glass didn't seem to find irritating or contrived, but apparently enjoyed answering in a crisp, dry and semi-professional tone of voice, as if preparing for the occasion, surely not far away, when she would answer similar or identical questions onstage, in front of an audience, at a well-attended literary event. Their conversations, and to some extent their relationship, had begun to take on the feeling of a *rehearsal*, Solomon Wiese realised, but it was a future performance by Phoebe Glass alone, not a future performance by himself and Phoebe Glass, that they were preparing for—his role was firmly that of supporting staff or stagehand, it became clear, Solomon Wiese said. He had also begun to suspect that the way they behaved at home, in Phoebe Glass's one-bed flat, was for some reason moving closer to how *others who knew about them would suspect they behaved*—in other words, that as a pair of so-called emerging poets, they were constantly discussing or debating the intricacies of the poetry world, the publication and performance of poetry, the poets who were on the rise and the poets who were going downhill—the thought of this made Solomon Wiese feel self-conscious and serious, so that the tone of their conversations became more self-conscious and serious—their conversations, even about Phoebe Glass's recent work, began to feel almost tense, Solomon Wiese had realised one evening, as if the interview he was conducting had become awkward and combative, after its relaxed and amicable opening phases. The relationship was still not without its happier and more natural moments, Solomon Wiese said, but increasingly the happy and natural moments only came about when Solomon Wiese and Phoebe Glass were united in condemnation of a particular poet or poem or poetry event, when their delight in *non-stop shit-talking* resumed temporarily and they were able to pass the time happily and naturally while *relentlessly shit-talking* said poem or poet or poetry event, *shit-talking it into the ground*—at these moments a true happiness and naturalness animated their voices again, that is, until one of them went too far in their *relentless shit-talking*, touching on a poem or poet or poetry event that in the opinion of the other was not an appropriate target for the *shit-talking treatment*, and stiffness and inhibition would return to their exchanges. They got on well, as long as they were *relentlessly shit-talking* a poem or poet or poetry event, Solomon Wiese said, otherwise their interactions had taken on the feeling of an ongoing rehearsal for actions in other arenas, specifically in the arenas of the poetry world, he thought, and when he realised this he saw little chance of saving his and Phoebe Glass's fundamentally *shit-talking relationship*. Sometimes he would believe that things were improving, only for Phoebe Glass to start talking excitedly about an upcoming symposium or poetry conference that the scholastici were preparing—they were organising another *symposium or poetry conference*, Phoebe Glass would report; just when Solomon Wiese had thought the non-stop programme of symposia and poetry conferences had come to an end for the time being, another symposium or poetry conference would appear on the horizon, and preparations would begin—in his new life there was apparently no escape from the symposium or poetry conference, barely a week would go by before Solomon Wiese would have to attend yet another symposium or poetry conference, would find himself once again listening to a whole day's worth of impenetrable narcissistic drivel, churned out by a host of dreary academics, who either didn't have any idea how to interact with an audience, and so simply read aloud from their impenetrable and narcissistic academic observations, or else seemed to be grooming themselves for a prospective career on state TV or radio, in which case they presented in the insufferable faux-jovial and condescending style favoured by the state's media platforms. The academic conference was an endurance test that it was only possible to survive, Solomon Wiese speculated, if you were anticipating delivering an academic paper full of your own impenetrable narcissistic drivel, this being the only chance that the socially inept academics, who could be relied upon to attend any symposium or poetry conference under the sun, had to present their dreary and irrelevant research to people who were guaranteed to at least feign polite interest. Over the series of symposia and poetry conferences that Solomon Wiese was obliged to attend, he encountered only one paper that was of interest to him, on the rise of so-called reading sickness, a problem that was now reaching the proportions of an epidemic, Solomon Wiese was intrigued to learn; every week thousands of researchers were entering something resembling a *hypnotic fugue state*, as the giver of the paper put it, at their desks, incapacitating them for up to three hours and making them unable to carry out their duties. The paper speculated on the possible causes of this *reading sickness*, which remained a mystery, but fell short of suggesting an effective remedy. This ten-minute paper was the only meaningful respite from the endurance test of the non-stop symposia and poetry conferences that Solomon Wiese was expected to attend, as a fledgling member of the scholastici and the companion of Phoebe Glass, their latest understudy. Soon the walls had started to close in on him, Solomon Wiese said—he had been unable to speak about this with anyone, least of all Phoebe Glass, but his inner life increasingly became one of desperation; he wanted nothing more than to escape the social prison he had allowed himself to be trapped inside, but as far as he could see there was no simple way to escape this social prison, without renouncing his successes in the poetry recital arena—people didn't simply retire from the ranks of the scholastici and continue with their lives as poets unhindered and uninterrupted, as Solomon Wiese was well aware. Any poet he could think of who was expelled from the ranks of the scholastici had been subjected to campaigns of abuse and accusation, until they had been forced to retire from poetry and public life altogether, Solomon Wiese said. At night, unable to sleep, he filled the hours by castigating himself with his interminable internal monologues, Solomon Wiese said, his internal monologues went completely out of control on these sleepless nights. As Phoebe Glass slept soundly beside him, he revisited every phase of his journey up to the current moment, condemning every decision he'd made in the strongest possible language; his internal monologue became an expletive-filled rant, with his own name as its object, Solomon Wiese said, and the culmination of this expletive-filled rant was the repetition of his own name *ad nauseum*, the repeating of his name as if hammering it with a metal object, until the associations emptied out of it like waste water, Solomon Wiese said, and the full ridiculousness and hollowness of his name became obvious—the social prison he was trapped inside then revealing itself as being *identical* with his own name, Solomon Wiese said, you'll always be Solomon Wiese, Solomon Wiese went on, there is no escape from being Solomon Wiese, Solomon Wiese had thought while lying in bed, Solomon Wiese said, Solomon Wiese is the name of your self-constructed social prison, and Solomon Wiese is likewise the journey that brought you here, with a bleak inevitability, Solomon Wiese had thought; the dismal fact *of* Solomon Wiese is where you've ended up, and Solomon Wiese is the only place you ever could have ended up with a name like Solomon Wiese, so ran Solomon Wiese's thoughts on these sleepless nights, Solomon Wiese said. When eventually he did sleep, the expletive-filled internal monologue having become a lullaby, and by which time dawn light brightened the curtains, he dreamed more than once that he was imprisoned with the poets he used to know in a kind of *creativity camp*, Solomon Wiese said, he couldn't think of a better way to describe it. In the dream he was living alongside his fellow poets in a facility that seemed to be somewhere between a hospital, a leisure complex and a theme park; there were café areas and turnstiles, waiting rooms and corridors, and all the inmates at this *creativity camp* were dressed in colourless gowns, although the members of staff, the people running the facility, were never seen by anyone. At intervals, each of the poets had to enter the inner areas of the facility, through the turnstile gates, and though none of them could remember what happened in these inner areas, they knew it involved *enforced creativity* of some description. When they reappeared they would be somehow depleted, Solomon Wiese said—their memories would be damaged, they would be missing fingers and toes, or their skin and hair would have aged, turning a strange silvery colour. The dream had clarified things, as his dreams had previously clarified things, Solomon Wiese said, in that it was true his current predicament was depleting him in ways that were directly analogous to losing fingers and toes, or whole swathes of memory, or actual passages of time, so that he woke up each day even more depleted than he had been the day before. He began to wonder how he had ended up in his position of ambiguous subservience to the scholastici, Solomon Wiese said, without anyone actually prescribing him that role. On some level we all wish to be dominated, if we don't wish to actively dominate others, he remembered thinking during this time, either we wish to dominate or we wish to be dominated, with a kind of weird fervour, Solomon Wiese added—admittedly at the current moment it seemed there were vastly more people who wished to be dominated than wished to dominate, in whatever sphere of human interaction, social, economic or sexual, though doubtless it was the case that in a *balanced* society those who wished to be *dominated* sexually, for example, were more likely to *dominate* in another sphere of action, their submission in the former arena being a kind of recompense for or transgression against their outwardly dominating character. But, at the current moment, the preference of most people was to be dominated, across *all* spheres of action, more often than not, it appeared to Solomon Wiese, which allowed those with an inclination to *dominate* a free rein, Solomon Wiese remembered thinking—if you wished to dominate rather than be dominated, you would have very little difficulty finding the opportunity to do so, whereas if you wished to be *dominated* the opportunities were few and far between, and in fact there was *brutal competition* for the opportunity to be dominated, Solomon Wiese remembered thinking. There seemed to be a critical imbalance, with a large majority of people wishing to be dominated, and a small minority willing to do the dominating, and as such they were left to dominate in whatever style they chose, unchallenged, as those seeking domination were too pathetically grateful, when the gaze of a potential dominator fell upon them at last, to question the character of that domination. He'd remembered his old friend as he thought about this, Solomon Wiese remembered, his only remaining London friend, who he had stayed with before moving in with Phoebe Glass, and beginning his programme of, until recently, unwitting domination at the hands of the scholastici. His old friend had realised, he had confessed to Solomon Wiese one evening, during a rare conversation that had managed to interest them both, that he was one of the few genuine *natural-born dominators* of his generation. He had had this realisation while watching a protest on television that turned unexpectedly violent—it was a net-neutrality protest, he remembered—as he watched the ranks of protesters clashing with the wall of armoured riot police, surging again and again against the immoveable barrier of riot shields and helmets, and as the police had regularly cut down the ranks of protesters with swift strokes of their truncheons, he had realised he wanted to be there, among the seething mass of protesters and police, but not, as Solomon Wiese would have assumed, given his old friend's background and political leanings, on the side of the protesters, but, to his own astonishment, as his friend confessed, *on the side of the riot police*, with their visors and helmets and transparent shields, raining down blow after blow on the unprotected bodies of the net-neutrality protesters. His friend had been astonished by this desire, when it had revealed itself to him, while watching the unexpectedly violent net-neutrality protests on TV, he said. Solomon Wiese had even relayed this story to Phoebe Glass one evening, as an indirect way of presenting some of his anxieties about their current situation, but this had been a catastrophic idea, he immediately realised. The story, he now assumed, had been reported back to senior members of the scholastici by Phoebe Glass. He didn't see this as the monumental act of betrayal it probably appeared to be, however, as part of him realised he must have known it would happen, given Phoebe Glass's loyalty to the scholastici, which he had observed at close quarters for around six weeks, Solomon Wiese said. By telling Phoebe Glass the story about his old friend, part of him must have wanted to sabotage his own position within the scholastici; it was a desperate attempt to extricate himself from their circle, he now thought—because there was only one possible way in which the scholastici would interpret the story, and that was as a reactionary statement intended to derail the scholastici's political efficacy, which although it was the subject of unending discussion and debate within the scholastici, was hard to define or provide a single concrete example of. But what he hadn't anticipated was that the scholastici would decide that this confession, of longing to join the riot police and bludgeon supporters of the net-neutrality movement with a truncheon, was in fact Solomon Wiese's *own confession*—in other words, that Solomon Wiese's old friend's confession, that he wished to stand among the ranks of riot police, dealing out indiscriminate blows with his truncheon to whoever happened to appear beneath it, *became* Solomon Wiese's confession; the confession was attached by the scholastici directly to Solomon Wiese, and was spoken about as if it had originated from him, and not from his old friend. Despite his careful efforts to explain, the scholastici failed to understand or refused to understand the distinction, Solomon Wiese said, and he eventually realised it was of no importance to them whether the confession was truly his confession or not, because he had been the one to vocalise it, so for all intents and purposes it *was* his confession, as far as the scholastici were concerned. His duplicitous involvement with the group was made clear by this single action and, he now thought, they had immediately started plotting his downfall. For this reason we should be careful whose confessions we listen to; we should be wary of the things we overhear, as well as those we confide in, Solomon Wiese went on, as these confessions have a tendency to attach themselves to us, to attach themselves to the listener, and, if repeated, in some cases, become intimately associated with the listener, and if repeated often enough, in some cases, they can even become part of the *listener's own experience*, so that the listener ends up believing that the events described in the confession happened directly to them, in some cases, when in reality they happened to an acquaintance or friend who had confided in them, and so they, the listener, end up taking on the consequences of this confession, as if they are one and the same person as the original confessor, when they were only ever the listener and repeater of the confession. They mistakenly come to view themselves as the confessor, when they were only ever the *handler* of the confession, Solomon Wiese said. The repercussions of this kind of delusion could be severe, in some cases, Solomon Wiese said. In a way, by your listening to *my* confession, I am making you the *bearer* of my confession—I am making you a part of the story of my confession, Solomon Wiese went on, sipping from an espresso that had appeared by the sleeve of his unseasonable winter coat, threaded with a lighter weave, that he was still wearing, despite the fact that the Travelodge bar was by now bathed in direct sunlight, though tens of poets continued to drowse on the long couches. And if you repeat my confession to anyone, it is only logical that on some level you *will* become the confessor—you will be positioned at the centre of the confession once you start to confess it, despite believing that you are only a figure on its margins, a passive onlooker, Solomon Wiese said. You might insist you are merely the repeater of the confession, but your listeners will begin to view you as the *true confessor* of the story, that is, the confessor of the *story of the confession*, as only you know the route the confession has taken to reach you, and how it will reach beyond you, which forms part of the substance of the confession, and so you are the only one who is able to confess it, in that scenario, Solomon Wiese said. I have almost unburdened myself of my confession, Solomon Wiese said—I am on the verge of completing my unburdening. But you are yet to unburden yourself of your confession, and in many ways that makes you a more unpredictable or dangerous component, in terms of the *story of the confession*, to those who might be concerned about the ultimate destination of this confession—because it is an unknown quantity when you will choose to unburden yourself and to whom; the only thing that's certain is that you will feel the desire to unburden yourself, at some point, Solomon Wiese said, that is, unless someone decides that you should be *prevented* from unburdening yourself, and takes steps to deprive you of that opportunity. In a way, it would be a simple matter to choose who should be *taken out of the equation*—someone who has literally just finished unburdening themselves of their possibly dangerous confession, or someone who has literally just absorbed this possibly dangerous confession, and will soon desire to unburden themselves of it, in their turn—to *pass on* the confession, and *pass on*, too, the desire to unburden, Solomon Wiese said. It should have been obvious to him what they would do, the scholastici, he said. They had all the tools at their disposal with which to quickly and effectively *take him out of the equation*, given his track record with the quantitative analysis and comparison system, Solomon Wiese said. In his view it hadn't taken more than a couple of days for the scholastici to submit the recordings or transcripts of his readings to the now publicly accessible QACS portal. And when the results came in, they had mounted his public excoriation, which everyone who had attended or viewed one of his spontaneous poetry recitals had added their weight to without a moment's hesitation, Solomon Wiese said. Phoebe Glass herself had led the public excoriation, it was a natural choice given her abilities, despite the fact they were still living together and maintaining a semi-functioning relationship—he would hear her tapping away at home in the adjoining room while he lay in bed, knowing she was refining some fresh condemnation or assault on his public profile, before she slid into bed beside him and turned out the light, Solomon Wiese said. He knew as well that Phoebe Glass viewed this public ordeal as a step on the way to his eventual rehabilitation, and the more brutal and thoroughgoing his excoriation now, the more assured his eventual redemption would be, in her estimation—but that didn't alter the fact that his girlfriend was the ringleader of his own public excoriation, Solomon Wiese said. He was a prime candidate for *alternative justice*, in Phoebe Glass's estimation, Solomon Wiese said. She had offered to chaperone him through the gruelling phases of the process, which would culminate in him voluntarily undertaking a quote unquote *self-nominated punishment*—this being the penalty agreed by the recently introduced *alternative justice system* that had been devised by the creative community for offences that fell, as his did, between legal and social transgressions; after his *self-nominated punishment* had been delivered, his name would supposedly be purged once and for all of its negative resonances, Solomon Wiese said. In the preliminary meeting, when she had accepted her role, Phoebe Glass had said it would be a *joyful privilege* to guide Solomon Wiese through the gruelling *alternative justice process*, Solomon Wiese said—that was her precise choice of words, a *joyful privilege*. They were still deciding on the nature of this quote unquote *self-nominated punishment*, Solomon Wiese said, though it was due to be carried out today, at noon. Today at noon he would receive his self-nominated punishment, so-called, Solomon Wiese said. You didn't want to be too lenient on yourself when suggesting a *self-nominated punishment*, Solomon Wiese went on, as the host of onlookers would feel you had got off lightly, so the temptation was actually to select an *excessively harsh self-nominated punishment*, to make sure that the view that you had got off lightly was all but discounted—but there were always people who would regard even an obviously *excessively harsh self-nominated punishment* as completely fair, Solomon Wiese said, so you had to go a step further again, in order to make certain no onlooker could imagine you had got off lightly. That you had not got off lightly had to be made self-evident by the excessively harsh nature of the self-nominated punishment, so-called, Solomon Wiese said. Throughout the process he had offered no resistance, Solomon Wiese said, he hadn't uttered a single word of protest or disagreement, he was well aware that any attempt at avoidance, for example an unapologetic statement or an unconvincing apology, would only add weight to his forthcoming and excessively harsh *self-nominated punishment*. He had remained completely passive as Phoebe Glass had guided him, with care and compassion, though also with professional rigour, it had to be said, through the phases of the *alternative justice process*. He had acquiesced. Not a word of protest had passed his lips. Metaphorically speaking, he knew that they would *take his hands*, Solomon Wiese said. It was clearly a metaphor, and he was still unsure what the reality of this metaphor was, the nature of the equivalent *self-nominated punishment*—*the taking of the hands* being the ancient punishment for thieves, of course, so he understood its appropriateness as a figure of speech, and although he remained unsure precisely what the actuality or interpretation of this metaphor, *the taking of the hands*, would be, he would find out today at noon—so not long now, Solomon Wiese said. The scholastici were one of the few groups of poets who would have nothing to do with the Festival of Culture, of course, Solomon Wiese said, so he was secure for the time being, here within the Festival of Culture bubble. The scholastici would not set foot within any venue that was used for the Festival of Culture during the Festival of Culture, which meant that here in the Travelodge bar he was safe. He should have known the public mood would turn against him, once the revelations of his QACS results were broadcast, most likely by senior members of the scholastici, Solomon Wiese said. He had considered disputing the results, when they had first been announced, as it was astonishing to him that the works of the unsung poets of the east of England should be traceable from his spontaneous poetry recitals, but as his image as a serial exploiter of poets became outlined with increasing emphasis, he had recognised it was hopeless. Stories about him emerged that had little or no significance on their own, but when placed inside this emphatic outline, which painted an image of Solomon Wiese as a serial exploiter and *pillager* of poets and poems, only enhanced its effect. In his view, though, it was only a matter of time before the unsung rural poets whose work he had pillaged would be revealed *themselves as pillagers* of previous poetic works, Solomon Wiese said—of that much he was certain. There was no way that the work of these unsung rural poets could be as derivative and middling as it was *without* pillaging from the work of previous unsung rural poets, or alternatively, from previous *well-known* rural poets, who were fortunate enough to have had their works *sung out*, in all senses, Solomon Wiese said, and if they couldn't be decisively proved as outright pillagers of these earlier unsung or sung poets, then they might as well have been, so pronounced was their debt to these previous rural poets. But he should have known that this was how it would go, knowing the people and the country of his birth, Solomon Wiese said. He should have known that once a weakness had been exposed in his public profile, the host of onlookers would try to probe at that weakness, to further expose it, knowing the English, and England, the country of his birth, Solomon Wiese said. He had known at that moment that the only thing he could do in the face of the non-stop assault on his public profile was *acquiesce* to the assault, endure it without a murmur of complaint or defiance towards his persecutors or the host of onlookers, who, as they hounded and mocked their solitary victim, became more and more *recognisably English.* The only thing that might eventually dampen the zeal of their vindictive attack on his public profile was if he bore the attack with complete passivity, Solomon Wiese knew—it is well known that the English demand meekness and deference from their victims, from all those that they hound and persecute, Solomon Wiese said. Anything else is intolerable to them. And if they are not content with the levels of meekness and deference on display, they will typically press their advantage, in other words, they will increase their vindictive zeal, in order to extract yet more meekness and deference from their victims. The English are a fearful and cruel people, Solomon Wiese said, this is known throughout the entire world. They are always afraid, and they are always prepared to mete out cruelty of the most uninhibited kind, whenever they have the opportunity. This fear and taste for cruelty is hidden behind the famous English *veneer* of civility, of course, Solomon Wiese said. The word *veneer* was probably adopted as a metaphor with the English in mind, in fact, Solomon Wiese said, so synonymous is it with the inherently duplicitous English character, the *veneer* of civility disguising the utter vindictiveness, cruelty and sensationalism that forms their substance, and the hysterical and baseless fear that powers the whole set-up. The English with their ducking stools, gibbets, whipping posts, stocks, dunce's caps and fox hunts, and above all with the *quintessentially English* taste for public humiliation that runs through all of their traditions, in all regions, at all levels of society. An island people, the English, who must kick someone off their island with sufficient regularity so that no one forgets for a second they are living on an island, hence the English obsession with borders and privacy, hence the *quintessentially English* phenomena of net curtains and privet hedges, gravel drives and walled acreages, all of which declare an ignorant and hysterical fear of the outsider, which in England includes one's own neighbours, as well as concealing a multitude of private perversions; hence the remorseless and *quintessentially English* appetite for mockery, cruelty and sensationalised public humiliation, hence the cruelty and vindictiveness directed at those members of society less able to defend themselves, hence the shameless celebration of the suffering of others that is hard-wired into the so-called English national character, which the English believe in above all else, actually taking a perverse pride in their reprehensible national character, with its track record of genocide and mindless oppression, in their stupidity and bull-headedness continuing to ascribe wildly inaccurate national attributes to their neighbours, while adhering with perverse pride to their own self-determined and thoroughly reprehensible *national character.* He had lived in England long enough to know exactly what to expect, to understand how he had to behave now, that is, with total passivity, meekness and deference, Solomon Wiese said. He had wondered, of course, how Phoebe Glass could have continued in this manner, that is, of calmly managing his public excoriation, Solomon Wiese said, of attempting to *perfect* him, there was no other word for it, in the eyes of the scholastici and the host of public onlookers, with a completely imperturbable countenance at all times. She had always claimed to have his best interests at heart, Solomon Wiese said, gesturing at Phoebe Glass next to him at the bar, where she still showed no signs of stirring. She had carried out her duties with an unmistakable steeliness, and there was never any suggestion of hesitation or doubt. Solomon Wiese could only put this attitude down to her old friend Jessica Lake, he went on—it was as if Phoebe Glass was hoping to redeem somehow the monstrous treatment of Jessica Lake by carrying out her duties for the scholastici, that is, by shepherding Solomon Wiese towards his *self-nominated punishment* with imperturbable steeliness. The connection might not be immediately clear, but this is what he thought she thought she was doing, Solomon Wiese said. He knew, of course, that I had been involved with Jessica Lake, years ago, Solomon Wiese said, not looking at me, but at the empty espresso cup in front of him, which he began to turn on the bar. Of course, you cannot be held accountable for what happened to Jessica Lake in the end, Solomon Wiese went on, turning the espresso cup on the bar. Nonetheless your actions did in a sense precipitate what happened to Jessica Lake, and therefore what happened to Phoebe Glass, in terms of her general outlook and worldview, and therefore it isn't too tenuous to say that your actions have a bearing on my situation, too. Jessica Lake was treated monstrously, as I have already said, Solomon Wiese said, his eyes on the espresso cup as he turned it on the bar—first by yourself, although the monstrousness of your behaviour pales when placed next to what she endured later on. It was your actions that drove her into the arms of a certain well-known poet, who treated her monstrously, Solomon Wiese said, we all know about the behaviour of poets in their private lives, and this one was no exception—and you all but forced them together, in Phoebe Glass's estimation, as by that time you wanted to wash your hands of Jessica Lake, having extracted all that you could from her, and being an essentially kind and decent person she gave it to you unthinkingly, Solomon Wiese said, and not least from her body, which had already endured its share of hardships, which you were happy to add to, according to your particular sexual mores, which are generally no less debased than other poets'—your successor not included.

The poet you pushed Jessica Lake towards was an arch-manipulator who sought to control her every move, making her life a daily hell, which she was able to escape only after several months of psychological torment, through the intervention of another young man—the well-known poet drove her, in turn, into the arms of this other young man, her would-be rescuer, Solomon Wiese said, and a very strange person indeed—the worst of the lot. She had hoped to escape from her monstrous treatment at the hands of the well-known poet, her daily hell of non-stop psychological torment, but she had received even more monstrous treatment at the hands of her so-called rescuer. I do not know the full extent of the abuses suffered by Jessica Lake at the hands of this third young man, a man with a pronounced limp, apparently, Solomon Wiese went on, but I do know that he ended up subjecting her to several *experiments*, there is no other word for it, in the house they shared, in Bury. He subjected Jessica Lake's essentially sweet and decent person and her damaged body to a series of *experiments*, at the behest of an anonymous client, apparently, Solomon Wiese said, his eyes on the espresso cup on the bar in front of him, once, that is, he had assured himself of his complete domination of her personality, so that when Jessica Lake was eventually found she looked twenty or thirty years older than she actually was—but I am not in possession of all the facts. Phoebe Glass was unable to help her. No one was able to help her. Whatever happened exactly of course had an irrevocable effect on Phoebe Glass, her closest friend, as I have already mentioned. Phoebe Glass, after discovering what had happened to Jessica Lake, was unable to feel anything towards the world other than disappointment and contempt, and obviously I am part of that world from which she cannot conceal her disappointment and contempt, even though I believe that Phoebe Glass does care about me, in her own fashion, Solomon Wiese said, and is demonstrating that care in the only way available to her, that is, by managing my passage through the *alternative justice system*. She has the idea that by doing this she will somehow safeguard the memory of Jessica Lake—this is what I have come to symbolise. Her project to *correct* me is nothing other that a vigil for her old friend, Jessica Lake. I have realised I am nothing more to her than a token in a larger equation—and you are at the other end of this transaction, with your tokens, Solomon Wiese said, still without looking my way. You are in possession of an abundance of tokens, it seems to me, from my place in the equation, on the other side of the equals sign. In a sense, the unfeigned affection that was shown to you by Jessica Lake, at your invitation, as you remember, is precisely the same unfeigned affection that Phoebe Glass has denied to herself and to all those who come into contact with her, due to Jessica Lake's monstrous treatment at the hands of a sequence of men, of which you were the first, Solomon Wiese said. It would be insane of me to believe that your treatment of Jessica Lake in any direct way prefigured the situation between myself and Phoebe Glass, he went on, without taking his eyes from the espresso cup, though he had ceased to turn it on the bar—even though one proceeded in every sense from the outcomes of the other, or to dwell on the thought that the unfeigned affection that I have come to value above all else, because it has always been withheld from me, is one and the same as the sweetness and decency that was shown to you by Jessica Lake, and that you soiled and devalued with the callousness of your actions, triggering her slide into misery and abuse. It would very probably be insane of me to believe this, but it still *doesn't altogether prevent me from believing it*, and therefore placing the blame, in a purely notional way, at your door, Solomon Wiese went on—I can *imagine* placing the blame at your door, I can feel the way I would feel *if* I placed the blame at your door, all without actually placing the blame at your door. That Jessica Lake was driven into the arms of this strange and unwholesome limping individual, with his so-called experiments, after being treated shamefully by a certain well-known poet, who you yourself drove her into the arms of, after taking advantage in every way of her innate sweetness and decency, is not in any *simple* sense your fault, and yet, by the same logic, it wouldn't have happened if not for your actions—those are the facts, Solomon Wiese said. In terms of the crude chain of cause and effect, it cannot be denied that really you are responsible, Solomon Wiese said, as it is hardly likely that this chain of events, at every stage of which Jessica Lake was treated monstrously, would have been set in motion if it wasn't for you—if Jessica Lake's view of romantic life hadn't been so dramatically tainted by her experiences with you as to have allowed herself to have been treated monstrously by a sequence of subsequent partners, then Phoebe Glass would not have suffered a similar process of disillusionment, and

I would not be in my current predicament—that is all. The feeling most *valued* by me in the world is symmetrical, if not identical to, the feeling profoundly *devalued* by you. The closer you look at it, the less different each of the monstrous participants in this situation seems, Solomon Wiese said—they come to appear interchangeable, that is the reality, when you've looked at the situation for long enough, one monstrosity becomes much the same as another, and it is of no consequence if one monstrosity comes to stand in for another monstrosity. Phoebe Glass was awake. Around us in the Travelodge bar all the poets were waking up—some cupped steaming coffees and teas in their hands, others chewed cautiously on pieces of dry toast, some had little bowls of cereal or fruit, and still others were applying themselves to massive fried breakfasts. Many bore the evidence of the previous night's excesses on their faces—I saw bruises and bloodied mouths, smeared make-up and shiny faces, but the mood in the Travelodge bar was a good-humoured one, kept afloat by a gentle babble of morning conversation. Without speaking, Phoebe Glass gestured at the clock, and Solomon Wiese looked up at last from his empty espresso cup. It was almost eleven. When they rose from the bar, I followed them outside, and we all paused on the street, by the large windows of the Embankment Travelodge. The morning was bright, the traffic was passing greyly and inconsequentially, the thin trees were shivering. I saw Phoebe Glass looking up into Solomon Wiese's face, then she took him by the arm and they turned to go, neither saying goodbye, but each showing an outstretched hand as they moved away, as if dismissing me at last from their concern. I watched them as they crossed Waterloo Bridge, until they became silhouettes, and then their figures seemed to disassemble, bobbing and melting, before disappearing into the scaled mesh of people and buildings. In the windows of the Travelodge bar, I could see that the poets were beginning to stand, unfolding themselves from the long couches, from their corners, from their positions at the bar. As they began to gather at the windows one by one, I reflected that I only had feelings or thoughts about these people, these poets, to the extent that I could see them or that I held them in mind, and yet I seemed to have feelings and thoughts about them constantly—I was like a house for feelings and thoughts about these forty or fifty people, who I could see gathering in the windows of the Travelodge bar, in that I was constantly occupied by feelings and thoughts about their lives and their activities, and I understood, as I watched them, that they were not dependent on me, these forty or fifty people, but that I was dependent on them, I was nothing but a house for thoughts and feelings about them, and that they had allowed me to express my thoughts and feelings about them, they had even welcomed and encouraged my feelings and thoughts about them, until the house of thoughts and feelings had emptied, and all of my problems and difficulties with these forty or fifty people seemed to disappear, now that I was confronted by them in person like this, massed together in the Travelodge bar, their outlines assembling in the windows like the expression of a single intelligence, as if they were the only outward expressions of my thoughts, but they were also where the *thoughts found form*, in that without them there would *be* no thoughts, so really my dependence on them was total, I realised, and I knew that if the forty or fifty people in the window were to turn away from me entirely, it would cause me to descend immediately into despair, to withdraw into my own endless complexes justifying my removal from the group of forty or fifty people, but equally, that if they had welcomed me into their ranks, and their ranks had closed around me, I would soon start to resent their proximity and their demands on my energy, and so I would also in that case withdraw into my own complexes justifying my removal from the group of forty or fifty poets—in other words the outcome would be the same, and it was clear to me then, I thought, that the only place for me was here, where I was standing, in front of a large sheet of glass that separated me from the poetry community, these forty or fifty otherwise quite unremarkable people, and at this safe distance, shielded by a layer of glass, I was able to praise and insult the group of forty or fifty poets who were gathered in the floor-to-ceiling windows of the Travelodge bar, their gazes beginning to click towards me, as I gestured towards them with friendly gestures and insulting gestures alternatingly, I knew that from this safe distance, while being able to observe the poets at full length, while *feasting my eyes* on this gathering of poets, nothing short of all the poets in the window collapsing to the floor would be enough for me, but this state of *nothing being enough* was precisely what suited me, I thought as I continued to pace and make gestures on the pavement outside the Travelodge bar, because I could feel the judgement that was coming towards us as if from overhead, it was falling towards us like a dark shape from the sun, and only if I could keep the poets in sight, in clear view at all times, as all of their eyes were connected to mine, or focused on an area around my neck, as I continued to gesture and pace on the other side of the glass, only then could I prevent myself from entering a state of absolute panic.

ACKNOWLEDGEMENTS

My sincere thanks to Anna Webber at United Agents for being the first to read this manuscript and for believing it to be a book, to Kendall Storey at Catapult for her generosity and energy, to Lettice Franklin at W&N for her enthusiasm and care, and to all three for their support, reassurance, advice and ideas. I also need to thank William Kherbek for his dispassionate scrutiny (and for "fauxetry"), and Emily Berry for her counsel on nomenclature. Thanks too to Nicolette Polek, Lucy Ives, Megan Nolan, Luke Kennard, Kate Kilalea, Jonathan Lethem and Laird Hunt for their time, kindness and advocacy. My very great thanks to the staff at the National Library of Scotland Reading Rooms in Edinburgh, where the majority of this novel was written. A thoroughly inadequate expression of gratitude, finally, to my family and friends for their constant and benign presences.

SAM RIVIERE is the author of three poetry books, *81 Austerities*, *Kim Kardashian's Marriage*, and *After Fame*, all published by Faber, and a book of experimental prose, *Safe Mode*. He teaches at Durham University and lives in Edinburgh, where he runs the micropublisher If a Leaf Falls Press.